The Place of Stones

Iosseini

The Place of Stones

A NOVEL

Curbstone Books
Northwestern University Press
Evanston, Illinois

Northwestern University Press
www.nupress.northwestern.edu

The Place of Stones and its characters are imaginary and any similarities with names or
places is coincidental.

Printed in the United States of America

10 9 8 7 6 5 4 3 2 1

ISBN 978-0-8101-3575-8 (paper)
ISBN 978-0-8101-3576-5 (e-book)

Library of Congress Cataloging-in-Publication data are available from the Library
of Congress.

In memory of Sa'adat Homayoun,
my young cousin who lost his life
in the Iran–Iraq War.

It's not clear
from what direction the wind is blowing but
from the ghostly fanfare of the palms
it's obvious that the anxiety of an incident is
playing with the village trapped in the green plain.

—MANOUCHEHR ATASHI

CONTENTS

PREFACE

This novel was published in Iran in 1997 under the title *Sangriz*, after more than a year of dealing with the government censors. It has subsequently been revised for publication in English. In Iran, then as now, writers have to cope with the Censorship Bureau of the Ministry of Culture and Islamic Guidance. I include at the end of the novel a letter to the Iranian publisher from the Ministry of Culture outlining a list of changes required before the book could be published. The page numbers refer to the mock-up of the Persian version of the novel. So as not to have any elements of the novel spoiled, readers may wish to view the letter after reading the book.

The censors were most sensitive in four areas: whatever appeared to them to indicate negativity toward the Islamic revolution and the war (the Iran–Iraq War); male–female relationships; descriptions of the human body, especially that of a woman's, including mention of breasts or anything they thought (even mistakenly) pertained to sexuality; and profanity. After consulting with a writer friend who had experience with the censorship office, I deleted certain things and reworded others; in other places I left the text unchanged in the hope that they would escape further scrutiny in the next reading, and that was the case.

ACKNOWLEDGMENTS

I would like to thank Deborah Woodcock for her encouragement and the translation of the poem by Omar Khayyám and Lee Miller for his thoughtful suggestions on the manuscript. Thanks also to Pamela Strauss, Paul Bates, and my agent, Valerie Borchardt. I would also like to acknowledge the encouragement of Alex Taylor of Curbstone Press and the following friends for their help with the Persian publication of the novel: my special thanks to Bahman Forsi for his encouragement and support early in my writing career, Ashkbous Talebi for his help with the Ghashghai phrases used in the novel, Shahriar Mandanipour for his help and assistance with censorship issues, and Majid Roshangar for his support. The comments of Lee Martin, who reviewed the book for the Press, are also appreciated.

NAMES OF THE MAIN CHARACTERS
WITH IRANIAN PRONUNCIATIONS

Haydar (Hay-*dar*)

Haydar's friend Jamal (Ja-*maal*)

Haydar's wife, Mehrangiz (Meh-ran-*geez*), and sister Golandam (*Gol*-an-dam)

Jamal's mother, Bibigol (*Bi*-bi-gol), and brother Jaffar (Jaf-*far*)

Mirza-ali (*Mir*-za-ali), a friend of the families from the nomadic Ghashghai (*Kash*-ka-ee) tribe, who still migrate seasonally in the southern and southwestern parts of Iran

Mirza-ali's son, Kubaad (Koo-*baad*)

Marafi (*Ma*-ra-fi), a friend of Jaffar's and Golandam's

Baraat (Ba-*raat*), the minibus driver

Danial (Daan-*yaal*) and Zomorod (*Zo*-mo-rod), a Gypsy couple who travel to the village once a year

Danial and Zomorod's son, Hatam (Ha-*tam*)

Rahbari (*Raa*-bar-i), an important landowner

Rahbari's son, Bahram Khan (Bah-*raam* Khan)

Amir Khan (Aa-*mir* Khan), a minor landowner with ties to Rahbari

Amir Khan's son, Sarferaaz (Sar-fe-*raaz*)

The Place of Stones

Part One

1

Haydar lay facedown on the ground, enjoying the warm spring sun on his tired body. Always when resting from his work in the fields, he would lie like this, hugging the ground and listening to the beating of his heart, its insistent throbbing seeming to be coming from the depths of the earth. He had just finished the lunch—naan with dates and yogurt—that his wife, Mehrangiz, and younger sister, Golandam, had brought him and drunk hot tea from the tin kettle and was going to take a short nap before starting work again, but today he couldn't sleep. He sat up on the hillside and watched his wife and sister walking back home to Sangriz through the wheat field. Golandam had taken off her scarf and her jet-black hair fell to her shoulders. She skipped along and circled ahead of Mehrangiz, the red and yellow of her skirt cutting through the dark green of the winter wheat, then waited for her sister-in-law to catch up and went off again.

Haydar kept them in sight until they got close to the village at the end of the fields and vanished from view. Seeing Golandam young and happy sent a joyful feeling through him, and he found himself thinking that it wouldn't be long before a young man would ask for her hand and take her away.

It was time to give up the pleasant sun. He put on his hat, grabbed his shovel, and walked down the hill to the edge of the wheat field. After checking the irrigation stream, he went back to the pit on the hillside and started to dig. He was so engaged in his task that he wasn't aware that someone was watching him from the top of the pit.

"Hey, Haydar . . . What's going on? You're digging as if you're only a few inches from the hidden treasure."

Haydar, startled, looked up and saw the tall figure of Jamal above him. He planted the shovel in the ground and then took off his hat and swept the droplets of sweat from his face.

"Eventually I'll find it," Haydar said, catching his breath. "One day I'll drag it out of the dark ground and let it shine in the sun." Then he grabbed Jamal's extended hand and pulled himself up from the pit.

"Do you mind the water at all?" Jamal asked with a smile. "Or do you leave it to run wherever it wishes while you're treasure hunting?"

"I checked it just before you got here," Haydar said. "My mind is always on the water. I've fixed it on the lower section of the field. It will be a while before it's all irrigated."

They walked over the scattered pieces of pottery that Haydar had tossed out of the pit over the past few days of digging. At the sound of their footsteps, a couple of field rats ran by and disappeared into their holes.

Haydar pushed a few shovelfuls of dirt into the holes and packed it down with the back of the shovel. "There are too many of them recently. They seem bigger and they're nesting all over the fields. They dig holes and the little water that the pump brings up is lost."

"Haydar," Jamal said, "how long are you going to search for the lost treasure? And how do you know that the Black Globe that you're after is hidden in this hill? It's only a fable. People like to tell stories from the past—you're wasting your time."

They reached the irrigation stream, a trickle of water running down the field. Haydar shifted the shovel from one shoulder to the other. "You've been bugging me more and more about this. I'll tell you something. It's been said that when Alexander of Macedonia defeated the armies of King Darius and was approaching Takht-e-Jamshid, the palace of Persepolis, one of the king's lovers ordered two of the palace guards to bury the imperial treasure in the nearby hills and then sent two other guards to kill them so that the location would remain secret. But when Alexander entered the palace, she lost her heart to him and to capture his affections showed him

6

where the treasure was hidden, all except for the Black Globe. Alexander didn't let her down. He took her and all the treasure and headed farther east."

"You're telling me that Alexander took all the treasure?" Jamal stopped in his tracks. "Then what are you looking for in these hills? Haydar, you always puzzle me!"

"And you never let a man finish his story. You're always in a hurry."

"You always exaggerate everything, my friend. Okay, I'll shut up."

"All the treasure did not equal that globe. The Black Globe was something unique. It was so dark and shiny you could see yourself in it. It's said that it was for this globe that Alexander attacked our country. If he had found it, he would have discovered the road to *aab-e zendagi*—the water of life—since one look into the globe was to confer eternal life. Alexander tortured the palace inhabitants, but no one knew where the globe was hidden except the woman who had been the king's lover and became Alexander's lover. He took her with him, not because he loved her—no, because he thought that someday, somehow he could get the information out of her."

Haydar pointed to a few low hills that rose here and there across the fields. "It's said that the globe is still here, hidden in one of the hills, probably not far from where we're standing."

"May God grant you some wisdom and me some wealth. Fine, but my dear friend, this story is more than two thousand years old. Do you understand what that means? It means that from then until now this land has been plowed at least once, and sometimes twice, a year. That makes several thousand plowings, right? And people have been all over these hills taking dirt to make mud bricks."

"So what? What are you getting at?" Haydar said.

Jamal scratched the top of his head and gave Haydar a smile. "Well, with so much plowing and other activity, how many hills could have been flattened? Besides, the gates of this country have been open to everyone during its long history. After the Greeks came the Arabs and then the Mongols, and . . ."—he was quiet for a moment—"even the Americans were here looking around these hills with their electronic equipment when we were little. Have you forgotten?"

"No, I haven't forgotten. I remember them very well. Especially the one who had a big dog that sat next to him in the car like a person. He used to come to the pump house—no, I guess it wasn't the pump house, there was no pump then. We used to draw water using a horse. He liked that and took pictures, do you remember? Anyway, he would come every day and fill up a big tank with water for the workers on his excavation site. He was very polite. *Ejazeh hast aab bebaram?* he would say—Is it okay to take some water?"

"Yes, I remember him. He knew a few words of Farsi—*Salaam Agah. Sohb be-khair.* Now after all that's happened around here, you're still trying to find the treasure? Whatever may have been buried here, it's gone, my friend. Don't waste your time. Where did you hear all these stories anyway—from your grandfather?"

"Of course, may God rest his soul. I've forgotten some of the things he told me. I was very small when he died. I think it was during the time of Ahmad Shah, or maybe it was Reza Shah, that the Western archaeologists came to Persepolis." He pointed toward the stone columns of the ruined palace that were barely visible on the distant mountainside. "My grandfather was six or seven years old and used to work at the excavation site as a water boy. He would carry jars of water from the river on a donkey for the men, who worked long hours during hot summer days and were always thirsty. The secret that he told me is"—he lowered his voice—"that when the sun is setting behind the palace, the shadow of one of the columns points toward the hill where the Black Globe is buried."

Jamal looked toward the ruins with amusement. "Okay, let's say he was right. But the problem is, first of all, that the columns were not just the ten or fifteen left standing. As you know, the palace had two or three hundred columns. Second, the area between here and the ruins is vast. Do you know how many acres of land we're talking about? All we can say for sure is that the treasure you're looking for could be buried somewhere within hundreds of acres."

"I know all that, Jamal. I've studied the area for a long time and at different times of the year. The way I see it, there's only one possibility. If you stand on the hill where I'm searching, you'll see the sun going down just behind the seventh column, no matter the season of the year. So I'm digging in the line of its shadow."

"Fine. Let's say you're right and you found the treasure, the Black Globe that you're after. What are you going to do with it? You won't be able to sell it, will you? The government will have you arrested and put in jail straight away. Like the poor farmer from the village of Khaaksar who ran up against a jar full of old coins with his plow. They didn't just take the treasure from him, they arrested him and threw him in jail."

Haydar stared at him from beneath his bushy eyebrows. "Well, I haven't got the Black Globe to be thinking about selling it, have I? I've got to find it in the first place, and if I ever do find it, I only want to take a look at it. I want to see it shine under the sun—that's all. I'll sneak a glance at it and then bury it in the same place." He pounded the ground under his foot. "I would like to touch something that has been in the hands of Darius the Great, the king of Persia. Then I'll put it back in its place where it's been buried under the earth for centuries."

"As long as I can remember, Haydar, you've been dreaming about finding a treasure, any treasure, but this is the first time you're telling me what you are specifically looking for, something that Alexander was after—the road to the 'water of life.'"

"Yes, *aab-e zendagi. . . ,*" Haydar murmured.

"I hope you'll give me a drop after you find it," Jamal said, laughing.

They were nearing the pump house and could hear the pop, pop sound of the motor.

"Do you hear that?" Haydar said. "The pump's been drawing water from early morning. It hasn't choked a moment all day." He moved aside the dried brush and tumbleweeds that had gathered on the stream, then struck the shovel into the ground and sat down next to Jamal, who had stretched out on the grass beside the stream. Haydar took off his hat and sat resting his elbows on his knees. In front of them a flock of quails landed, disappearing into the green wheat, and another flock took off across the sky.

After a while Haydar stretched out as well. They were quiet. Both had grown up on the vast plain at the foot of the Zagros Mountains and learned to work the land from their fathers. They knew in their bones the hard labor of harvesting wheat and rye in the high heat of summer and digging out sugar beets during the frozen chill of winter. They were children of the land and had learned to farm at an early age. Jamal, in his twenty-four years of life, had never been as close to anyone as he was to Haydar, who was two years older than he. In the ups and downs of their lives, they had been together like brothers. For the past ten years, they had been working the land for Mr. Rahbari, who lived in the city of Shiraz, eighty miles or so beyond the mountains, and owned most of the good land near the village of Sangriz.

Jamal sat up. "Well," Haydar said, recognizing his uneasiness, "aren't you going to tell me about your trip to the city? What happened? Were you able to persuade that little brother of yours to stay?"

"No, I couldn't make him understand. Jaffar is becoming a stubborn boy. He doesn't want to stay in the city and doesn't want to go to school."

"Did you bring him back, then?"

"Yes. If he won't go to school, I can't leave a twelve-year-old boy at Baraat's, can I? Baraat is always on the road between the city and the villages, and his wife hardly manages with four children."

"If you hadn't brought him back, maybe he would have changed his mind after a few days and gone back to school."

"No matter how much I tried, the stupid kid wouldn't budge. I almost tied him up to make him stay. He jumped up and down like a chicken with its head cut off, crying and asking me not to leave him there. He begged me so much I gave in." Jamal looked up at a flock of quails circling close by. "Do you remember when he finished sixth grade at the village school, how happy he was to go to the city and start seventh grade? Now he says that he doesn't like the city, that it's closed up and crowded. I think he missed his mother and his friend Marafi."

"*Ay baba!* There are kids his own age in the village who can manage a pump house and irrigate acres of land by themselves. Mirza-ali's son, when he was younger than Jaffar, took care of two hundred sheep during the winter and summer. Jaffar has it too good, staying in the city with a nice family. What could be better than being with Baraat and his wife? Bring him over here to help

10

with the farm. Then he'll realize what life is about." After a few seconds, Haydar regretted his words. "But it's a shame if he doesn't continue with his schooling. The misery of many of us, including you and me, is from lack of education. At least I thought this boy would know better."

"And that he would take advantage of his situation," Jamal added, lowering his head and looking at the ground. Close to his feet, an ant was moving between the blades of grass. It climbed all the way to the tip of one blade and then turned around and reversed its path. Then it started up another and did the same thing, as if it were confused and couldn't figure out where to go.

After a long silence, Jamal looked up and turned to Haydar. "As you know, two years ago, when my poor father was on his death-bed, all he asked of me was to make sure that this little brother of mine got an education. That was his last wish. Now what am I sup-posed to do? My father didn't want Jaffar to end up like me, who ran away from the mullah's madrese."

"I'll talk to him," Haydar said. "I'll try to convince him to go back to school. Anyway, what's he going to do in the village? Become a farmworker? Or a shepherd?" He laughed aloud. "That mullah, he wasn't a teacher. He was a madman. I believe we did well in tolerating his stinging stick. Enough for a lifetime."

They both laughed, and Jamal said that after all Jaffar wasn't to be blamed, that when they were in Baraat's minibus coming back home, he had managed to get it out of him. At first Jaffar had been too embarrassed to admit it, but eventually he'd told him. Haydar had gotten up, ready to go back to the pump house, but sat down again. Jamal was still following the progress of the ant. "The city kids, those sons of bitches, are to blame," he said. "They've caused Jaffar lots of problems. They laughed at him, teasing him that he was a country boy. A country boy who had come to the city to be a city boy. They teased him that he had a country accent, stuff like that. After the Nowruz holidays, when he went back to school, the crotch of his pants was ripped. He was embarrassed to ask Baraat's wife to stitch it for him, so what does he do? He goes to school in his pajamas. After everyone, including the teachers, had had their laugh, the principal sent him home to dress properly. After that, no matter how Baraat and his wife tried, Jaffar wouldn't go back to school and wouldn't tell them what had happened."

"Well, no wonder," Haydar said, shaking his head in dismay. "Those city boys are something else. May God help a shy kid among those sons of bitches. Have you forgotten Bahram Khan, the landlord's son? When he was a boy and used to come to Sangriz, even the village dogs would run away from him."

"I feel sorry for Jaffar. After all, there're only a couple of months left in the school year. And I haven't told my mother yet—she thinks he's back on vacation. If she finds out, she'll have a fit."

"Don't worry yourself," said Haydar, "I'll try to find a way to persuade him to go back."

"That would be good. He likes you and he'll listen to you."

The sun had reached the peak of the mountain and an afternoon breeze was cooling the air. Haydar grabbed his shovel and they walked toward the pump house.

"Now at a time that I have all this going on," Jamal said, "Mirzaali, may God rest his father's soul, stops me at the village entrance and asks me when I'm going to shape up. I think my mother went to him again and complained that she's getting old and I haven't been thinking of getting married."

"Have you forgotten three years ago when he wouldn't leave me alone?" Haydar said. "Every afternoon he would stop me and remind me that I should get married. I would ask him to let it be and say that when it was time I would let him know and he could look for a bride for me. Eventually, I caved in and became Mehrangiz's suitor."

When they got close to the pump house, Jamal's horse, Abrash, which was grazing in the pasture, perked up her ears and looked their way. Jamal whistled and she came, her mane flying and her gray coat glinting in the sun. Jamal walked over to the horse and ran his hand along her back. Abrash rubbed her face against Jamal's hip, snorted, and snapped her long tail in the air.

Jamal pointed to Haydar's motorcycle leaning against the pump house. "Haydar, what do you say? Shall we have a race again?"

"You don't rest a minute, do you, Jamal? You always have to have something going on. I'll show you, though. I've repaired the motorcycle. This time I'll leave you in dust."

12

Jamal smiled. "We'll have to see it first, then we can talk about it."

"Okay," Haydar said. "Let's have a bet, then. If I win, I'll take that one-year-old ram of yours. Tell me what you want if you win."

Jamal looked at Haydar. "If I win . . ." He lowered his eyes. "If I win . . . I'll ask for . . . Well, I'll tell you later."

From the shy look that came over Jamal's face, Haydar could guess that he was thinking of Golandam.

2

Jamal bent low over the horse's neck, his thighs tight against her warm skin, urging her to run faster. His arms moved up and down like two wings with the motion of the horse and his sleeves danced at his sides. Abrash, her reins relaxed, took in the cool afternoon air and raced on. Jamal, humming to himself, would turn once in a while to see how far he was ahead of Haydar but could hardly see through the thick dust kicked up by the horse. Near Sangriz he came up behind a group of women and young girls with water jars and pots atop their heads on their way back to the village who scattered to either side of the road when they heard the pounding of the horse's hooves. Jamal pulled the reins and leaned close to the horse's ear. "Whoa—easy, easy. Don't you see Golandam? Look, the prettiest one, the one with the sky-blue scarf."

As they went by the women, Jamal's gaze sought Golandam's. Although many glances had passed between them, it was as if he were seeing her for the first time, and a feverish warmth rushed to his heart. For a moment he felt dizzy and was afraid of being thrown from the horse right in front of the women's eyes, but then he broke off his gaze and dug his heels into the horse's sides. *Yallah*, he called out, and Abrash sped away.

At the entrance to the village, Jamal jumped off the horse and looked back down the road, but he could see only the group of women in the distance. There was no sign of Haydar, and when he listened, he couldn't hear the sound of the motorcycle.

As usual Jamal and his horse had left Haydar and his motorcycle in the dust.

Jaffar, seeing the horse and rider, got up from the adobe stand in front of the village school and ran to meet them. His friend Marafi picked up the Koran and the *Shahnameh—The Epic of Kings*—which he always carried in his worn-out satchel, and followed behind him, limping and murmuring his everlasting song—*da, da, da . . . la, la, la*. With each step, his old cotton shoes slipped halfway off his feet, brushing a line in the dirt.

Jaffar took the reins from Jamal and stroked the horse's forehead and ears. Abrash lowered her head and sniffed Jaffar's sleeves.

"Can I take her home?" Jaffar asked.

"No, not yet. Walk her for a while," Jamal said.

Jaffar pulled on the bridle and walked beside the horse, murmuring to her. "I know you'd like to give me a ride and take me around Sangriz, but not now. It wouldn't be fair. You're hot and sweaty the way Jamal has ridden you. Don't worry, I'm not going back to the city. I'll be home with you and I don't care if Jamal is unhappy with me for quitting school."

Past the entrance, which was nothing but a wide opening in the old village wall, the huge wooden gate being long gone, was the village square, a small area with dirt alleys that angled off from it and snaked through the village. At the end of the square, Mirza-ali was standing next to Baraat's minibus in front of Sayed Ayoub's shop, the only one in the village. Baraat was under the bus, struggling with something, trying to fix it. When Mirza-ali saw Jamal, he shifted his walking stick from one hand to the other and went toward him, his old dog, Gorgi, following him. For the past few days, Mirza-ali had been after Jamal. "Let's throw a celebration for you," he had said. "Why don't we go to Haydar's house and ask for Golandam's hand." Each time Jamal had politely refused. He had in mind talking to Haydar himself, but every time he had an opportunity to say something, no words came to him and he shied away.

Mirza-ali stopped by the horse and called out to Jamal—*Nechon ati, bohdar ghchir chabdo rirang?*

"What are you saying in your Ghashghai tongue, Amu Mirza-ali?" asked Jamal.

16

"I said, 'Why do you run the horse so much? Are you trying to kill the poor animal?'"

"Don't worry, Amu Mirza-ali, nothing will happen to her."

Mirza-ali turned to Jaffar. "Hey, kid, don't let the animal stand still. She'll catch a cold. Walk her, walk her."

Hearing voices, Baraat pulled himself out from under the bus and straightened up. His fuzzy hair was dusty and his hands were blackened by motor oil. He walked to the others and threw down a metal object covered with grease. "This miserable piece of shit," he grumbled. "Is this the time for the dog arm to break on me? I have to go back to town. Hopefully I can find a mechanic to weld it. If I'm lucky, I'll find a used one. It'll probably cost me a bundle."

Mirza-ali tapped the metal part with the tip of his walking stick as if he were examining a dead animal and frowned. "What did you say is broken? The *dog arm*? What sort of thing is this? It doesn't look anything like a dog's arm."

"Yes, *amu joon*. It's called a *dog arm*. It attaches to the steering rod."

Not all the villagers knew exactly where Baraat was from, but his dark skin and accent suggested he was from the Persian Gulf area. He'd moved to Shiraz long ago and for the past few years had been carrying passengers between the city and the surrounding villages. Because of his gentleness and warmth, he had found his place among the villagers and often stayed at Haydar's or Jamal's. When he talked, his black eyes smiled, giving him a childish look. At any time, even in the middle of the night, the door of any house in the village would be opened to him.

"Where's Haydar?" Baraat asked Jamal as he picked up the metal object from the ground. "Is he still back at the pump house? I may need to borrow his motorcycle to go to town."

"He was right behind me," Jamal said, stepping up onto the adobe stand by the entrance to see better. "I don't know what happened to him." He jumped off and, before starting down the road to find out about Haydar, called out after Jaffar, who was still walking the horse. "That's enough. By the time you get home, she'll be dried off. Take her back and add a cup of rye to her alfalfa."

"Amu Mirza-ali, did you tell Jamal?" Baraat spoke softly as he wrapped the part in a piece of an old cloth. "Did you say that we were planning to speak with him about going to Haydar's to ask for Golandam's hand?"

"No, I haven't had the chance yet."

Jamal passed the group of women and girls on the road without paying much attention to Golandam, whose eyes were seeking him. He could see Haydar a couple of hundred yards down the road. He was holding the handlebars of his motorcycle with one hand and the back of the seat with his other hand, pushing the motorcycle forward as if it were an angry ram that wasn't happy to be handled.

"What happened, Haydar?" Jamal said as he approached him. "Are you all right? Did you fall off?"

"Today's bet is not a bet at all," snapped Haydar.

Jamal put his hands on the back of the motorcycle to help push. "Why isn't it a bet? Just because it broke down on you again?"

"If this damn piece of shit hadn't run out of gas, you would have been left all the way back at the pump house."

"Now you can see that the old ways are much better," Jamal said teasingly. "Be proud of your noisemaker. *Tocka-tocka-tocka.*" He mimicked the sound of the motorcycle and laughed. "One day it's out of gas, another day it has a flat tire, then there's something wrong with its motor. I do admire my horse. My poor Abrash eats only a cup of rye and a handful of hay and if you wish will take you all the way to Shiraz with no problem."

"Well, I guess this isn't the vehicle for me after all," Haydar said.

When Baraat saw Haydar and Jamal by the entrance, he wrapped the broken metal part in a piece of cloth, then quickly wiped off his hands and ran up to them. "Is there a problem?" he asked.

"*Na, baba*—nothing." Jamal laughed. "He had us all worried for nothing."

"Haydar," Baraat said, "I'm glad you're here. My old minibus has broken its dog arm. I was hoping I could borrow your motorcycle to go to town and have it welded."

"Baraat, is this the time for you to tease me as well? A dog arm?"

"Why should I tease you? It's a part of the steering mechanism."

"Oh, well. Here, take it," Haydar said. "Put some gas in it and go anywhere you want."

"You should stay and have dinner first," Jamal said.

"Thanks, Jamal, but I need to hurry before the mechanic's shop closes. If I hadn't run into this problem, Mirza-ali and I were planning to come to your place." He turned to Mirza-ali.

"Amu," he said, "why don't you go to Jamal's place and tell him and his mother our thoughts?"

"*Khali khob.*" Mirza-ali nodded. "I'll try, but I think between both of us, we would have had a better chance reasoning with this young man." He looked at Jamal and smiled.

Baraat took the motorcycle and parked it beside the minibus. He retrieved a piece of old plastic hose from under the seat of the minibus and pushed one end of it into the gas tank. Then he twisted the cap off the motorcycle tank and grabbed the other end of the hose and started to suck on it. As soon as he felt the flow of gas, he quickly took the hose out of his mouth and pushed it into the motorcycle's tank. The sharp smell of gasoline filled the air. Baraat coughed a few times and spit on the ground. He wiped his mouth with the back of his hand and bent over the motorcycle. All his attention was on the tank. When it was almost full, he pulled out the hose from the minibus and held it up to drain the last of the gas into the motorcycle. Then he wound up the hose and put it back under the seat. After tying up the broken dog arm on the motorcycle's back rack, he got ready to leave. He had to push down on the foot crank a few times before the motor turned, its sudden *tocka-tocka-tocka* sound making Gorgi, Mirza-ali's old dog lying by his foot, jump. A cloud of gray exhaust rose into the air as Baraat gave the motor more gas and drove away.

3

The sun was gone and darkness, like a slow-moving liquid, seeped steadily into the alleys of the village. Lanterns, one after another, began to twinkle from the houses. The smell of straw fires filled the air and the jingle-jangle of bells of the animals returning from the fields could be heard throughout the village. Haydar, before leaving to go home, wished Mirza-ali and Jamal good night. Mirza-ali, stick in hand, followed by old Gorgi, went with Jamal, who had already guessed the purpose for the evening visit.

Jamal's mother, Bibigol, was pleased to see Mirza-ali walk into their house. Her eyes sparkled with happiness because she knew that this time Jamal had agreed to the matchmaking. Bringing Mirza-ali home with him was the evidence. Otherwise, he would have made an excuse and sneaked away from him.

"Welcome, welcome." She greeted Mirza-ali with a smile. Then she turned to Jamal. "Where's Baraat? Why didn't you invite him?"

"He had to go back to the city to get some parts for his minibus," Jamal said.

"His bus has broken its *dog arm*," Jaffar said, laughing.

Bibigol, not paying any attention to her younger son, invited Mirza-ali to come in and sit down.

Mirza-ali took off his cotton shoes and put them next to those of Marafi, who had been hanging around Jaffar all afternoon and rather than going home had followed him to Bibigol's. He was bent down over his old copy of *The Epic of Kings*, sitting in the amber light of the lantern with his mouth half open and reading the story of Bijan being rescued from a well, a story he read over and over whenever he got a chance. Mirza-ali sat down cross-legged on a cushion and leaned against the wall.

Jamal, still standing at the door, gestured toward Marafi and spoke to Jaffar. "Did you tell his mother before bringing him here?"

There was no answer from Jaffar.

"Run and let her know before the old woman starts to wander the dark alleys looking for him. Then go to Amu Mirza-ali's house and tell his wife he's having dinner with us. Come on, hurry up."

Jamal took the water jar from the bench by the door and went to the middle of the yard to wash up. Bibigol, feeling a sudden energy in her old bones, started with the preparation of tea and dinner. She checked the pot of stew boiling on the fire in a corner of the yard, singing a wedding song under her breath. During the past year, every time she got a chance, she had talked to Jamal about getting married. She had even asked Mirza-ali to talk to him. "Amu," she had said, "I can't get through to him, no matter how I try. See if you can put some sense into him."

"My dear son," she would say, "it's every mother's wish to see her son as a groom, to put henna on his hair. I'm longing for that. I long to hold your child, to carry your child through the village. How long do I have to wait? I'm getting old and I'm afraid I'll die before seeing my grandchildren."

Now she thought all her pleadings had borne fruit. The first step had been taken. Jamal had decided to ask for Golandam's hand. In her imagination, Bibigol could see Jamal and Golandam in their wedding chamber and her grandchildren running and playing by her side. She was totally submerged in her thoughts when Jaffar returned. She asked him to take the *sofreh* and the naan, then picked up the pot from the fire and went inside. Jaffar spread the *sofreh* in the middle of the room, and everyone sat around it. The smell of the steaming stew made old Gorgi, who was lying by the door, open her eyes and sniff the air.

Bibigol took only a small amount of food and ate slowly so that there would be enough for her guests. Once in a while she looked at Jamal and then at Jaffar, feeling pleased that on this night her younger son was home.

Jamal glanced at Marafi. It had been years since the incident, but he couldn't free his mind of thoughts of the fall afternoon when they were released from the mullah's teaching and he and Marafi, Haydar, and the other boys ran happily out of the madrese. He had thrown his books in a corner of the yard and, out of sight of his mother, had grabbed a small sack and run to the village square. Haydar was already there, a rope coiled in his hand. It didn't take long before Marafi arrived, his satchel still hanging from his shoulder.

"What's this?" Jamal snapped at him. "Why are you bringing your satchel with you?"

"It's okay," Haydar said. "Let him be, Jamal. You know he never goes anywhere without his satchel. Let's get going before it gets dark."

The sun had reached the crest of the mountain above Sangriz and the shadow of the mountain was stretching out toward the village when they got to the old well in the foothills of the mountain.

"Marafi," Haydar said. "You're the smallest and lightest. Why don't we tie the rope around you and send you down the well?"

"No, I'm afraid."

"What do you mean, afraid? There's nothing to be afraid of. Come on."

"No, the old wells have jinns."

"Jinns, what jinns? Jinns wouldn't be in the well during the daytime. They go in at night. Let's get going, don't be afraid. It'll take only a minute."

"No. Why don't you go in yourself?"

"You're lighter than we are," Jamal said. "Come on. If you get scared, we'll pull you up right away."

"If you go in," Haydar promised, "whatever we find, half is yours."

Marafi gave in, and Jamal tightened the rope around his waist. Haydar examined the knot and, before hanging the sack around Marafi's shoulder, reached for the boy's old satchel but was stopped short by Marafi's protest.

"No," Marafi said. "If you want me to go down the well, I have to have my satchel with me."

"Okay. You and your old books," Haydar said. "Why didn't you leave them at home?"

They moved closer to the mouth of the well.

"Keep your eyes wide open, okay?" Haydar said. "Whatever you find, put in the sack."

Marafi nodded.

"You have to look in the crevices—that's where ancient treasure is hidden. We'll lower you down slowly, and when you see an opening or a crack in the wall, call out and we'll hold the rope. Okay?"

Marafi nodded again.

Jamal pulled the rope tight. Haydar stepped behind him and grabbed the rope as well. Marafi sat at the edge of the well with his legs dangling down. The sack was hanging on one side of his small body and the satchel on the other side. He gazed down into the darkness, hesitating, but then, with a smooth push from Jamal, slowly slid forward. Jamal and Haydar tightened their grip. Soft earth from the rim of the well started to pour down. The rope stretched out and Marafi's bony figure hung in the open mouth of the well.

They released the rope more and Marafi disappeared into the well. Seeing nothing except darkness, his eyes widened and his heart, like a captured bird, started to beat wildly. As he was lowered further, more dirt poured down, falling into the depth of nothingness, then suddenly with a loud explosion of flapping, a flock of birds brushed against Marafi and flew up toward the sky. Marafi's cries echoed loudly. "Pull me up, pull me up. Spirits, jinns. Hurry, pull me up!"

"Calm down. They're only wild pigeons," both Jamal and Haydar, who were startled by the flight of the birds, called out to Marafi.

"No, pull me up," Marafi yelled louder. "Pull me up!"

In confusion and panic, Jamal and Haydar hurried to pull up the rope. They were covered with sweat and the rope was burning their hands. As another column of dark shapes that could have been a group of bats shot out of the well's mouth, Marafi's cries gave way to screams.

"Hold on," Haydar called out, "hold on."

Jamal and Haydar tried pulling the rope, but no matter how hard they pulled, it slipped between their fingers as if hands from the bottom of the well were pulling it down. Suddenly the rope went loose and there came a sound, a thumping sound like a sack thrown down from a roof onto the soft dirt of an alley. More dirt gave way at the rim of the well. A few seconds later a gray fog coiled up from the well's mouth and fanned into the late afternoon air.

They knelt down at the edge of the well and called into the darkness, "Marafi . . . Marafi . . ." Their calls echoed over and over—"Marafi . . . Marafi. Marafi . . . rafi . . . rafi . . . rafi . . ."—and slowly drowned in the mysterious stillness that seemed to rise from the well and sit on their hearts. Terrified, they rushed toward Sangriz as fast as they could.

It was night by the time the villagers, carrying lanterns, came to the hillside. Jamal and Haydar couldn't remember which old well they had gone to and went from well to well until they found the right one and someone went down with a lantern and a rope, and then Marafi was pulled up. He had broken his leg and was in shock. Marafi's mother's cries shook the night.

"Oh, my poor child. They've killed my son. Did you want treasure to bury in your father's grave?" she yelled at Jamal and Haydar. "Did you want treasure to put at your mother's feet? May God never forgive you. May you never see a happy day in your lives for what you've done to my dear, sweet son."

Jamal's train of thought was broken by hearing his mother praising God for the food and for their guests. She gathered the dishes and picked up the *sofreh* and asked Jaffar to take Marafi back home and on the way let Haydar and Mehrangiz know they were coming to visit. Then she went to the back room to get the turquoise necklace given to her by her mother when she got married. The necklace had been bought years earlier from the Gypsy family that came to the village every fall. She asked Jamal to bring the lantern and the box of sweets he'd brought from the city. As they stepped out into the alley to walk to the opposite side of the village, Mirza-ali whispered a prayer. "Dear God, grant us your blessing, we are going for a good deed."

At Haydar's they sat drinking tea and enjoying the sweets that Golandam offered while Mirza-ali talked about the winter and how it had seemed colder and longer than usual, saying that he hadn't had enough feed for his herds and they had barely survived. He was happy that spring was here and he would be able to take his animals to graze on the mountainside. Then he began to talk in earnest, saying that he had known both families for many years and seen them support each other during hard times. Above all, he was pleased he had been friends with both Jamal's and Haydar's fathers, may God rest their souls. Two men who were helpful to him from the first day he came with his family to live in Sangriz. Two men he could always count on. Finally he said that he had come in good faith for a pleasant deed that would bring the families even closer together. He praised Jamal as a good, honest, and hardworking young man and Golandam as a beautiful and clever young woman and said that, God willing, they would make a very nice couple.

Golandam blushed and when she glanced at Jamal and saw him looking her way, lowered her eyes. She had guessed from the beginning why they had come. The notion that Jamal was interested in her and any day would ask for her hand had been in the air—both Bibigol and Mehrangiz had talked to her about it—but she had been too embarrassed to say a word. She knew that someday she would be married like the other girls in Sangriz but couldn't believe how quickly the time was arriving.

Bibigol said that nothing would please her more than having Golandam as her daughter-in-law, that she loved her as a daughter and would come to love her even more. She was sad, she said, only that Golandam's mother wasn't alive to see this day but knew she would have approved. Haydar said Jamal was like his own brother and that he would be honored to have him as an in-law and was sure Jamal would love Golandam and take good care of her. He added that if his parents were alive, they would have happily approved of the engagement.

Jamal cleared his throat and in a low voice thanked Haydar and said that he looked up to him as an older brother and would be honored to be accepted as part of his family, adding that he loved Golandam and nothing would please him more than making her happy.

Then Mirza-ali brought up the subject of the dowry, indicating that since both families knew that neither was wealthy, Jamal had said he would offer five gold coins. Repeating the offer, Mirza-ali said it was his wish that this could be agreed upon by the families.

The dowry was far more than any family in the village had offered for a bride. It was usually a couple of copper pots or, on a few occasions, one or two gold coins. Five gold coins for a dowry was far more than anyone in Sangriz had heard of.

Haydar was pleased to accept and said that the dowry didn't matter, he was just happy for his sister to marry Jamal and have Bibigol as her mother-in-law. It was just a month earlier that he had turned down Amir Khan's offer of two hectares of land when he had come asking for Golandam's hand for his son, Sarferaaz, an easy decision since he didn't want his sister to be married into such a family in spite of all their wealth.

Mirza-ali was satisfied that his efforts had not been in vain. Nothing made him happier than the happiness of a young couple and two families that he liked and respected. He praised God, *Inshallah mobarak-e*, and congratulated the families on the happy occasion.

Bibigol wiped her eyes and went over to Golandam to kiss her and hang the turquoise necklace around her neck. "My dear," she said, "I've been waiting for this day."

Part Two

1

Bibigol sat crouched against the village wall, her elbows on top of her knees and her head resting in the palms of her hands. She looked toward the road that curved beyond the low dirt graves of the village cemetery and waited for Baraat's minibus to show up. A month had passed since the engagement of Jamal and Golandam, and she was going to the city to buy a few things she needed for the wedding.

Golandam, Jaffar, and Marafi were a short distance away, sitting by the school wall. Marafi had *The Epic of Kings* open on his crippled leg and was showing Golandam a drawing—in miniature style—of Sohrab and Gordafarid locked in battle. Gordafarid's hand was hooked into Sohrab's belt, and Sohrab's hand had knocked off her helmet, and the heroine's long black hair was showering down. Marafi was trying to explain to Golandam that Sohrab hadn't known he had been fighting a woman. He pointed to the drawing and repeated, "Da, da, da . . . la, la, la . . . ," then held his breath and shook his head.

"Yes, yes . . . I understand," Golandam said, smiling. Marafi, with his bulging eyes and half-open mouth, always looked as if he had seen something fearful or had been trying to say something but had forgotten what he wanted to say.

Jaffar was absentmindedly drawing lines on the ground with a twig. Once in a while he glanced at Golandam, finding it hard to believe that she was the same little girl who had been his classmate at the village school until two years ago. Now she was taller than he and engaged to Jamal. He thought about the time years ago when he had been pushed into confessing his feelings for her. At night he and his father, lantern in hand, would go to the school and sleep there so the young teachers who came from the city wouldn't be afraid. Everyone would sit and listen to his father's stories. One night when he was nodding, trying not to fall asleep, one of the teachers asked him to tell them which one of the schoolgirls he liked the best.

Jaffar blushed and his heart beat faster. He lowered his head and thought to himself how rude the teachers were. Weren't they ashamed to ask him that in front of his *baba*? How strange these city people were.

The teachers' scrutinizing didn't stop that night and they wouldn't let up. "Well, Jaffar, you didn't tell us the other night. Tell us now, come on. You're a smart boy—come on, flatter us!"

Jaffar, embarrassed, would glance at his *baba* and wonder why he wouldn't tell these shameless teachers to leave him alone. Maybe Baba was wondering as well, wondering what sort of teachers they were to tease him like that.

One night, Jaffar, thinking that he might be able to put an end to their pestering for good, nervously lowered his head and softly said, "Gol . . . Golandam."

"You naughty boy," one of the teachers burst out.

"You've picked the most beautiful flower," the other teacher said. "All this time we thought of you as a shy and naive boy. You fooled us all."

The teasing didn't stop and took on different patterns as time went on.

"What a clever boy this Jaffar is! Tell us how you stole Golandam's heart? Tell us, so we can learn, too!"

"You sneaky devil. Didn't we see you yesterday in the corner of the school yard holding Golandam's hand? Come on, tell us."

Jaffar would sink within himself, crumpling his small body like an airless ball. He couldn't understand why his father sat there so quietly. Not only didn't he tell the teachers to leave him alone, but he insisted that Jaffar go with him to the school every night. Maybe he didn't want to be alone with these city people. Now he could guess why, after recess, when the teachers would send them out to play and keep the girls inside, the boys would return to find the girls sitting on their benches, red-faced and nervous.

Jaffar looked at Golandam. He wondered why he had given her name that night but knew he always liked to be with her and had been feeling that way even more since he came back from the city.

Bibigol was counting her money and thinking about what she should be buying for the bride in the city bazaar when she saw Mirza-ali coming out of the village. He was dragging the dead bodies of a sheep and a small goat behind him. With his head down and his body bent more than usual, he held the back legs of the animals in his hands and struggled on. The bodies swept the soft dirt and left two broad parallel lines stretching back toward the village. The green eyes of the sheep, fixed in eternal sleep, were like two glass marbles. The goat, its mouth open and its lips pulled back, seemed to be grinning at the group of village boys following Mirza-ali. One of the short, newly grown-out horns of the goat made a thin incision in the wider swath line left by her body. Old Gorgi, her head held low, followed, along with Mirza-ali's four-year-old grandson, who had his grandfather's walking stick and was dragging it behind him.

Bibigol bit her lip in sympathy and hurriedly put the money back in the corner of her scarf and tightened the knot around it. "Amu Mirza-ali," she said. "May God keep bad events away from you. It looks like you've lost more of your herd."

Golandam was startled to see the dead animals, but collected herself. She and Jaffar and Marafi watched Mirza-ali stop and straighten his back. Gorgi, who seemed unable to take another step, lay down beside the dead animals and rested her head on her paws. She watched as the boys came closer and, when they poked at the dead animals with their bare toes, growled at them without moving.

"Yes, I've lost more of my herd," Mirza-ali said, turning to Bibigol. "It looks like God has opened the corner of the sky to rain down disease over my few animals." His voice shook and his eyes grew moist. "Stop bothering them, *baba joon*," he said softly to the boys. "It's not nice. They haven't done you any harm."

33

His animals were dear to Mirza-ali, and seeing the children toying with them made him feel that they were poking at his own body. Even after he left the dead ones outside the village wall to become food for vultures and the village dogs, they remained alive to him.

Jaffar rushed to the boys and snapped at them to get lost. The boys, laughing, ran into the village, scattering a group of hens and roosters that were scratching the ground near the entrance.

"May God keep your children healthy, Mirza-ali," Bibigol said. "God always shows mercy. Don't worry yourself so much."

"I've seen many ups and downs in my long life," Mirza-ali went on in a dry voice, "but what can I say of these times?" He looked away from Bibigol toward the dead animals. "What can I say? From the day the government made our tribe stop our yearly migration and we settled in this village, day turned to night for us. God doesn't have anything against poor animals—it's we humans who bring about disaster. Animals need feed. At this time of the year, they should be on a green pasture up in the mountains. In this arid land no one can raise a herd. Animals have to migrate from pasture to pasture. Goats and sheep aren't cows that you can tie down in a corner of your yard." He shook the leg of the goat. "This baby goat, her mother died ten days ago and now she's dead. Bibi, there's not enough feed for them. Not enough feed. What can I do? A herd that doesn't have good pasture, doesn't have feed, grows weak. And where there is weakness comes disease."

Mirza-ali let go of the goat's leg and it stood sticking up in the air. He walked over to Bibigol and sat down next to her against the village wall. His grandson sat beside him. He wiped the boy's runny nose with a corner of his shirt. "Why are you barefoot, dear boy?" he said. "That no-good mother of yours couldn't put shoes on you?" Then he turned to Bibigol.

"I was hoping that my animals would be allowed to graze in Mr. Rahbari's field after the wheat harvest, but Bahram Khan, that no-good son of his, put a match to the field right after the harvest and burned the hay to ash." Mirza-ali took his time and talked slowly.

"If my poor animals would have gotten a few mouthfuls of hay, maybe they could have survived. This son of Rahbari, now that his

34

father is ill and can't get out anymore to look after his property, thinks he's in charge. Someone should tell this incompetent young man to wait until the old man is in his grave before he starts galloping around."

"I know, Amu," Bibigol said. She looked anxiously up the road to see whether Baraat's minibus was coming. "But I can't understand why he would do a thing like that."

The old man raised his head to the morning sky. "*Allah blesin gechemsin*—May Allah never forgive him . . . Bibi, I don't understand it either. I was there. There were other shepherds and their flocks, not just from Sangriz but from the nearby villages as well. The combines had just finished—the animals could have grazed for days, maybe even for a week or more. I saw Bahram Khan's jeep and a group of people down by the pump house and thought maybe there was a problem, that maybe someone had fallen in the well. When I got there, I saw Jamal there with Haydar, Mash Najaf, and some other elders. They were trying to reason with Bahram Khan. When I heard what he was up to, I begged him. 'Khan,' I said, 'don't do it. Your father never did that. Neither did your grandfather. They always had respect for tribal people like us. They always let us graze our animals on their fields.' Do you know what he said, Bibi?"

Bibigol shook her head.

"He said, 'I don't care what they did, times have changed. Burning is good for the land.' " Mirza-ali shook his head. "Amir Khan was there, too—that man! I asked him to say something, to help us. But he was as silent as this wall." He turned to touch the wall behind him.

"I know," Bibigol said. "Jamal told me."

"Well, anyway," Mirza-ali went on, "I thought there was only one person who might be able to stop him, and I hurried back to the village as fast as I could on my old legs to ask Sayed Ayoub to get his Holy Book and come with me. We were halfway back when I saw flames and smoke sweeping over the field." Mirza-ali was silent for a moment and then spoke in his tribal tongue. "*Oot doshdi choleh, oot doshdi choleh*—The whole field was on fire. Panicked animals were running every which way, and people were rushing around trying to herd them away from the fire."

35

"We all saw it," Bibigol said. "Remember that night when a high wind coming down the mountain fanned the flames closer and closer to the village? People were watching from their rooftops and praying. For days my nose and throat itched from the smoke. Finally the wind died out, thank God, otherwise the whole village would have been swallowed by the flames. From that day on, my heart has been heavy. May God forgive this faithless young landowner, Rahbari."

Mirza-ali lit his pipe and his face disappeared behind a cloud of smoke.

"I know, I know," he said. "It was no one's fault except that stupid son of Rahbari. He may burn the fields this year as well. They say that the Agriculture Department has advised the farmers to burn, because the ash is good for the land, it's like fertilizer. But I believe that there's something else, Bibi—I think they're trying to make it harder for the nomads to migrate and find pastures for their animals."

Bibigol called out to Jaffar and Marafi, who were standing by the dead animals. "Stop fooling around over there, both of you." Then she turned to Mirza-ali. "I know, Amu. When I was a young girl and not yet married, there were many nomads who would come and camp in the Sangriz fields." She looked off in the distance as if she could see them passing in front of her eyes. "The fields would be covered with hundreds of black tents, and I loved to look out from our rooftop in the evening when there was a fire in front of each tent—hundreds of small fires shimmering all around the village. It was amazing to see. And then at dawn, the roosters would erupt in crowing, the village roosters from the rooftops and the nomads' roosters out in the fields as if they were in competition."

"Those days are gone, Bibi," Mirza-ali said. "And there are fewer and fewer of us. My family was one of those that camped by Sangriz. It's twenty-five years since we were forced to stop our migration. Twenty-five years. I wish I hadn't ended up here. My whole livelihood, what's left of it, has disappeared right in front of my eyes. And now if they burn the fields, the few sheep and lambs that I have are likely to die. If it weren't for my young son Kubaad

36

and his little boy"—he stroked the boy's head gently—"I would gather the few things I have and go to some other cemetery."

Bibigol, who had been totally absorbed in listening to Mirza-ali, caught sight of the minibus coming toward the village, dust rising behind it. "Amu Mirza-ali," she said, standing up, "may Allah take care of you and your children. Don't upset yourself so much. God is merciful."

"Jaffar," she called out again. "Stop whatever you're doing over there. Get Marafi away from the dead animals and send him back home. Let's go. Come on, the minibus is here."

Baraat passed the dead animals and stopped. He stuck his head out the window. "Is anyone going to the city? I'm going to the next village to drop off a barrel of kerosene and then I'll be back."

"Just us," Bibigol said. "We've been waiting since sunrise. May God grant you a long life, Baraat. Try to get back as soon as you can."

"As long as there have been animals on earth," Mirza-ali went on after the minibus was gone, "they've grazed the land and given their dung back to it. This city boy doesn't understand, and I doubt if the people in the Agriculture Department who advised him understand either. They don't understand that animals graze the land and fertilize it at the same time. What can we do? He just doesn't understand."

Baraat wheeled the minibus around and drove off in a fountain of dust. Bibigol sat down again. "That sort of thing," she said, "putting fire to a field, I mean. That sort of thing takes the blessing away from the land."

After a few more puffs, Mirza-ali shook out the ashes from his pipe and put it inside his tobacco pouch and back in his coat pocket. He slowly pushed himself up and, after brushing the dust off the back of his pants, walked back to the dead animals, his grandson following.

"Amu," Jaffar said, "let me help you." He stretched his arm out to grab the sheep's leg.

"May you live a long life, young man," Mirza-ali said, letting go of the leg. They dragged the animals through the graves until they reached a large pit at the end of the cemetery. Standing at the rim, Mirza-ali let go of the little goat and it slid down the slope all the way to the bottom. Then Jaffar pushed down the sheep, and as it tumbled down, dust and a sharp smell rose from the bottom of the pit. A group of dogs feeding on the carcass of a lamb that Mirza-ali had thrown down a couple of days earlier ran out opposite them. The boys who had followed Mirza-ali crooked their necks and looked down into the pit. Mirza-ali held his grandson back from the edge and Marafi, fearful, turned around and limped on, his crippled leg circling out beside him as he made his way.

"Amu?" Jaffar asked, "why don't you give them to Gorgi?"

Mirza-ali took off his hat and wiped his eyes and rubbed his neck and wrinkled forehead and with an old handkerchief. "Not Gorgi," he said. "She wouldn't eat them. Gorgi is a smart dog, she was fed human milk. Don't look at her as old and tired. She's a sheepdog. She's been with the herd for years and has learned to protect them, not to eat them. She's a lot smarter than many people, smarter than that son of a bitch Rahbari boy."

He took his walking stick from his grandchild. "Let's go, my boy." His back looked more curved than ever. "Jaffar, right now I don't have the heart to tell you the story of Gorgi, but if one day I get the chance, I'll tell you how she was saved when she was a puppy by drinking human milk after her mother was killed by a wolf. That's why I called her Gorgi—Wolf—because of what happened to her mother."

Bibigol felt her heart grow heavy seeing Mirza-ali with his dead animals. She didn't know what to do. She felt sorry for the old man and at the same time was upset with herself. "These dead animals are an omen," she said quietly. "I wish I'd never left home in the first place, but going back would be bad luck. May God put everything in its right place. If only Baraat had shown up earlier, I wouldn't have ended up in the middle of this."

Mirza-ali came back and sat down beside her again. He took out his tobacco pouch and refilled his pipe. Jaffar and Marafi were in the graveyard, and a couple of boys were still standing above the pit throwing stones at the snarling dogs that had returned to feed on the animals.

Bibigol, seeing the dust rising in the distance beyond the cemetery, stood up and stared toward the road for a moment and then called out to Jaffar. "Come over here. It looks like Baraat is finally returning." Then she asked Golandam to hurry and get their things together. "May God grant Baraat a long life," she murmured. "It's almost noon and we're still here."

The minibus stopped by the entrance. It took a while for the dust to settle. Baraat, his head and shoulders covered with dust, stepped out from behind the wheel. He opened the passenger-side door and asked the women and children to gather their things up and make room for a few more people. "Whose sack is this?" he said, pushing it aside. "There, Bibi," he said. "Let's go."

As Bibigol was about to get in, Mirza-ali took out his money bag and held out a bill to her. "Bibi, if it's not too much trouble, could you buy me a pipe head and some tobacco? If the money isn't enough and you could add to it, I'll pay you back later. This five-toman note is all I have right now. Have a good trip. I hope you'll find pretty clothes for the bride."

Golandam, who had blushed and lowered her head hearing the word "bride," moved past Bibigol and got into the minibus.

"It's not any trouble at all, Amu." Bibigol smiled at Mirza-ali. "I'll find you a pipe head so beautiful you'll admire it every time you look at it."

Jaffar again pleaded with his mother to let Marafi come with them, saying that poor Marafi had never been to the city and that he would watch out for him himself.

"I've been telling you no since early this morning," Bibigol said. "Words don't stay in your head, do they? How much do you like to torment me? Years ago he went and fell in a well and everything was blamed on your brother. His mother is still cursing us, and now you want to bring this tongue-tied creature to the crowded city. What if he gets lost? Then what am I to do? Get in before I raise my voice."

2

It was past noon when the minibus reached the Koran Gate above Shiraz. Below in the valley, the city seemed to be napping in the heavy air of the summer. The turquoise dome of Shah-eh Cheragh shrine was a beacon to every eye. Baraat, in a gesture of tribute, tapped on the brake, construing the momentary slowing of the car as a kind of bowing, and called out, *A Salaam-o alekom, ay Shah-eh Cheragh*. The passengers, straining to see the dome, loudly repeated the tribute to Imam-zadeh as the minibus passed under the arched gate. Bibigol closed her eyes and held up the palms of her hands. "O Shah-eh Cheragh," she prayed, "please make everyone's good wishes come true, and don't forget my family, Haydar's, and Mirza-ali's as well, and keep his herds healthy." Then she opened her eyes, looked at the gleaming dome, and brought her palms down across her face. All the passengers, including the children, did the same.

A short way into the city, Baraat stopped at the corner of Esfahan Square. Most of the passengers got off quickly and hurried toward the Bazaar Vakeel. Bibigol, as if she had gained energy, urged Golandam and Jaffar on past the crowd of noisy peddlers through the passages of the bazaar toward the shrine of the Imam-zadeh. This was the only way Bibigol knew to get to the shrine. Whenever she traveled to Shiraz, she made sure not to miss a pilgrimage to the shrine. This time, though, it was special because she had more to ask of the Imam-zadeh—for a blessing of the coming marriage between Jamal and Golandam.

In the courtyard of the shrine, she bought two packages of candles, one for Golandam and Jamal and one for herself and Jaffar. As she went on praying under her breath, she lit the candles and put them in the candleholders by the entrance. They took off their shoes, holding them under their arms, and tried to find their way in through the crowd of people going in and out. The shrine was saturated with the smells of burning candles and rose water, the odor of the pilgrims circling the tomb, and the noise of reciters, who, for a small coin, would deliver verses from the Koran and other religious books under the mirrored dome.

Golandam was searching her childhood memories for the day she and her mother and Bibigol had made a pilgrimage to the shrine—how she wished her mother were alive and there with her. She remembered how the mirrored walls and dome had dazzled her eyes and not being able to reach the padlock on the grated enclosure of the tomb amid all the hands stretching out to touch it. That day it had seemed more crowded than now. Her mother had picked her up and held her above the crush of adults so her face was almost against the lock. "Kiss it, my dear," she had said. "Kiss it." Golandam could still feel the cold metal lock against her lips and hear her mother's prayer. "O Imam-zadeh, please help us. Please keep illness away from my little child. I don't want to lose her like my first child. Please help her to grow up, to become a bride, and every year both of us we'll come to you, we'll come to kiss the ground of your tomb."

After circling the enshrined tomb seven times and praying for the bride and groom, Bibigol was feeling dizzy from the heat and the smells. She nudged Golandam and Jaffar forward, and they struggled to find their way out. They passed people pleading to the Imam-zadeh and those selling candles or begging and hurried toward the Bazaar Vakeel. It was crowded and noisy in the bazaar as well, but in the cool shade of the tall arched ceiling, Bibigol went patiently from shop to shop, looking at merchandise and haggling with the shopkeepers.

A few hours later, Bibigol had finished with her shopping and they were resting in the shade of trees in the nearby city park.

She had bought two boxes of sweets, a couple of kilos of raisins, two cones of sugar, and a copper pot. The colorful cloth to make dresses for the bride was in a new suitcase together with a pair of shoes—she had made Golandam try on at least ten pairs before they selected one—and she had wrapped the china pipe head she bought for Mirza-ali in the cloth to shield it from movement of the minibus and put the bag of tobacco in the bottom of the suitcase. She had also taken care of the rings, earrings, and bracelet that she had bought for the bride by tying them in a scarf and putting them in the inside pocket of the suitcase. In her mind she was still calculating the prices and the money she had paid and took out the jewelry and examined it again. Even though Jaffar had done the calculations for her several times, she still was unsettled. Once more she untied a corner of her scarf and took out a few old bills and coins, counting them and doing calculations on her fingers to figure out how much she had spent. Then she frowned. "Maybe those faithless shopkeepers have cheated me," she whispered as she started another round of counting.

Jaffar and Golandam were sitting on a bench not far away, eating halvah and fresh naan *sangak* and talking and laughing. Jaffar had bought a ballpoint pen and a book of the odes of Hafez from a bookstore in the bazaar to give to Marafi. He had bought a copy of the book for himself and was showing it to Golandam. Then he closed the book and asked her if she would like to know her fortune. Telling that Hafez tells the future, he inserted his fingernail at random between the closed pages.

"Don't open it yet," she said excitedly. "Let me make a wish first." She closed her eyes for a few seconds, her lips moving, then looked intently at Jaffar's hands on the book.

He opened the book and read:

> Since we have given our heart and vision to misfortune,
> Let the flood of sadness wash away the house from its foundation.

Jaffar read the ode to the end before looking at Golandam, who was rapt with anticipation. "I can't understand the hidden meaning of the poem," he said. "The poet seems to be talking about some changes coming . . . They say there's always mystery and mysticism in Hafez's poems. Marafi knows the whole book by heart. It's too bad he can't say anything. When we go back home, I'll ask him to write down his interpretation with the pen I bought him." He grew quiet and then asked Golandam whether she thought Marafi would like the book and the pen.

She smiled. "Of course. Why wouldn't he?"

Bibigol, sitting away from them, had fallen asleep. After the pilgrimage in the noisy shrine, going up and down the crowded bazaar bargaining with shopkeepers, and keeping track of Jaffar and Golandam, she had no energy left. She had put her head on the suitcase and closed her eyes to rest for a few minutes, but had fallen asleep.

Jaffar had been wanting to take Golandam and show her the school that he used to go to, but Bibigol wouldn't chance letting the future bride out of her sight in the big, crowded city. He reached for Golandam's hand, and with light steps, they moved away from Bibigol. Golandam was nervous but followed Jaffar even though she didn't know what he was up to. When they were farther away, Golandam turned and looked at Bibigol. Where were they going? she asked Jaffar. And what if Bibi wakes up?

Jaffar promised that they wouldn't go too far, only to the end of the park and back. The park was hot and almost empty, but as they walked along the park's main avenue heading for the gate, more families with children were coming in. The sycamore and maple trees rose high into the sky, their leaves seeming to be seeking one another's shade to survive the summer heat. Jaffar and Golandam, holding hands, passed through the rows of trees and left the park. A few streets away they stopped by the big iron gate in front of the high school. Through the rails, Jaffar pointed toward the large yard with a garden and lemon trees. Golandam put her face between the iron bars, which were warm from the sun, and gazed into the garden, surprised by the number of bright-yellow lemons on the trees.

Jaffar said that he missed his school and, God willing, would go back in the fall. He explained that he had made a big mistake by quitting last spring and it was Haydar who encouraged him to go back, telling him that if he wanted to do anything good for himself and have a good future, it wasn't going to happen by staying in

Sangriz, in the first place, and trying to go without an education, in the second place. And that he was a hundred percent smarter and braver than any city boy.

"Oh," Golandam said, "I'm so happy you listened to Haydar and have decided to go back to school."

He went on to tell her that this time he would know exactly what to do with those city boys if they gave him a hard time. He said they were a bunch of cowards and full of empty talk. He knew how to deal with them now because he'd had the whole summer to think about it. In the fall when the Gypsies came to Sangriz, he would buy one of those small looped chains from Danial, the old Gypsy, and when he was back at school and those rascals heard the chain rattling in his pocket, they would run to find a rat hole to hide in. He would snap one on their fat hips so fast they wouldn't know where it came from and would squeal with pain as if struck by a snake.

"I'm telling you," he said, excitedly, "those sons of bitches won't ever dream of making fun of me again."

He laughed and moved his hand as if snapping a chain. Golandam wasn't paying attention. She had her face between the bars and was still looking into the school yard. "What big lemons," she said. "Why don't they pick them?"

"When school starts, the kids won't leave one of them on the branches. It's funny, those city boys can't even climb a tree. They throw their books at the lemons." He laughed again. "I can go up a tree like a cat. Wait until I come back to school. I'll pick ten of these lemons and give them to Baraat to bring to you. Would you like that?"

"Sure."

Jaffar suggested they stop at a nearby ice cream shop he knew. Although she was elated at the idea, Golandam was worried about getting back to the park, but Jaffar assured her it would take only a few minutes. The shop was big and filled with families and noisy children and cool with the three big ceiling funs turning full speed. A song by the popular pop singer Gogoosh was barely audible above the talk and laughter. As they waited their turn in line, Golandam watched the group of young boys ahead of them who were talking about the movie they had seen and imitating a fist-fight. At the tables girls and boys were talking and eating their ice cream and *falodeh*. They all looked so different from the people she had seen at the shrine or in the bazaar. Everyone seemed to be enjoying themselves and happy to be in a cool place on a warm summer afternoon.

When it was their turn they ordered two cones of saffron ice cream. Golandam took a bite from the top of the cone. She wished that Bibigol were with them, thinking how she would have enjoyed the cool, sweet ice cream.

"Next time we come to the city," she said, "we have to bring Bibi here. I think she will really like this place. I don't know if she's ever been to an ice cream shop."

"Yes, she has," Jaffar said. "Last year when she came to visit me, I showed her my school and brought her here. I don't know what's going on with her on this trip. I think she has too much on her mind, maybe because of all the shopping and expenses. Do you know what her favorite thing was when we came here?"

"No, what?"

"A mix of ice cream and *falodeh*. I'd get her some, but I'm sure it would melt by the time we get back to the park."

Golandam suddenly became aware of the time they had been away. "Let's go before Bibigol wakes up," she said, even though she would have loved to stay longer. "Do you know which way to go?" she asked nervously.

"Of course I do," Jaffar said, reaching for her hand. "I know the city like I've lived here all my life," he said. "I walked all over this area last year." He looked around and suggested they cross the street. Cars, buses, taxis, and motorcycles zipped by. They crossed carefully and started back toward the park. He told Golandam he was happy to show her the school and how the thought of going back to school thrilled him. His plan, he said, was to work all summer. He would go to the fields and help Jamal and Haydar with the harvest and save whatever he made so he would have money to spend when he returned to school in the fall. He would bring gifts to her and Jamal and his mother every time he came back to Sangriz for a visit.

"Did you know that parents in the city give their children pocket money every day to buy sweets at school?"

"Really, is that true?"

"Why should I lie?"

"Are there girls at your school, too?"

"No. They have their own school."

Golandam was surprised to hear that. "In Sangriz," she said, "we went to the same school as the boys, and we even sat together."

"Sure," Jaffar nodded, "because there weren't any women teachers and we had only two men teachers, one for each grade."

"I wish I would have continued and finished sixth grade," Golandam said. "How long do you think you will go to school, Jaffar?"

"Until twelfth grade. I want to get my diploma and become a teacher. I'd like to teach in a school in Shiraz. Maybe Jamal will come to the city and find a job after you get married. Wouldn't that be nice?"

Jaffar squeezed her hand and looked into her black eyes. Golandam blushed. She couldn't even imagine having a husband, let alone living in a big city. Every time she thought about marriage, a cold shiver ran down her spine. She wished that time would slow down and the childhood days would stop going by and she could always be with Jaffar, like today. It was so easy to talk to him and to laugh and tease him. She didn't think about Jamal very often, but when she did think about getting married, she wished she had a better understanding of what it all meant. She didn't know Jamal well and wondered if things would become clearer as time went on. Their families were close and Jamal and Haydar were good friends and worked together. Jamal was close to ten years older than she was, and even though the families would visit and go for picnics at the pump house, and in times of need would take care of each other, she still couldn't say how Jamal would be as a husband or what it would be like to be a wife and be with him for the rest of her life. She thought, though, of the way he always smiled at her and seemed happy she was around.

"We'll bring Mother to the city, too," Jaffar went on. "We'll all live together. There're so many places to go in the city—the cinema, the parks. Do you know what's really nice about being in the city?"

Golandam shook her head.

"It's very nice in the evenings when everybody is out. The streets and the shops are all lit up, full of families who've come to shop or eat or just walk around and enjoy themselves."

"I'd like to see all that, but what I'd really like is to go to the cinema. I can't imagine what it's like."

"Sure. When I am back at school, maybe you can come and stay for a couple of days and we can go see a film, maybe a funny one."

"*Khali khob*. Now let's hurry back before Bibi gets all worried about us."

3

Bibigol was still sitting on the same bench, sound asleep, when they reached the park. Close by a couple of soldiers were sitting on the grass in the shade of a willow tree. They had taken off their boots and were happily playing cards, drinking Pepsi, and eating nuts. Jaffar and Golandam walked past them quietly and went to a nearby water tap to wash up. Jaffar splashed water on her and laughed, and Golandam filled up her hands and went after him. Jaffar, keeping his eyes on her, started to back away, but, laughing, she suddenly jumped closer and tossed the water at him. Jaffar ducked and turned to move away and in doing so tripped over the suitcase next to Bibigol and went down on the ground. Drops of water hit Bibigol, and, startled, she opened her eyes as if awaking from a bad dream. At first she didn't know where she was. When she saw Golandam and Jaffar running after each other and laughing, she stood up and retied her scarf.

"What is the matter with you two?" she said as she walked to the water tap. "Being in the city is getting to you? Dear girl, go pick up our things. We need to get going. Come on hurry—you, too, Jaffar."

Jaffar and Golandam stopped and did what they were told. Bibigol washed up and dried her hands and face with a corner of her scarf. Then she grabbed the bundle and the copper pot. Jaffar took the suitcase and Golandam picked up the rest of their things, and they walked toward the park entrance. The weather had cooled off a bit and a light breeze was starting. The streets seemed even more crowded with people, cars, and vendors.

"Fresh grapes. Hurry, hurry—they're going fast."

"Oranges, oranges. Fresh oranges."

"Move over, watch out. Move over . . . ," a man pushing a cart called out.

Bibigol, alarmed, moved out of the way of a donkey pulling a cart. They could smell onions and lamb and liver kebab being cooked over an open fire. "Delicious kebab," the boys called. "Come and get it . . . Come on . . ."

Bibigol turned to Golandam and Jaffar. "Are you hungry, kids? Why don't we buy some kebab, have a bite and take some home for the rest of the family? I hate to go back with nothing for them, especially Mehrangiz."

After they bought the kebab they hurried through the crowd and went up the street to the cinema where Baraat had asked them to wait.

"Keep your eyes on our things," Bibigol said after they put down their belongings. "I'll be back in a minute."

She walked over to a vendor who, without taking a breath, was calling out, "Sale, sale . . . Beautiful socks on sale . . . hur-ryyyyyyyyyyyy . . . half priced . . . imported socks from *Omrica*."

Bibigol took a pair and started to examine them. "Don't stretch them, ma'am," he said. "Are you interested in buying or not? Imported socks . . . ," he yelled out to some passersby. "For ladies and for gentlemen . . . hurryyyyyyyyy, before they're all gone."

Bibigol picked out two pairs—one for Jamal and one for Golandam—and bought them after bargaining on the price. She went back, opened a corner of the suitcase, and pushed the socks in. Then she sat down and leaned against the big glass wall in front of the cinema.

A sermon was sounding from the loudspeaker of the mosque on the other side of the square. Black-and-green banners flapped above the minarets. In front a crowd had gathered and people were going in and out. Bibigol thought there must be a funeral and prayed for the poor departed soul.

Close to half an hour had passed without any sign of Baraat. It had been a long day and Bibigol was anxious to get back home. She watched the crowded street impatiently and kept her eye on Jaffar and Golandam, who had walked over to look at the movie posters showing cowboys in a gunfight.

Just at the moment that Bibigol saw the minibus in the busy street and got up to get ready, a group of men came out of the mosque shouting, *Allah-o Akbar, Allah-o Akbar* and ran into the street without paying any attention to the traffic. The voice from the loudspeaker sounded more agitated. Traffic stalled and people stopped, trying to find out what was going on.

Bibigol called out in dismay. "Jaffar, Golandam, what are you doing, watching a circus? Come on, let's get away from this place. The minibus is here."

Jaffar went over to his mother and had grabbed the suitcase to carry it to the minibus, which had pulled up to the other side of the street, when the crowd, still shouting, *Allah-o Akbar* and "Death to the Shah," rushed toward the cinema, and a rain of stones began to fall against the plate glass windows, shattering them to pieces. He ran to the minibus, threw in the suitcase, and turned back to get the rest of their things, then he heard his mother scream in pain and saw a piece of brick, turning and tumbling, land beside her.

Jaffar picked up the brick and, confused, stood for a moment facing the crowd before cursing and throwing the brick back at them. His mother collapsed on the sidewalk holding her head, blood seeping between her fingers. Golandam, seeing the blood, let out a cry. A young man tried to help Bibigol get away. There were more shouts of "Burn it—burn it" and "Down with the Shah." People began to smash the doors of the cinema and a Molotov cocktail arced over their heads and landed inside. A second one fell short and smashed on the sidewalk with a loud puff of flames and smoke—a couple of young men tried to kick what was left of the burning cloth inside the cinema. The sounds of sirens and gunshots echoed across the square. "Run, run. The police are here." "The bank," someone else shouted out, and another person shouted, "Hurry, everyone, let's get to the bank on the corner. It's being attacked. Let's burn all the *ghrabi*—Western—symbols."

Jaffar and Golandam were frightened and didn't know what to do or where to go. They hovered over Bibigol, trying to protect her from being trampled by the crowd. "What's happening?" Bibigol moaned. "What's happening? Take me away from here." Finally Baraat reached them. He put his hands under Bibigol, picked her up, and, watching the crowd, waited for a chance to get to the minibus. Smoke and flames had engulfed the cinema. It looked as if the whole block was going to go up in flames. At the sound of approaching police sirens, the crowd started to dissipate and turn back toward the mosque and Baraat started across the street carrying Bibigol and calling to Jaffar and Golandam to get their things and follow him.

They zigzagged through the crowd and reached the minibus. Baraat put Bibigol on the back seat and Jaffar tossed their belongings in back. One of the other passengers brought Bibigol's bloody scarf, which she had picked up from the sidewalk, and took Golandam by the hand to help her get in.

The streets were packed with cars, people, and police with shields and batons who were hitting anyone in their way and arresting anyone they got their hands on. A few stones hit the minibus as Baraat inched his way along. He was muttering to himself, "I told them—I told them there was trouble in town these days and they should be careful." A few blocks away he stopped on a quiet street, got out of the bus, and ran into a bakery, returning with a glass of water for Bibigol, who was sitting bent over and panting with her hand on her head. "I should have known it wasn't my day," she said. "Early in the morning dead animals appeared in my way—I should have known it was a sign."

Jaffar anxiously watched his mother and stroked her shoulders. He was wondering who those people were and why they had attacked the cinema. He had walked past that cinema on his way to school every day the year before and had seen movies there several times. And now these crazy people, shouting *Allah-o Akbar* and "Death to the Shah," had set fire to it. Golandam, still shaking, started to cry quietly.

"Here, Bibi," Baraat said, holding the glass out to her, "have some cold water. It will help you feel better. Come on, have some water."

One of the women took the glass from Baraat and brought it to Bibigol's lips. Bibigol raised her head and, without opening her eyes, took a sip, wetting her lips with her tongue. The woman took

Bibigol's wrist and moved her hand away from her head. Blood had dried on Bibigol's fingers and her gray hair.

"What happened to my scarf?" Bibigol said in a panic after she realized she didn't have it on—she couldn't say if it had slipped off by itself or she had taken it off.

"Here, Bibi, I have it," the woman said, handing it to her.

Bibigol hurriedly ran the scarf through her fingers until she found the corner with the knot where she had tied up the old bill and a few coins that were left after her shopping. She let out a deep sigh and, holding the scarf on her lap, let herself be inspected by the woman, who carefully drew back the strands of hair and examined the wound. A few of the passengers stretched their necks to see. Baraat also took a look. Golandam covered her face with her hands.

The woman announced that the bleeding had stopped and started to wrap the wound with Bibigol's scarf. Bibigol, who was breathing more smoothly now, straightened herself up and took the water glass.

"What happened?" she asked. "Was there a fight?"

"No, Bibi," Baraat said.

"Then a piece of brick fell from the sky and hit my head?"

"There's been trouble in the city the past few days," Baraat said. "If I'd made it there only a few minutes earlier, we would have been out of there before it all happened . . . May God forgive me, there's so much to do. I went to get a few crates of Pepsi-Cola for Sayed Ayoub's store. That's why I was late."

Baraat, seeing that Bibigol was recovering, took a deep breath.

"Where's your brother's bride?" Bibigol asked Jaffar. "Is she all right? Nothing happened to her?"

Golandam took her hands from her face and from the next seat showed herself to Bibigol.

"Did you bring everything?" Bibigol asked.

Both Golandam and Jaffar nodded. The woman helped Bibigol lie down on the back seat. Baraat tried to convince Bibigol to go to a doctor, but she wouldn't agree.

"Dear Baraat," she said, "I don't want to. Just take me out of this hell. Take me back so that if God is planning to take my life, he'll take it in my own house."

Hearing Bibigol's pleading, Jaffar started to cry. He had never seen his mother so broken and hurt. Golandam was quiet and didn't know what to do. Since the time of her mother's death, Bibigol had been like a mother to her. She cried softly and thought about the spring days when she would go with her mother and Bibigol out of the village into the fields to collect wild mint.

Everyone was quiet on the way back to Sangriz. The passengers' heads nodded involuntarily as the minibus went up and down over the bumpy road. Golandam and Jaffar turned constantly to look at Bibigol.

Bibigol's eyes were closed and her eyelids trembled. Droplets of sweat sat on her forehead and behind her earlobes. Heat was nesting under her skin and her head hurt. It was as if a handful of needles had been thrown inside her skull. Her whole body and all her joints were throbbing. She couldn't tell if she was asleep or awake. She wanted to say something but her tongue wouldn't move. She saw her husband in bed, crumpled in pain. She saw Jamal and Haydar in the middle of a dry and hot field, plowing away. She saw a volume of black vultures circling in the Sangriz sky, descending down into the huge pit by the cemetery and tearing at carcasses of sheep and goats that Mirza-ali had thrown down . . . The fire under her skin seemed to be burning her up. The pain started from her navel, struck at her spine, and traveled all the way up to her head, beating at her temples and making her shaky and dizzy. It reminded her of the strange pain, that pain that had to be obeyed, when she was pregnant with Jamal.

Part Three

1

The old village of Sangriz, a blind knot of low adobe houses and narrow, crooked alleys, clung to the hillside, looking as if it had clawed itself to the rocks and bushes to keep from sliding down the side of the mountain whose shadow fell heavily over the village. A kilometer or so away stood the columns of the ruined palace of Persepolis. Below were the vast happy green fields of Dashtak, belonging to the landlord. Above the village lay the arid fields of Sangriz that slowly merged into the bare dark mountain. This uneven ground with its numerous ups and downs belonged to the villagers and was divided into narrow strips, a piece of land as dry and wrinkled as if the creator in his wrath had showered down shapeless dark stones upon it.

When the people of Sangriz—the place of fallen stones—were asked about their village and its origin, they would proudly explain that when Alexander of Macedonia invaded Persia and was on his way to the palace of Persepolis, the soldiers of King Darius III rained down fiery stones over them from the mountaintop in the direction of the village. Another tale was that the attackers were Moslem armies and the stone throwers the soldiers of King Yazdegerd III, the last king of the Sassanians.

From early morning, Haydar and Jamal had been gathering stones on their strips of land. They were working close to each other, humming as they dug into the earth, picked up the stones, and threw them on the piles accumulating here and there. Haydar's imagination would often take wing in the heat of work when there was no conversation between him and Jamal. He would see his father, Mash Safdar, rising up to his full stature in front of him and stomping the ground, telling him not to be stubborn and to take the baby lambs and goats to the field so they could graze on the few blades of grass growing among the stones before they starved to death. Haydar always remembered that image of his father, with his high cheekbones and his teeth yellow from smoking, who knew only the land and how to labor on it. He worked all his life on this strip of land, a land that, with each plowing, produced more stones than anything worth harvesting.

During the Shah's land reform—the White Revolution—the land of Sangriz had been divided, with one-half going to the landlord and the other half split among the peasants. A year before the land reform took effect, Mr. Rahbari, the landlord, decided to dig an artesian well on the best land on the plain of Dashtak. Mash Safdar, when he heard about it, went to the village square, where people had gathered and were talking about the well. "What wise man would dig a well in a field that can be irrigated with the God-given water of the river?" he wanted to know. "Why would he add unnecessary expense for himself?"

It didn't take long before the villagers found out the real purpose of digging the well and constructing the pump house. With this trick Mr. Rahbari, like other landlords throughout the country, changed the status of the best land of Sangriz so that it could be excluded from the land reform, since the land now had its own water and didn't need to be irrigated by the common water from the river. That same year Mr. Rahbari gave a few hundred acres of good land to Amir Khan, his representative in the village, to gain his support in the upcoming land reform. The small pump house that Amir Khan constructed on the land brought him wealth and new pride. The arid Sangriz plain was divided among the peasants, but whether they owned it or not, the outcome was the same—it produced very little.

Haydar remembered it well. He was a boy of fourteen, and Golandam, his little sister, was barely walking when his father and a few of the peasants made repeated trips to the Agriculture Department in Shiraz to represent their case to the government that they

58

had been cheated and their land taken from them unlawfully. These trips were not only fruitless but led to Mash Safdar's arrest and his ending up behind bars for fourteen months. He returned from jail a middle-aged man, his hair and beard turned white. For one year he managed to stand being bad-mouthed by people like Amir Khan, who had taken sides with Mr. Rahbari. Then he fell ill, no longer able to leave his house, let alone go to the fields, before giving back his life to the creator.

Haydar straightened up. His eyes twitched. In the distance the shape of Dashtak plain shifted in the haze of a cloudless sky as if the souls of the past generations who had worked the land were wading through the shimmering heat to rise to the light of the upper world. He thought about his father and the days and nights he had helped him irrigate the wheat fields. One night in particular had stuck in his memory. It was when they were just starting to have problems with Mr. Rahbari. A cool breeze was coming down the mountain and he remembered how he had to put his hands in his armpits to keep warm. His father was telling him about the land and cultivation with great passion, as if he could feel the wheat growing and see the grains filling out. He had picked up a handful of soil and held it out to him. All their lives were attached to that dark soil, his father had said, holding it under the low lantern light next to them, and if they were separated from it they would die. All they knew was how to work the land—nothing else. Then he let the soil pour out through his callused fingers. That's what Mr. Rahbari is aiming to do with us, he went on, separate us from our livelihood. But I'm not going to stand aside and let it happen. I'm going to fight it. I may be alone and I may not succeed, but it's the right thing to do. I want you to remember, it's the right thing to do. I'll fight it and some God-fearing deputy at the Agriculture Department may listen to me. Then he talked about Mirza-ali and how the poor man had been forced to abandon his tribal life and settle in the village, where he felt strange and out of place. It wasn't Mirza-ali's fault, his father believed. It was because he didn't know about village life. He wasn't a farmer, he was a herdsman and knew all about sheep, goats, and horses. His roots were in his tribe and his livelihood the herd that he needed to take from pasture to pasture. If a man lives with virtue in a place where he has roots, Haydar remembered his father emphasizing, and if he's good to people, then when he's sick, everyone will ask about him, and when he dies, everyone will mourn him.

Haydar knew how good-natured his father was and how he loved life. He knew that he didn't die of the pain of going to jail or the sarcasm of the people who talked behind his back, some who didn't have the guts to stand up to the landlord and stop him from rubbing them out of their land. It was being cut off from his soil, from his land, unjustly. That was the pain that won out over the old man.

After that, many of the peasants working on the lands of Sangriz gave up farming and went to Shiraz as laborers. But Haydar and Jamal and a few other stubborn ones would throw some seeds of rye or wheat over their fields, look up at the sky all winter in anticipation of a few drops of rain, and then in the height of summer try to harvest whatever strands of grain had emerged among the stones. Often the harvest wouldn't amount to the winter feed for a few goats or a donkey or horse.

A few years later, Haydar and Jamal were hired to work on the landlord's Dashtak fields. Haydar loved the land and hoped that someday he would be able to get back his share that he thought Mr. Rahbari had taken from his father by using his connections and cheating the law. Jamal, however, was satisfied to work for Mr. Rahbari as a laborer. "This way," he would say, "the headache of running a farm is much less and a person doesn't have to worry about water, seeds, or fertilizer or the end-of-year harvest. He'll get a wage no matter what and can go on with his life."

Haydar would disagree. "The landlords are a bunch of hyenas," he would say. "Others do the laboring, they do the enjoying." He especially didn't trust Bahram Khan, the son of the landlord. It was late in the season and the young khan was postponing renting a tractor to plow the fields. The Dashtak fields should have been ready to sow, and Haydar thought for sure Bahram Khan was up to something.

"What could he be up to?" Jamal replied, smiling. "He likes to act like a khan, like a landlord, since his old father fell ill. He wants to pretend that he knows all about farming, plowing, sowing, and harvesting—whatever it is. Have you forgotten how much trouble he caused us during the last harvest? The way he burned the field after the harvest and didn't let the village animals on it? Poor Mirza-ali—I felt sorry for him the way he begged Bahram Khan not to burn the field."

Haydar had been there the day that Bahram Khan, just after his father became ill, had come to the farm with several city men he had never seen before. They had looked around, studied the area, and left. Haydar guessed there was some sort of relation between the burning of the wheat field after the last harvest, the postponing of this year's plowing, and the coming of the strangers. But he couldn't figure out what it was, and this bothered him even more.

Past midday Haydar combined all the small piles of stones he had collected into one big pile. He sat in the shade of the rocks to drink some water from the water jar. Jamal stopped working and called over to him. "Say, Haydar, look up the mountain road. Who do you think is coming this way?"

Shading his eyes, Haydar stood up and gazed at a shadow appearing at the far edge of the fields. "How should I know?" he said, grumbling. "Maybe it's the ghost of my father running from his grave to come and find out what they've done with his land."

He sat down on the rock pile again, took off his hat, and wiped the sweat from his forehead with his index finger, the droplets vanishing quickly as they touched the hot, thirsty ground. He grabbed the water jar again and drank eagerly, threads of water running from the corners of his mouth and down his neck.

Jamal, not taking his eyes off the person on the road, walked over to Haydar. "Who could that be in this heat and on foot?"

Haydar passed the water jar to Jamal, and they both watched the man stop in the lower part of Mash Nasrolah's field and stand there for a short time before turning and coming toward them. They heard him say something and thought he was calling out to them, but as he got closer, they realized he was singing and could make out the figure of a broad-shouldered young man in a military uniform.

"Why are you staring?" asked the young man, who was drenched in sweat. "It's me, Goodarz."

"Goodarz of Mash Nasrolah?" asked Jamal, surprised.

"Yes, who else?"

"I saw you stopping by your field," said Haydar, "but couldn't imagine who it was, let alone recognize you."

They hugged and kissed each other on the cheek. Haydar stepped back and joyfully looked the young man up and down. "When they took you away for your military service, you were only a kid. Now look at you. May God bless you, you've grown so big and strong. It must be the military's free food."

"Free and plenty," Goodarz said, laughing. "Haydar, my guess is that you haven't found the treasure you've been after all these years."

"Why do you say that?"

"If you had, you wouldn't still be trying to farm this accursed land that even a horse can't walk over."

They all laughed.

"You're right, young man," Haydar said, patting him on the shoulder. "It's because God hasn't cooperated so far, but I'm more stubborn than he. I'm not giving up so easily. Eventually I'll find it."

"How many days' leave do you have?" Jamal asked as he held out the water jar to Goodarz.

"Until the end of my life, God willing," said Goodarz and laughed.

"You mean you deserted?"

Goodarz drank some water, wiped his mouth with the back of his hand, and sat down on a rock.

"Well, kind of," he said.

"I always knew they wouldn't be able to keep you for long," Haydar said, smiling.

"They did long enough," Goodarz said. Then he asked if they had heard about the problems in the country.

Both Jamal and Haydar nodded.

"There are riots in the capital and the other big cities," Goodarz said. "It may not be long before things get completely out of hand. The military is falling apart already. Officers aren't showing up at their posts. Most of the barracks in Tabriz, where I was stationed, have emptied out and the soldiers have gone home. I left with four other soldiers a week ago, and we had lots of problems on the road. The buses aren't running and the roads are getting dangerous. The others were from Khozestan—I hope they make it back home." He fixed his eyes on Haydar and Jamal. "In the capital things are even worse. Protesters have set fire to banks and cinemas and some government offices. There's a curfew in many places."

Jamal was surprised. "We haven't heard all that. Why is this happening? Why are people suddenly so unhappy about the government and angry at the Shah?"

"Well, they say it's all to do with a mullah in the city of Najaf in Iraq—Ayatollah Khomeini, who was forced out of the country by the Shah years ago. Now he's coming back and is really mad." He laughed.

"Our own Shiraz went through some rioting a month or so ago," Haydar said, "but it quieted down fast. Just yesterday, though, Baraat said it looked like it was picking up again. People were demonstrating and shouting, *Marg bar Shah*—Death to the Shah."

"Well, who knows what will happen," Goodarz said. He stood up and walked away a few steps before turning around. "I ought to come and clean the little field of mine and sow some wheat or something this fall."

Inshallah, said Haydar and Jamal at the same time. Then they watched as Goodarz walked down the hill heading for Sangriz.

It was close to sunset when Jamal and Haydar saw a cyclone of dust rise by the mountain road and recognized Bahram Khan's blue jeep turning in the direction of the pump house. They stopped picking up rocks and headed for the pump house. A group of women and young girls had gathered around the small pool that the water was pumped into on its way to the fields.

When they got there, Bahram Khan was walking leisurely by the little pool, a cigarette between his fingers. The women and young girls, Golandam among them, were washing their dishes.

Jamal and Haydar greeted Bahram Khan and asked about his father, Mr. Rahbari, who had been homebound for more than a year and unable to come to the farm. Jamal spread a kilim next to

63

the pool under the shade of a willow tree, and Bahram Khan lay his long body down.

Haydar lit the small kerosene stove and went to the pool to fill up the kettle to make tea. He noticed that the women and girls, unlike on other days, weren't chatting and seemed to be in a hurry to fill up their jars and pots and leave, but he didn't pay it much attention, thinking that they were just shy having a strange city man walk in the midst of their activity of washing and talking. His thoughts went back to Bahram Khan. How is it, he wondered, that today he doesn't have his friends and a bottle of arak with him?

Bahram Khan was calmer and quieter than usual, although he seemed preoccupied and kept looking toward Golandam and the women at the pool. Haydar and Jamal, on the other hand, were talkative. They inquired further about the health of his father and expressed their concern about postponing plowing the fields and getting them ready for the fall cultivation. They were anxious to know about the surveyors who had come by a few days earlier, checking things out and doing some measuring around the pump house, but Bahram Khan wasn't willing to say much.

"In the past few days," Jamal said, "the pump has been giving us problems. It doesn't start easily. The motor is old and may be on its last legs. A newer and stronger one would make things much easier and would draw more water."

"This morning it gave us a hell of a time," Haydar said. He rubbed his arm and shoulder, which were still sore from turning the motor and glanced at Bahram Khan, who seemed to be agitated.

Bahram Khan propped himself up on his elbow and took a sip of his tea. "This is the last watering the sugar beet field needs. If you manage it well, we should be done in, say, fifteen or twenty days at the most. Then we'll see." When he talked, his Adam's apple moved up and down and his voice sounded as if he had water in his throat.

"It's going to take longer than that," Jamal said. "At least a month or so. And in the meantime we should have the upper fields ready for the winter wheat."

"We're not cultivating any winter wheat this year." Bahram Khan drank the last of his tea. "When the watering of the sugar beets is finished, the pump will be put to sleep."

"Put to sleep?" Haydar asked, stunned. "What do you mean?"

"We are not going to draw water anymore. That's what it means."

"But why?" Haydar asked. "For what reason?"

"We're not seeding the field this year. For now, you guys can think about hiring a few helping hands so that we can start harvesting the sugar beets as soon as possible. I want the first truck of beets that enters the sugar factory to be ours." He lit another cigarette and looked at the girls and the women, who had gathered their dishes and balanced pots of water on their heads and were walking away. "It doesn't make any sense," Haydar said, raising his voice, "I don't understand. We're not going to seed the field this season?"

"Khan," Jamal said, "what are you going to cultivate, then?" He seemed disappointed as well.

Bahram Khan, who never liked to say much, let alone go into detail, answered without looking at them. "At this time, nothing. We have a lot to do this fall. After the sugar beet harvest is over, I plan to start the construction of a brick factory on the land."

Jamal and Haydar looked at each other, not believing what they were hearing.

"Then the visit of the surveyors was for that reason," Haydar said. "I'd guessed they were up to nothing good."

Haydar's thoughts went to the village of Khaksar, a village halfway between Sangriz and Shiraz. He could picture the earth-digging machines, bulldozers, and dump trucks moving the dirt around and the Afghan workers in baggy pants who labored there. Trying to keep calm, he turned to Bahram Khan. "God won't forgive those who take the fertile soil and burn it in a kiln to make bricks." There was an insistent note in his voice.

"Many people from Sangriz," Jamal said, "earn their daily bread by working on this land. What would they do?" He gestured toward Haydar. "And what would we do? Making bricks isn't our occupation. We're farmers. Farmers, sir, not brick makers."

"There will be work for everyone," Bahram Khan said calmly before asking for another cup of tea. "With better pay. And when the brick factory gets going, we'll pave the road, God willing, and ask the government to help with running water and electricity for the village. We'll give workers free bricks to build new houses so they can get out of those small mud huts full of bugs."

Bahram Khan went on with his musings while Jamal and Haydar, puzzled, looked at each other and then at him. Haydar started to speak quietly, as if he were trying to stop a small child from doing something dangerous. "Sir, have you traveled to the village of Khaksar recently? Have you seen the brick factories there? Khaksar has been turned to hell. Its fertile fields are lost—gone. A brick factory would be the death of farming." He waved his hand toward the Dashtak plain, where the ruined columns of Persepolis far beyond the fields were barely visible in the afternoon haze. "Sir, how will your heart accept running bulldozers over this beautiful, happy field?" He moved closer and faced Bahram Khan. "Does your father know what you're up to?"

Bahram Khan's patience was running out. "That's no business of yours," he said, standing up.

Jamal and Haydar stood up as well. Jamal tried to indicate to Haydar that he should calm down and not say anything more, but Haydar wasn't paying any attention. "Of course it's my business," he responded. "I'll go to your father early tomorrow morning to see if he has any idea what you're trying to do here."

"What's it to you, you stupid villager," Bahram Khan yelled, "the land is ours and you dare tell us what to do with it?" He raised his hand but then, seeing Haydar's burning eyes gazing at him, lowered it and quickly stepped away.

Haydar ran for his shovel. "You're a godless creature," he shouted. "I'll show you who the land belongs to. Your father cheated and took it away from us and now you think you can keep us off it, too. You think you can push us around like the old landlords, that you can tie the peasants up and whip them the way your shameless father did! Haydar won't stand even God's hand raised to him. How dare you. I'll show you." Images of long ago, when he was a little boy, crowded his mind. He could see the peasants pleading as Mr. Rahbari ordered them to take their shoes off and told Amir Khan, his representative, to put their feet through the leather strap and pull it tight around their ankles. It was in the Rahbari summerhouse in the village, in the middle of the yard, beside the small pool where Mr. Rahbari used to wash up and say his daily prayer to Allah. Haydar watched everything through the crack in the gate. Amir Khan had picked up one of the twigs floating on the top of the pool. Whoosh . . . whoosh . . . whoosh . . . the twigs cut the air and the peasants whimpered. "Agha, forgive us. Agha, we made a mistake. We won't take from the field anymore . . . we'll keep our animals away from the fields."

Haydar, raising the shovel, shouted again. "I'll show you, you son of a bitch. You think you are like your no-good father and can push us around."

Bahram Khan turned to run for his jeep, but stumbled and fell to the ground.

"No, Haydar, no," cried Jamal, grabbing Haydar by the arm.

Bahram Khan looked up at the shovel hovering above him and managed to crawl out from under Jamal's and Haydar's feet and start for the jeep. Haydar was right at his heels, but Bahram Khan again stumbled and fell as Haydar's shovel came down sharply, splitting the air and missing his head by only an inch.

2

As the sun moved lower, the patches of clouds above the mountain peak went from orange-yellow to red and drifted apart and the shadow of the mountain grew darker as it crawled toward the village. The wind, seeming to carry the warning of a harsh autumn, was beginning to bellow against the village wall. To the "Hey, hey" and whistling of the shepherds, herds of goats, sheep, and cows entered the square, separated into small groups, and headed into different alleys to go home. Dust and the smell of wool and dung hung in the air, making it difficult to breathe.

Sangriz had put the hot summer behind it. Those farmers who had sown the arid fields had harvested the sparse, short stems of wheat and stored them away for winter feed. And now, with not much to do, they sat in the village square in the lazy autumn sun chatting and napping, trying to regain their energy and awaiting the arrival of the Gypsies, who would come and put up their black tents outside the village by the graveyard as they had done as long as anyone could remember. The villagers would have their tools and plows shined and repaired so they could take them back to the fields again and continue their ancestral routine.

A group of young men were gathered around Goodarz, who had just arrived back home that afternoon after leaving his soldier's duties in the northern part of the country. They hadn't seen him for more than a year and were hungry to hear about his time in the military. He told them about the troubles and uprisings he had seen in the cities and soon launched enthusiastically into his stories. He rubbed his hand over his short hair and in a mixed half-city, half-village way of speaking talked about places the villagers may have heard of but had never been to, the excitement in their eyes egging him on.

"What a night we went through," Goodarz was saying. "I wouldn't wish it on even a desert wolf. We were five soldiers and a captain from Khorasan—what a nice man he was. Two of the soldiers were Kurds and one was from Kerman. The snow was up to our knees and the wind blew so cold in those mountains of Azerbaijan and Kurdistan that the stones would shatter. We'd been sent to watch a remote border area because of some guerrilla activity. We had to keep walking. There was no way to sit or stand still for long unless you wanted to freeze to death. As God is my witness, before the sun was up, I saw my own death in front of my eyes at least ten times. I thought I'd never see Sangriz again and no one would know what happened to me. In the morning when we went to the armored car and opened the door, the captain sat frozen behind the wheel, as hard as a rock."

A little distance away from Goodarz and his listeners, a group of boys sat around Mirza-ali. Among them was Jaffar, who had returned from the city on Baraat's minibus that afternoon. He had gone back to school at the beginning of the fall and put a month behind him with no problem and now was home for a couple of days on school holiday. Mirza-ali, breathing heavily, coughed and wiped his lips with an old handkerchief and then, after taking a strong puff on his pipe, asked, "Where was I?"

"At the point when a wolf attacked," one of the boys said excitedly.

"Ah, yes. But not one wolf, a pack of them." The boys gathered closer. "Wolves always attack in packs . . . sometimes packs of three, sometimes packs of seven. Our camp was by Black Mountain, about a day's walk from here." He pointed to the mountain in back of the village. "Black Mountain has many wolves and I've seen many of them there with my own eyes. They're beautiful and brave animals, but vicious. Anyway, one late afternoon just as the sun was going down, I was driving the herds and was only a stone's throw away from where we'd set up our tents when they attacked, three of them, wounding a sheep, two goats, and several lambs. We had a black dog—what a great dog she was. I've had a few dogs in my life, but none as courageous as she. It was a big loss." Mirza-ali was quiet for a moment and sucked on his pipe. "That dog was the mother of Gorgi." The old dog lying beside him, hearing her name, raised her head, perked up her ears and looked at Mirza-ali, and then put her muzzle down on her paws and closed her eyes.

"That day the black dog attacked the wolves and wounded one of them, but she was badly injured herself and died soon after. The bite of the wolf is deadly. There's no remedy for it."

Jaffar was listening to Mirza-ali, but his eyes were on the village entrance. He was watching for the return of Golandam, who had gone to the pump house to fetch water with a group of women, and was anxious to see her after being away for almost a month. When he saw the group of women and girls coming with jars and pots on their heads, Golandam was in front. With each step, some water ran over the rim of the pot and splashed down her shoulders and chest. There was a sense of agitation among the women, the way they were hurrying, almost running, as if they had come across a wild animal at the pump house.

Goodarz saw the girls approaching and stopped talking, his eyes following Golandam. In the past few months, she had grown taller and her face was fuller, giving her the look of a beautiful young woman ready to be married. Goodarz was about to say something when Sarferaaz, Amir Khan's son, noticed and broke the silence. "You're too late, my friend," he said. "She's going to be warming up Jamal's bed any day now."

Goodarz asked who she was. "Golandam," someone said. "Haydar's sister."

"Oh," he murmured, a sad feeling coming over him. "She was only a little girl when I left for my military duty."

"I know," replied Sarferaaz, a bitter note in his voice. "We've been watching her grow up in front of our eyes." It hadn't been long since Haydar's family had refused the offer of marriage that his father had made on his behalf, further souring the relations between the two families.

Jaffar was about to get up and follow Golandam home, but Mirza-ali started to talk about how it happened that Gorgi was fed human milk. Jaffar remembered the summer day he had helped Mirza-ali drag his dead animals to the pit outside the village and how he had said that someday he would tell him the story of Gorgi. So he thought he should wait a bit longer and listen.

Mirza-ali went on, saying that Gorgi was only a month-old puppy when her mother was wounded by the wolves and died and that Gorgi meant "wolf" and he had given her the name because of the incident—a familiar story that he had told the boys often, although they were always ready to hear it again. She didn't drink goat's or sheep's milk, only human milk. He had been able to get some milk every couple of days from a relative who had given birth a few months earlier. Of course, Mirza-ali explained to the boys, who looked at him with astonishment, tribal people sometimes, if they had the chance, would feed a bit of human milk to a new puppy, believing that it would make the animal grow up to be smart, but in Gorgi's case it was different. She was smarter than any dog, because she had been fed only human milk.

As soon as Mirza-ali finished the story, Jaffar decided to go home to get a few of the lemons he had picked from the school yard trees to give to Golandam, but he changed his mind at the last minute and started for Haydar's house. Marafi threw his satchel over his shoulder and limped after him. At Haydar's, Jaffar waited at the gate for a second. As he pushed it open and stepped into the dark passage leading to the yard, he heard Golandam's voice and stopped in his tracks.

"It was Bahram Khan." Golandam was talking to her sister-in-law, Mehrangiz. "He came to the pump house in his jeep . . . We hurried to finish washing our dishes . . . and . . ." She hesitated.

"Well go on," snapped Mehrangiz. "What happened?"

"He came to the pool and asked for a drink of water." She sniffled. "I filled up a bowl and, as I was giving it to him, he asked who I was. I told him I was Haydar's sister. He drank the water and when I reached for the bowl, he held it and wouldn't let go."

Jaffar stepped closer to hear better without letting himself be seen.

"I was scared. I couldn't move and he . . . he just held on to the bowl and stared at me. I didn't know what to do. Then he saw Haydar and Jamal coming and let go. By the time we had washed our dishes and filled up our jars and were about to leave, he was sitting under the tree, drinking tea and talking to Haydar and Jamal. We hadn't gone very far when we heard them shouting at each other—I don't know what about, maybe it was because of me."

"Were they fighting?" Mehrangiz asked nervously.

"I think so. We heard them . . ."

Mehrangiz stood up suddenly and rushed out of the yard. She was startled to see someone standing by the gate. Then she realized it was Jaffar. "When did you get here?" she burst out. "Run to the pump house to see what's happened to Haydar and Jamal."

Jaffar wanted to go to Golandam but turned around and ran down the alley to go home and grab a stick. Bibigol was in the yard releasing a mousetrap to get rid of a dead mouse and talking to herself. "No matter how much I poison or trap these filthy creatures, it doesn't make any difference. They keep coming out of their holes." During the past few days she had been cleaning the house in preparation for Jamal's wedding. Although she had recovered from the head injury she had received on her trip to the city, she still had bad headaches once in a while, especially if she did too much housework. She felt guilty that her son's wedding had been postponed because of her and was struggling to get well so the wedding could proceed.

She saw Jaffar rush in and snatch a stick from the corner of the yard.

"What's going on?" she asked. "What are you doing with that stick?"

"Nothing," Jaffar said. "I'm going to the pump house. I'll be back soon."

Bibigol, alarmed, dropped the mousetrap and ran to the alley and watched Jaffar disappear around the bend. She had a feeling something was wrong and decided to follow him. The first person she came to, she grabbed his shoulder. "What's happening?" she demanded. "What's happening?"

"Da, da, da . . . la, la, la" was the only reply. Realizing it was Marafi, she let go and hurried on toward the square.

A few people were still listening to Goodarz when they saw a woman run past them and go out of the village. A few minutes later footsteps echoed again and someone, stick in hand, came

73

rushing from the upper alley after her. In the evening twilight, no one could realize that the woman was Mehrangiz and the person following her was Jaffar.

"Whoever he was," someone said, "the way he was going after her didn't look good. We have to stop him."

Jaffar clenched the stick between his fingers and jumped over rocks and ditches on the narrow shortcut to the pump house. He could still hear Golandam's whimpering as she told Mehrangiz what had happened. He wondered what Bahram Khan had done that caused Haydar and Jamal to fight with him. He switched the stick from one hand to the other. "I'll show you, you son of a bitch," he repeated. "I'll hit you so hard that you'll run all the way to your mom in the city and never come back to Sangriz again. You've forgotten how stupid you were those summer days you came to the village and how you would beg me to show you things?"

He remembered one summer when he was six or seven years old and Bahram Khan was ten or twelve. Bahram Khan was afraid of animals—horses, donkeys, dogs—and loved to throw stones at them. One day they took Haydar's white donkey out to the fields—this was before he sold his donkey to the Gypsies and bought a motorcycle—and Bahram Khan had begged him to help him ride. But the donkey had thrown him off and he'd cried and run to his mother at their summerhouse.

"Now, you come here and cause problems for Golandam," Jaffar said out loud. "I'll show you, you son of a bitch." Then he saw Mehrangiz ahead, her skirt flapping in the air as she rushed toward the pump house, and he felt embarrassed, thinking that she may have heard him. He passed by her and had gone only a little distance when the headlights of a car by the pump house cut the darkness. Jaffar ran to the main road and stood in the middle, holding the stick tightly with both hands. "Come on, you son of a bitch, come on," he said. Blood was rushing to his head and he could hear his heart pumping against his ears. He wasn't sure what he was doing, but he wanted to bring the stick down on Bahram Khan's head. The headlights bobbed up and down, and as the jeep came closer Jaffar swung the stick and aimed at the windshield. Suddenly there was the sound of a horn blowing and glass shattering. Mehrangiz's

74

scream echoed into the night. But Jaffar didn't hear a thing, not the continuous blowing of the horn and not Bahram Khan yelling, "Get the hell off the road, you stupid villager" as he wheeled the jeep past him. Nor did he hear Mehrangiz's screams. He only felt a sharp pain in his wrists as the stick snapped in half and the jeep sped away with only one headlight.

Terrified and covered by the rising dust, Jaffar started to cough and spit, then rubbed his wrists and went to Mehrangiz, who stood frozen on the other side of the road.

"Have you gone out of your mind to stand in the middle of the road?" Mehrangiz said. "If he'd run you over, what could we have done? Don't you know what these people are capable of? . . . God knows what he could have done to Haydar and Jamal."

Mehrangiz hurried up the road again. The thought that something might have happened to Haydar frightened her. She wasn't at all happy with herself. In the past few days when her husband came home for the midday meal, she had watched him eat a piece of naan *o most* in silence and return to the fields. She knew something was wrong but hadn't tried to find out what was bothering him. She'd considered the possibility that he might at last have found the treasure he'd been after but dismissed the idea. "I doubt it," she'd told herself. "We're not that lucky." Then she had thought maybe he was upset at the way people talked and laughed behind his back, calling him Haydar Ganji—Haydar the treasure hunter—and said his mind had been afflicted by the spirits of the ancient hills.

No word passed between Haydar and Jamal as they walked toward Sangriz with Abrash, the horse, following behind. They were like shadows on the road, moving slowly, their minds preoccupied with what had happened at the pump house. If Jamal hadn't put himself between Haydar and Bahram Khan, the shovel surely would have split Bahram Khan's head in half, but before Haydar could try again, Bahram Khan had managed to get to his jeep. "I'll show you," he had shouted as he drove away. "You raise your shovel to me—I'll show you, you stupid man."

They were halfway home when they ran into Mehrangiz and Jaffar on the road to the pump house.

"What are you doing wandering around under the darkness of night?" Haydar asked Mehrangiz.

She was about to answer when Jamal recognized Jaffar in the darkness. "When did you get back?" he said, going over to him. "Have you run away from school again?" Before Jaffar could open his mouth, Jamal grabbed the end of the broken stick, causing Jaffar to lose his balance and fall. "What are you doing carrying a stick? You think you're a man now?"

"Leave him alone," Mehrangiz pleaded, grabbing Jamal by the arm. "Is this what he deserves for coming out to see what could have happened to you? Why take your anger out on him?"

Jaffar got up and left for the village ahead of them. Mehrangiz, seeing that Haydar and Jamal were okay, said nothing more. Here, in the dark with the fields all around them, wasn't the place to ask her husband any questions. She would wait until they were under the roof of their house to find out what had happened. For now she kept quiet as they walked shoulder to shoulder toward home.

In the village people had gathered outside when they heard the horn of the jeep blowing continuously as it stopped by the graveyard. Amir Khan and his son, Sarferaaz, had run over to the jeep. Bahram Khan talked to them for a few minutes, telling them what had happened, without getting out of the car.

Amir Khan addressed the curious people gathered around him after the jeep drove away: "Now Haydar Ganji has gone too far." He went on in his old slow way of talking. "Every day he's up to something. For sure he must have lost his head in the hills to raise his shovel over the landlord and try to split young Rahbari's head. Someone needs to remind him that he's a peasant who doesn't own even the shirt on his back. He needs to be reminded of what happened to his own father after he made trouble for the landlord."

The people of Sangriz knew about Amir Khan, his son, Sarferaaz, and his lackeys. They were aware of Amir Khan's past dealings with the senior Rahbari. They also knew of the trips that Bahram Khan and his friends took to Amir Khan's farm and orchard. They even knew that Bahram Khan brought prostitutes there and that they drank arak and smoked opium. Kubaad, Mirza-ali's son, swore

76

that one day he had his herds grazing close to the orchard and had seen all of them drinking and smoking opium, Amir Khan and Sarferaaz included.

On the bridge over the small canal just outside the village, Haydar, Jamal, and Mehrangiz ran into Bibigol and Golandam, and the other villagers, including Goodarz, Kubaad, and Marafi, who had come out when they thought there was trouble. They all quietly headed back to the village, walking past the square where Amir Khan was still speaking to the group gathered around him.

Amir Khan stopped talking as they passed, his eyes following them until they turned into the upper alley and the light of their lantern vanished.

3

The silver bowl of the moon was rising in a corner of the San-griz sky, drizzling a bluish light over the mountains and fields. The wind had died down and the smell of straw fires from the yards was in the air. Once in a while the cry of a child, the *bahahahahahah* of a sheep, the barking of a dog, or the yowling of jackals beyond the village broke the silence. Here and there on the flat rooftops of the houses, mosquito nets cast milky shadows against the dark mountain. In the distance, the stone columns of Persepolis were slowly becoming visible in the moonlight.

Most of the villagers, tired from their daily work, had eaten their supper—a piece of bread and yogurt or a bowl of watery soup—and drunk a cup of strong tea and were getting ready to stretch out in anticipation of a good night's sleep when the voice of a dervish rose above the rooftops.

"O Imam Ali," the dervish sang, "king of righteousness . . . beloved of the universe . . . bless us all . . . bless the people of Sangriz . . ."

Everyone knew that the voice came from the roof of Sayed Ayoub's house. Whenever a religious man like the dervish, an amulet writer, or a stranger happened to come to Sangriz, Sayed Ayoub's door was open to them. He believed that, as a descendant of the Prophet Mohammad, it was his duty to be kind to strangers. Every day he sat behind the counter of his small shop in the village square, his head covered by a green cotton hat and his white beard reddened by henna. The middle of his high forehead was slightly callused—a badge of devotion from putting his head down on the praying *moher* five times a day. With sharp eyes he watched the activity in the square from sunrise to sunset, praying under his breath and helping his customers who came in to buy beans and rice, black pepper and turmeric, hard candies, and bottles of Pepsi-Cola and Canada Dry. When school was in session, he would sell notebooks, pens, and pencils to the students.

As the dervish sang, the village children started toward Sayed Ayoub's house. Each household, depending on their devotion and situation, would send a coin, a cup of sugar, or a bowl of wheat or barley to the dervish.

Bibigol was sitting on the roof of their house with Jamal, Jaffar, and Marafi, who had been hanging around Jaffar since he arrived that afternoon. She was listening to the dervish and drinking a cup of tea. She opened the wing of her scarf and took out a coin that she gave to Jaffar to take to the dervish so he could pray for the family. She nodded toward Marafi. "Many years ago on summer nights, Marafi's father, God rest his soul, would recite from the *Shahnameh*, the book that has been in their family for generations. You wouldn't believe it. He had such a beautiful and powerful voice and recited the stories so passionately that you felt the sorrows of the kings and heroes. It always brought tears to my eyes. Wealthy people from nearby villages would invite him to go and recite for them."

Marafi, absorbed in the dervish's singing, looked toward Bibigol, his eyes sparkling as if he were hearing his father's voice and remembering the days when he was a boy and his father taught him how to recite. He loved the old book and knew all the epics written by the great poet Ferdowsi centuries ago.

Jamal was stretched out half asleep listening to the dervish, but his heart was heavy with the events of the day. What Haydar had done was not a small thing and he was worried about the outcome. They'd never confronted the landlord like that, although at times they had thought about it. They knew many stories about conflicts between peasants and landlords, but what had happened today was different. To Jamal it was obvious that this wasn't the end of it and only God knew the consequences. He had the coming of his wedding on his mind as well. He'd hoped it would happen before winter, but if they weren't going to plow the fields . . . if the landlord was planning on starting a brick factory . . . if Bahram Khan took some action against them for what Haydar had done . . .

Jaffar was uneasy as well. He was still upset at the way Jamal had gotten angry at him and sorry that he had come home for a visit and was thinking about leaving for the city the next morning and never coming back again. He took the coin from his mother. "With your permission, Mother," he said, "after going to Sayed Ayoub's, I thought I might drop by Haydar's for a while."

"Listen to this," Jamal said. "He's been in Shiraz only a month and already he's talking like a city boy. And look at the crease in his trousers and his shiny shoes."

"Leave him alone, for God's sake, Jamal," Bibigol said bitterly. "Why do you have to tease him? Can't we listen to the dervish in peace?"

Jaffar was hurt by Jamal's comment but ignored him and was going down the stairs, followed by Marafi, when he heard his mother call after him.

"Jaffar, would you ask Golandam to come over early tomorrow morning so we can make some bread for you to take when you go back to school?"

Khali khob, he answered, before picking up his bag at the bottom of the stairs and starting to go across the village.

On Sayed Ayoub's roof, the dervish, leaning against a pillow, sang with his eyes closed. The lantern cast an amber shadow on his face and white beard and hair. He reminded Jaffar of a picture he'd seen in one of his schoolbooks of Amu Nowruz, the fairy tale character who appeared at the time of the Persian New Year. Jaffar dropped the coin in the *kashkool* that the dervish had set in front of him. Marafi sat down across from the dervish and stared at him in fascination. Jaffar, who knew that Marafi would sit there as long as the dervish was singing, waved good-bye and left for Haydar's house.

Haydar, Mehrangiz, and Golandam were on the roof of their house. Haydar was listening to the sad singing of the dervish, but

81

his mind was busy with what had happened that afternoon. He was facing a dilemma. Should he wait until the son of the landlord, the young Rahbari, pushed him off the land, or should he leave Sangriz altogether and go to the city to look for a job the way many of the villagers had ended up doing? He had the feeling that something was in the air and with a heavy heart ran through the events, old and new, that he thought had happened for a hidden reason—the coming of the Westerners to the ruins of Persepolis years ago, the coming of Mirza-ali to the village, the land reform, the building of the pump house by the senior Rahbari and his grabbing the best land of the village. And now there was talk of a brick factory to be built on the land by the junior Rahbari. In addition to all that, there was trouble boiling in different parts of the country and riots and uprisings in the cities. Were all these things related in some way? And how would they affect his future or that of his little sister, who was about to be married?

He thought about talking to Mirza-ali. His friendship with him and his father went back years, even before Mirza-ali settled in Sangriz. When Haydar was three or four years old his father had taken him to Mirza-ali's camp, a day's walk away near the Black Mountain. It seemed that it took forever to get there. They started before sunrise and didn't arrive until evening. They had crossed a river on horseback, and he still remembered the way the water rose all the way to the horse's neck and they'd had to dry themselves out after reaching the other shore. In the camp there were dozens of black tents and hundreds of lambs and sheep, horses, and camels. The visit had left a strong impression on him, especially the night when everyone sat around a big fire in front of Mirza-ali's tent, drinking tea and listening to the elders talk and show off their rifles. They talked about the hard time they'd had that year crossing the river with all the herds. The water was high and they'd had to inflate hides that they had brought along for this sort of occasion and tie the tent poles on top of them to make rafts. One raft had been lost in the rapids with a dozen of baby lambs and baby goats on top of it. A man, blind in one eye, played his reed flute and sang as everyone quietly listened. Now and again someone would sing a sad song about someone looking for his lover. Haydar didn't know he had fallen asleep until he woke up to the sound of dogs barking and saw the shepherds helping the women and young girls to milk the ewes before they drove them out to graze. Haydar didn't remember how many days they were there but remembered that when they were leaving, Mirza-ali had given him a baby lamb, a white-faced lamb with big black eyes and long ears, that he held in his lap all the way back to Sangriz. It was a few years later that Mirza-ali came with more than two hundred sheep and goats and ten horses and settled in the village. His son Kubaad was only four or five years old and would ride his horse around the village square with such speed and skill that all the villagers would watch in awe. Jamal's horse, Abrash, was a descendant of one of Mirza-ali's horses. In those days Mirza-ali would give cheese and yogurt to the villagers. Now he was left with only a dozen skinny sheep and goats and no horses or camels. He used to have two shepherds tending his herd. Nowadays his son Kubaad was the village shepherd.

The more Haydar thought, the more confusing everything became. He wanted to figure things out, to understand the secret behind everything that was happening. He wanted to get up on the roof and call out as loud as he could, call out above the singing of the dervish that was now filling up the ears of the villagers. He wanted to shout the way his father had that summer's day, when he had run to the square barefoot and with no hat, crying, "Hey, people . . . Thieves, thieves—they're here, they're on the Dashtak plain, they're taking our land. We have to stop them . . . Stop, thieves!" People had gathered around watching him until, drenched in sweat, his mouth going dry and his voice hoarse, he collapsed on the ground hardly breathing. The same damp summer night, Mash Safdar left this world.

"Salaam."

Haydar came to with Jaffar's greeting.

Jaffar sat down beside Golandam and Mehrangiz on a carpet and took out the lemons from his bag and put them down in front of Golandam. Smiling, she picked up one of them and smelled it. Mehrangiz was pleased to see Jaffar and knew it was good he had come. Now Haydar wouldn't be so withdrawn and would talk with him.

Jaffar told them about his school and the city, the uprising that had intensified to a point that the military and tanks had been called in, and the curfews that were in place to keep the protesters from gathering, especially after dark.

"You should only be paying attention to your school," Haydar said. "You shouldn't get involved in anything like that, young man, you hear? My guess is that the city boys don't dare cause you problems anymore. I'm proud of you. Come here and tell me about it."

"There's so much going on at school," Jaffar said, moving closer to Haydar. "The students write slogans on the school walls and recite satirical poems about the Shah and the military." He told them about how his school had participated in the demonstrations. The teachers had walked in front and the students behind them, carrying signs and shouting, "Death to the Shah." One day they walked all the way to the shrine of Shah-e Cheragh, where soldiers with guns were everywhere.

"This afternoon we saw Goodarz coming back," Haydar said. "He's left his military duty.

He said that a mullah from Najaf has a *fatwa* that the Shah must leave the country."

"Yes," said Jaffar, "Ayatollah Khomeini—he's gone from Najaf to Paris. At school we listened to the tapes he sends into the country."

They all looked on as Jaffar talked excitedly.

Soon the dervish's voice died down and they could hear Amir Khan's radio coming from the second floor of his house. Haydar turned to Jaffar. "I'm telling you again, don't get involved in anything that keeps you away from your schoolwork." Then he kissed Jaffar on the forehead. "Be good. I wish Sangriz had ten young men like you."

Jaffar was embarrassed and glanced over at Golandam.

Haydar stood up and was about to enter the mosquito net at the far end of the roof. "Well," he said, "that explains it. It's because of the problems in the city that the village teachers haven't shown up recently. It's been about two weeks now, and the children have been doing nothing except to wait for the teachers and play in front of the school."

Mehrangiz filled a bowl of water from the jar, but before taking it over to the mosquito net, said to Jaffar that if he would like to sleep there, Golandam would bring him a couple of blankets.

Jaffar nodded.

When Golandam got up to make up Jaffar's bed, the village was silent and most of the lanterns on the roofs had been put out. Jaffar stretched out on the blankets a few feet away from where Golandam was going to sleep. He stared at the stars over Sangriz and soon fell asleep but before long was awakened by low, muffled sounds. At first he thought he was in the city but then saw the stars shining above him. A moment passed and then he heard low talking and could see figures inside the mosquito net, silhouetted against the bluish glare of the moonlight. He strained to hear better, holding his breath and watching the shadows intermingle as they whispered and their breathing rose and sank in harmony.

Perplexed and fascinated, Jaffar forgot himself, all his attention on the shadows playing on the mosquito netting. He watched until they stopped and his own heart started to rest. Soon he heard Haydar's snoring and turned on his back and looked at the stars again. He couldn't say what was happening to him. He felt uneasy and didn't know why. He tried to go back to sleep, but wasn't able to. After a while, he got up and grabbed his shoes. Close by the stairs, he saw Golandam sound asleep, her chest moving softly. He looked at her round face in the moonlight for a few minutes before heading downstairs and going home.

The moon was long gone and dawn was approaching when a woman's cry woke up the village. Jamal jumped out of bed and looked for his shoes. Jaffar, who had just stretched out and was half asleep, sprang up, grabbed a stick, and ran out of the house barefoot. Bibigol sat up in confusion and turned up the lantern. "What's happening?" she asked.

Jamal ran out into the alley and went toward the direction of the cries. Everyone, old and young, men and women, had come out of their houses. Some were watching from their roofs, trying to find out what was happening. The dogs were barking. "Thieves, thieves," someone called out. "There are thieves in the village."

People had gathered in front of Haydar's house and were trying to find out what was going on. Jamal pushed his way to the front. A gendarme with a revolver in one hand and a flashlight in the other was standing at the entrance. Beside him, four more gendarmes with guns were watching the crowd. Two gendarmes brought Haydar out of the house, his hands in handcuffs. Golandam, carrying his shoes and softly crying, knelt down by her brother and put them on his feet. Mehrangiz put her husband's hat on his head. Haydar's fists were clenched and his eyes sparked with rage.

Jamal stepped closer and was about to ask a question when the head gendarme yelled out, "Quiet everyone," and put his hand on his revolver.

Goodarz kept himself behind the crowd and tried to hide from the gendarmes' gaze, thinking that they might recognize him. One of the gendarmes shouted at the people: "What do you want? Go back to your homes. Get lost. Everyone."

The crowd stepped aside and followed as they took Haydar toward the square. Golandam and Mehrangiz followed, wailing, their cries rising as Haydar was pushed into a jeep. When the jeeps drove away, the villagers, mumbling uneasily, headed back to their houses in confusion. Absent from the crowd were Amir Khan and his son, Sarferaaz, who watched from the second floor of their house as the jeeps drove away and their red taillights grew faint in the darkness.

Part
Four

1

For a week Sangriz lived in fear and panic. From the time the roosters crowed, the ground-digging machines shook the houses and stole the sleep from the eyes of the tired villagers. People got up earlier than usual and unwillingly started their daily work. Dogs barked and children drove their animals outside the village entrance to hand over to Kubaad, the village shepherd.

The sun was rising behind the Zagros Mountains to throw spears of light at the night-chilled air of the valley when Mehrangiz ran out of her house and hurried toward Bibigol's. Her face was red from the morning cold and tears were slipping from the corners of her eyes, but she wasn't paying attention to the cold.

Bibigol, a cup of tea in hand, was startled to see Mehrangiz suddenly appear in the doorway, blocking the morning light. She wondered if something had gone wrong or if Golandam wasn't well again—she hadn't been herself since the day they took Haydar to prison. Mehrangiz greeted Bibigol in a dry voice and sat down on the cold ground by the door. The smoke from the fire in the corner of the room curled up toward a hole above the doorframe. Bibigol gave Jamal his tea and then turned to Mehrangiz.

"What's the matter?" she asked. "Why are you squashed down in the doorway? Come sit by the fire."

Mehrangiz wiped her eyes with the end of her scarf. "It's fine right here, Bibi." Then she turned to Jamal. "To whom should I go to beg?" Her voice was full of anger. "Whose help should I seek to free Haydar? I don't know night from day anymore."

Bibigol offered her a cup of tea, but she pushed it away.

"Why are you upset with us now?" said Bibigol.

"I'm not upset with anyone, Bibi. I'm upset with this life of mine. Everything is becoming one big confusion. What has Haydar done that is so bad that they won't let him come back home?"

It had been two months since the night the gendarmes took Haydar away. On Fridays, Mehrangiz and Golandam, and sometimes Jamal, would go to Adel-Abad prison on the outskirts of Shiraz to visit him. A feeling of loneliness always surrounded the jail, a loneliness that seemed to have been there for ages. It choked Mehrangiz and Golandam every time they went. The grimy walls of the small waiting room hadn't been painted in years and were covered with dates, poems, and the names of visitors or inmates. Some of the graffiti had been scratched out by the tip of a knife or some other sharp object. On visiting days, the room would fill up with women and children, old and young, carrying bags of fruit, food, and cigarettes. Anticipation, hope, and sadness lay heavily on the hearts of the visitors. Softly crying and praying, they would watch the heavy glass windows separating them from the room the prisoners would walk into. At first sight of the first prisoners behind the windows, an uproar would rise as the visitors stood up to see their loved ones.

When Haydar, head shaved, eyes sunken, his bony figure looking taller in the striped prison uniform, appeared on the other side of the window, Golandam and Mehrangiz would rush to pick up the telephone receiver. Their visit was always full of tears and sadness as they passed the receiver between them and took turns talking to Haydar, but their anxiety would slowly give way to smiles and hopeful gestures.

Haydar, looking for the slightest change in Mehrangiz, would notice the tiredness and loneliness in her eyes. He wished he could hold her tight in his arms, brush her hair and kiss her, and calm her down and ask about everything that was going on. Mehrangiz would look back at him, reading the pain and frustration in his eyes. She wished she could break down the glass with her fists, free her husband, and take him away from there.

When it was Golandam's turn to talk, Haydar wouldn't be able to hold in his emotions. At the sound of her voice, tears would fill his eyes. He was afraid for her. Having her visit the jail when she should have been married and happily starting a new life was the most upsetting thing for him. He would think of the days she and Mehrangiz would bring lunch out to the field to him. How happy Golandam was, laughing and running through the fields of wheat. He didn't like it that they were faced with this unfortunate situation. He would say they shouldn't come to the jail anymore, that it was too upsetting for them, but then every Friday he would be waiting for them impatiently. Often he would curse Rahbari and Amir Khan for what they had done and advise Mehrangiz not to ever go to them. They weren't the people to ask for anything, she shouldn't trouble herself . . . God willing, he would get his chance to deal with them.

At the end of the visiting hour, which they always thought came too quickly, they would hold up the bag of fruit, sweets, cigarettes, and whatever else they had for him and give it to the guard to take to him. Mehrangiz would curse all human existence that she didn't know what to do or how to find a way to free her Haydar. She couldn't understand why her life had become so twisted and her Haydar had ended up there. Just because he stood up to the landlord. After they left, they would sink within themselves, struggling with their memories and lost in a whirlpool of hope and despair.

Bibigol poured two more cups of tea and put one in front of Jamal and the other in front of Mehrangiz. Jamal had put on his shoes and was getting ready to leave. He turned to Mehrangiz. "What do you suggest I do? Climb up the sky?" He looked up at the smoke-covered ceiling and raised his hands. "If I could, I would climb up to God himself . . . More than ten times I went to that bastard Bahram Khan. I asked him, I begged him to have Haydar released from jail. What else can I do?"

Mehrangiz wiped her eyes again. "Today I'm going to the city to see the senior Rahbari. I'll go and tell him what his son has done to us. I'll go to his house and raise all kinds of hell . . . Maybe someone will listen to me."

"Go to that senile old man?" said Jamal. "It's no use, Mehrangiz. No use at all. Didn't I go there myself the first day? He doesn't recognize anyone anymore. He's a bag of old bones in a wheelchair wetting himself day and night." He shook his head. "A fitting end for someone so merciless. One day he was on horseback, pushing people around, now he's crumpled up in a wheelchair. There's no good end in being cruel." Jamal put on his coat. "Now that stupid son of his is in charge. A young man with his head in the clouds. He'll be coming to the pump house today to see the progress of his destruction. Can't you hear?" He gestured toward the hollering of the bulldozers that came from the fields. "He'll come and I'll ask him again to pardon Haydar."

Jamal grew quiet for a moment, then hit the palm of his hand with his fist. "I told Haydar a hundred times that nothing is achieved by quarreling. Quarreling only brings on more quarreling. A man must proceed slowly and cautiously. Fighting only makes things worse. He wouldn't listen, though. Besides, as far as I'm concerned, Sangriz and all its land can go to hell. Should it be only us who have to worry about the land? There's the whole village. Why should we be the only ones offering our heads to the wind?" Jamal's sharp gaze fell on Mehrangiz and then his mother. His voice, his talk, betrayed years of accumulated hardship and frustration. "But would Haydar listen? He always wanted to do things his way and was impatient and wanted things to happen at the moment he desired . . . and look where we are. To hell with the land reform, to hell with farming. If our fathers had been able to get a piece of land fifteen or twenty years ago, that would have been something, but nowadays the godless gendarmes, the godless landlords, the godless agriculture office, the court system—they're all alike. They've made a pact. How can we, a few shirtless, unknowing villagers, get our land back?"

"Why are you upsetting yourself, son?" said Bibigol. "Nobody's blaming you."

"Oh yes they are. My heart is torn up over this. Every time I told Haydar to be calm, he got upset and accused me of not giving a damn. That I only cared about a paying job, not the land . . . And he's right. Am I a donkey brain who doesn't understand anything? Am I to put myself in the way of a raging bull? And who for? For the lazy and worthless people of Sangriz? Now that Haydar's been thrown in jail, which one of them has even bothered going to visit him, let alone taken a step to see if they could do something? To lend a helping hand. Not even one of them would put a simple question to Rahbari and ask why he's destroying the best land of Sangriz. Even if ten of them came, we could go to the Agriculture Department and at least let them know we're concerned about what's happening here, but they don't want to have anything to do with it, not one of them—except Goodarz, but he's afraid he might get in trouble because of running away from the military. All the rest, after they saw what happened to Haydar, crawled under their wife's chadors."

Jamal moved toward the door and then stopped. "Haydar has been like this as long as I remember, from when we were boys. Every time we wanted to do something, he would take charge and start some kind of commotion. Marafi is the way he is because of Haydar, but I was the one blamed."

Mehrangiz squeezed to one side of the doorway to let Jamal pass. After he had left, she hit her chest with her fist. "Bibi, it's these sorts of words about Haydar that pour salt on my wounds."

"Don't take his complaining to heart," Bibigol said as she gestured to Mehrangiz to drink her tea. "He's upset that his hands are tied and he can't do anything. I know he's constantly thinking about a way to get Haydar out. He wants to bring home his fiancée and start their new life. He's tired and upset with everything that's going on these days. You heard him—he's upset with everything."

At the sound of Abrash neighing, Mehrangiz turned to see the horse's tail whipping the air as Jamal rode out of the yard and into the alley. She moved closer to the fireplace. "I know, Bibi. Jamal's been very attentive. He's been coming over, asking if we need anything. He stays for dinner and tries to cheer us up. He and Golandam are more relaxed with each other. They laugh and tease each other. The other day he brought her a beautiful scarf that she likes and has been wearing. But I have to confess, Bibi, it reminds me of our engagement days. Haydar would come to our house every day. It was pomegranate season, and he would bring a big crate of pomegranates. We would sit around eating and laughing. My mother, God rest her soul, was so fond of him." She stopped and looked away for a moment, then reached for Bibigol's hand. "Bibi," she said, "I haven't been able to sleep for nights. The roar of these machines is one thing and the nightmares something else again . . . I've been awake since midnight. I'm terrified, Bibi. What am I to do?"

Bibigol looked at her sympathetically. She hated to see her so upset and worried and wanted to comfort her. She was aware of all the pain and difficulties Mehrangiz was going through, but she herself was not in any better situation. The threads of their lives were tangled in knots. It was as if everything were heading in a direction so that her son's wedding wouldn't take place. She thought of the day she had gone to the city to buy wedding things and the attack on the cinema and touched her head where the brick had broken it. Now she believed that the whole thing was a bad omen. Just when her wound started to get better and she was hoping the wedding would take place, Haydar was taken to prison. And now she was concerned for Golandam. Ever since the night the gendarmes took Haydar away, she had been upset, crying and eating little or not at all for days. She had no heart for anything.

"Bibi," Mehrangiz said, putting down the empty teacup, "you know very well the reason they accused Haydar. They were waiting for an excuse and in the end found one. They said he'd found treasure in the hills and not turned it in to the government. It's all Amir Khan and his circle's doing. That old hyena won't die and let this village live in peace. Now the gendarmes, the judges, and the prison guards have all sharpened their teeth. They think that Haydar has found a treasure and that soon they'll have their hands on it . . . I kept telling him to stop searching the hills, to stop talking about hidden treasure, the Black Globe, and things like that. People will think you really have found something. Now he's in trouble for nothing . . . We're doomed, Bibi. I'm afraid they might not let him out. What am I to do?"

Mehrangiz turned toward the yard and raised her voice. "Hey, you nonbelievers, you misguided ones, come and see how Haydar's house is full of treasure, how we have locked away gems and gold coins . . . Come and see how we are in need of our daily bread. Have we found the treasure in Amir Khan's father's grave? . . . May those who brought this upon us be met with bullets in their hearts."

94

When Jamal and Mehrangiz had gone to the city to ask Bahram Khan to forgive Haydar and have him released from jail, their request had been met with a harsh reply. "What can I do? This has nothing to do with me," he had told them coldly. "It's nothing to do with Haydar's stupid fight with me. It's to do with treasure that he found. The court's order is that he stay in jail until he tells them where he found it and what he's done with it. There's nothing that I can do."

Mehrangiz knew that Bahram Khan was a dishonest man and thought he was responsible for Haydar's being arrested and was trying to excuse himself. "I could see in his eyes that he was lying," she said to Jamal after they left Rahbari's house. "He thinks we don't understand, that we're stupid. That we don't know he's made a pact with Amir Khan and his son, Sarferaaz. He thinks we don't know. Well, all the people of Sangriz know. They know that Amir Khan testified in court against my husband. That he said that he'd seen Haydar in the middle of the night going to the hills with a sack and then in the early morning hop on his motorcycle and take something to Isaac the jeweler in Shiraz . . . May those who lied and gave wrong testimony never see a happy day in their lives."

"Well, Bibi," Mehrangiz said. "You tell me, what have we done to Amir Khan? Did we sell him wet firewood that he's exacting his revenge? I know he never liked us, but must he be our enemy and do this to us just because Golandam refused to be engaged to his son? I'm glad she did. He's a wicked man. He stands on the square and eyes any woman and young girl who passes by and says bad things behind their backs. They're not kind people, Bibi. God only knows what else they may be up to. I'm afraid that in the end we may have to pick up our few belongings and leave Sangriz. I don't see how Haydar could raise his head in this place again."

Suddenly Bibigol's tired eyes, which had years of patience stored in them, sparked. "What are you saying, woman? What has he done that he won't be able to raise his head? He stood up to bad people. Against wrong. That's not anything to be embarrassed about. If the people of this village had a drop of Haydar's blood or his father's in their veins, they wouldn't let someone like Amir Khan or that old wolf Mr. Rahbari cheat them. I don't want to hear any words like that again. What nonsense, he won't be able to raise his head!" She coughed and then glanced at Mehrangiz. "Baraat was here a day ago. Do you know what he said?"

Mehrangiz shook her head.

"He said there was trouble in the city—lots of rioting and that it might get out of hand. Whoever has done wrong in the past is fleeing or has gone into hiding. That no-good Rahbari at the time of the land reform cheated the government and the peasants. We all know that he paid a bribe so that the Dashtak plain wouldn't be included in the land reform. Now that things are changing, they're trying to cheat people like us again. Rahbari's son is worried things will turn around for him here, and he's in a hurry to build the brick factory on the Dashtak plain before we can lay claim to the land. I heard it from Baraat and Jamal. If they change the land from farming and build a brick factory, they'll say it wasn't good farmland in the first place and that they've created jobs for people. Baraat says he's heard that in some parts of the country, villagers are taking back their lands. But we know that the Rahbaris are related to an important mullah. And they say that the mullahs are taking control of everything."

"To hell with their land and their jobs and whatever they're building or not building," Mehrangiz said quietly. "May the brick factory tumble down on their heads. What's going to become of Haydar?" She stared at Bibigol. "Bahram Khan and Amir Khan aren't going to let him go free. They know, after what they've done, that if he's free, he'll go after them and try to get his land back—Bibi, when he's out, I have to keep him out of trouble."

Bibigol took the empty cup in front of Mehrangiz and spoke calmly. "Now, my dear, don't upset yourself. Don't let all that weigh heavy on your heart. What will we do if you fall ill? All you need to do is to take care and run your household. Haydar will be free, God willing, he'll be free. Because he's done nothing wrong. He's a good man and God is on the side of good people. Don't be hurt by what people say. You can close a village gate but not the mouths of people. Let them say whatever they want, that's not our concern. We've always been like a patient stone and need to be so. Have another cup of tea and go back home and ask Golandam to come over. I'm very worried about her. I'm afraid she'll be ill or lose hope. She's young and doesn't have the will for this sort of trouble. She's stressed by all that has happened. You need to pay attention. Don't worry her by talking about Haydar and what people say. And don't let her out of your sight, you hear? These are bad days, difficult days, and we must be strong and pray that they pass soon. Come back this afternoon and help me to make some sweet bread to take to Haydar. I'd like to come with you and Golandam this coming Friday when you go to visit him. I miss him and would like to see him. We'll go to Baraat's and give Jaffar a visit, too. At least my younger one is away from all this and doing well at school now. Praise Allah for that blessing. I think Golandam would be happy to see Jaffar. I think it will do her good. I'm sure of that. They're fond of each other, as you know."

Mehrangiz nodded and took the cup of tea from Bibigol.

"People . . ." Bibigol went on after a while, "the people of Sangriz are like camels that eat a handful of tumbleweeds and carry loads all their lives."

Mehrangiz put the teacup down in front of her and stared at the smoke snaking above her head toward the hole above the door. "Bibi," she said after a while, "I had a nightmare last night and couldn't sleep. I've been shaking ever since. That's why I came so early. I just needed to talk to you, to see what you think. I didn't want to start all that with Jamal. I thought he would be gone by this time."

"Don't worry about Jamal," Bibigol said in anticipation. "Let me hear your dream. *Inshallah* it's all for the good,"

"It was a terrifying dream, Bibi. I've never had a dream like that . . . I was in the storeroom getting a bowl of barley to make soup. It was a cold, icy day and I thought Haydar would like that when he came home from the fields. When I opened the sack and took a handful, it was all worms." She cleared her throat. "Tiny worms, the size of barley grains, wiggling all over one another and falling out of the bowl. The sack was full of them. I dropped the bowl and ran out of the house. I went toward the Dashtak plain to find Haydar. The road and all the fields were covered with ice and a cold wind was blowing so hard it cut to the bone. There were

97

huge crows and vultures, hundreds of them, flying over Sangriz and going to the pit outside the village to feed on the carcasses of Mirza-ali's herd. I ran toward the pump house looking for Haydar and Jamal, but I couldn't find them . . . Nobody was there. I could hear sounds but couldn't say where they were coming from—from the sky or the bottom of the earth . . . *groomp* . . . *groomp* . . . *groomp*, it went on and on, echoing all around me. I called and called Haydar's name, but I could only hear my own voice and the wind. When I turned back to come home, there were these animals blocking my way. They were white and gray and blended with the air and ice, as if they weren't there, but they were, I could see their yellow eyes staring at me . . . I was sure they were wolves . . . a pack of them, Bibi . . . seven of them coming from the ruins of Persepolis . . . I started to run and called out, 'Haydar, Jamal, where are you? Who would go out in this icy weather, who would sow wheat in this frozen land the way you're trying to?' "

Mehrangiz stopped talking. She swallowed a few times, and as she bit her lip, reached for Bibigol's hand. "A pack of wolves, seven of them . . ." She tightened her grip on Bibi's hand. "I saw them . . . I saw them and they had human arms and legs in their jaws and ran off into the mountains . . . I collapsed. I couldn't take another step . . . then I heard someone calling and calling my name. It was Golandam. She was standing beside me, calling and trying to shake me awake."

Bibigol held Mehrangiz's hand for a moment and then turned to stir the fire. "May God help us all and forgive Rahbari," she said softly. "May God save Sangriz." Then she looked at Mehrangiz again. "It was just a dream, my dear. Don't upset yourself. Get up and bring me a handful of rue and alum from that bag in the corner of the room. I'll throw it on the fire to drive away the bad spirits."

Mehrangiz stared into the yard. Bibigol spoke to her again. "Don't worry, my dear, don't upset yourself. It was only a bad dream. Come now, go get me a pinch of rue and alum to throw on the fire and drive away the bad spirits."

Mehrangiz stood and walked over to the sack, a heap of worms wiggling in front of her eyes. She hesitated for a moment, then nervously opened the sack and grabbed a handful of rue and alum. Bibigol took it from her and, repeating the name of Allah and the Prophet Mohammad, threw it into the fire. Sizzling blue smoke rose from the fire as she blew on the embers.

2

When the bulldozers and dump trucks first came to Sangriz and started to rumble around and shake the village, everyone thought that Bahram Khan was planning on digging another well and building another pump house. Everyone was fascinated and watched through the rising dust as the earth-shaking machines tore up the ground. Soon a rumor started going around that oil had been discovered under the Dashtak plain and an oil well was to be drilled.

"Our village, God willing, will be prosperous," someone said. "Just think of it—first an oil well, then a refinery, and then good-paying government jobs."

"We'll have running water," added another.

"Electricity," said someone else. "A paved road and a better school. Maybe a clinic with a doctor."

Sayed Ayoub had his dreams as well, and from the day the work had begun he had started thinking about enlarging his shop, adding a shaded area in front with chairs and tables and maybe even opening a restaurant or teahouse. "With God's help," he remarked, "I will hire some help and feed the hundreds of workers who come to work here."

This frenzy was at its height when, a few days later, the Gypsies arrived and put up their tents by the graveyard. Every year their coming brought pleasure and excitement to the village. The peasants would take sickles and shovels, axes, and other old tools in need of repair and pile them up in front of Danial's tent. The village women would bring knives and scissors to be sharpened and copper pots and pans to be re-tinned. Some would even bring broken china and teapots to be glued back together. The fire would flame in front of the tents and pieces of blazing iron would be made into axes, sickles, and plows under the skillful hammering of Danial and his son Hatam. The children, entranced, would watch Danial grab a red-hot ingot with a pair of tongs and drop it into a bucket of water, causing a sudden sizzling and bubbling and rising of steam that made them step back and laugh. Around another fire in front of another tent, the women and young girls of the village would hold out their palms for the Gypsy women, waiting to hear their fortunes, which the Gypsies, by their manner of looking and asking questions, would sprinkle with positive predictions. In another corner, some village boys would set spinning the brightly colored wooden *ferfereh* they had just bought from the Gypsies and make bets about whose would go the longest.

During the two or three weeks of the Gypsies' stay, daily life in the village would change totally. It wasn't just the rusty old tools that were repaired and shined anew in the hands of the Gypsies, but also the tired souls of the villagers were revived through conversation and evenings sitting around the fire listening to them sing and tell stories.

This year, instead of four or five families of Gypsies, only Danial's family came, and a month earlier than usual. Their arrival didn't hold its usual excitement, and fewer people gathered around their nightly fires. Danial, his face more worn than the year before, repaired and polished the few tools that the villagers brought to him in a couple of days. Then he sat smoking his pipe and talking to Mirza-ali and a few other elders as the big machines roared on the opposite side of the village.

"The world is changing every day," Mirza-ali said. "People as well. You don't need to go too far. Just take a look around you. From the day that these iron creatures appeared in Sangriz, young and old go and stand watching them. With all the dust, mud, and noise, is the tearing up of the land something to watch?"

"It's the same everywhere, Amu Mirza-ali," Danial said. "I guess our time has gone by. Why do you think we're here sooner than

102

usual? There was nothing much for us to do in any of the villages we've gone to this year. No sooner did we arrive and put up our tents than we had to take them down and move on. There's no need for people like us anymore. It's all agricultural machinery—tractors, combines, disk cultivators—you name it. There are no sickles, plows, or other tools for us to repair. Machines are doing everything nowadays. They plow, sow, and harvest. There's no need for old farming tools anymore. You know what I'm saying, Amu? Those days are passing by and will soon be gone."

"Yes," Mirza-ali said, sucking on his pipe, "you're right, Danial. The world is getting to be full of machines. I was a small boy when our tribe was on the route of spring migration and camped not far from here, by the ruins of Persepolis. Saalaar, the *saarebaan*—caravan man—may God rest his soul, although he was an old man by then, in his youth he had traveled all over the country, taking camel loads of merchandise from the port of Bushehr on the Persian Gulf north all the way to Tehran and beyond Tehran to Mazandaran by the shore of the Caspian Sea. One hundred or more camels and each trip, going and coming back, taking eight to ten months. We children would gather around and listen to his stories. 'You see those trucks?' he would say. 'See the dust rising high behind them? They want to let God know that they're here and let us know that they will ruin the caravan business. In a few years we won't be needing camels or horses.' People would say that Saalaar the old *saarebaan* had gone out of his mind, that he didn't know what he was talking about. How could a few trucks do that?" Mirza-ali let out a dry laugh. "Now I see that good man Saalaar was quite right. He saw the future as clear as day . . . Of course, I must say, with the coming of machines, many things are easier nowadays. We can go all the way to Tehran in a day. Imagine that. I wonder what Saalaar would think if he were alive."

Old Najaf, who was cleaning his nails with a knife that Danial had sharpened for him a few minutes earlier, spoke up in a broken voice. "It's true . . . it's true . . . things are easier . . . no question about it. But the prosperity and blessing of the land have been lost." He scratched the tip of his nose and wiped his wrinkled face with a handkerchief. Then he gave everyone a questioning look. "What portion of the harvest with these new machines is scattered away and lost, would you say? . . . Twenty percent? . . . Thirty percent?"

"Maybe even more, Amu Najaf," Mirza-ali answered. "I've had my herds grazing the field right behind a combine as it was harvesting the wheat. I saw with my own eyes how much of the crop it spilled. I didn't need to drive the animals from field to field. I could leave them in one area and soon they would have enough and with their bellies filled would lie down to rest and chew their cud."

Mirza-ali shook his head and then hit his knee with the palm of his hand. "But this year, like the year before, Bahram Khan shamelessly set fire to the field after the harvest was over, not letting any animal graze on the land. He put Haydar in jail and, as you can see for yourselves, is tearing up the fields with those bulldozers for no good reason and no one is doing anything about it. If Haydar were here, I bet he would be the one to stop him."

"Oh, Haydar," said Danial, sighing. "I heard about his trouble. What a nice man. He was always good to us when we came around. May God be with him wherever he is and may he come back to his family soon."

Old Najaf nodded. "His fate was like that of his poor father, Mash Safdar. What did they gain fighting the landlord? The same thing! A trip to prison. You can't win if no one is behind you, if no one raises a hand to help you. That's the truth. That was the problem with the father and the son. No one was with them."

Danial finished sharpening the old sheep clippers that Mirza-ali had brought to him. "Here, Amu, as sharp as a razor."

Mirza-ali took the clippers and ran his thumb against the blades. "Excellent," he said, "*dast-e tu dard nakoneh*—may your hands never ache—it'll do fine for the few sheep I have. You wouldn't believe how many sheep I've sheared with these old clippers." He was silent for a moment and then put his thumb and forefinger through the finger rings and opened and closed the blades a few times, listening to the snipping of the blades. "There was a time when I used to shear more than two hundred sheep a season."

"My only job of the day," Danial said as he gathered up his tools. "This year no sooner do we get to a village than we have to hurry on to the next, hoping to find some work. Only our womenfolk have been able to make a few toman by selling some knitting and telling fortunes. We men crouch beside a cold fireplace and sharpen a few knives and scissors. That's all."

Danial talked in a gloomy voice, a frown spreading across his face, a face spotted with the marks of childhood smallpox. "It won't be long before we have to let go of our blacksmithing and settle in a town. To stop our wandering and, if lucky, become laborers in some corner of the country, like some of my relatives who have already done it and don't come this far anymore. Some of them are in towns doing odd jobs and some stay south and pick fruits at orchards at harvesttime—lemons and oranges, or grapes and figs, things like that."

Another old man spoke as he knocked the ashes from his pipe. "In the past few years many of the youngsters of Sangriz have left for the nearby towns searching for work."

Mirza-ali, shaking his head, turned to Danial. "You talk about stopping your migration and settling down in a town. Well, that may work for you, because you have no herds, but it was a disaster for nomadic people like us."

Across the plain, a Land Rover could be seen speeding toward the tent, but no one moved except for Marafi, who got up to watch the approaching car. Since a month earlier, when news came that rioting had been increasing in big cities throughout the country and especially in the capital, the villagers had been seeing more military jeeps coming to the area. They were used to seeing military officers come around looking for draft dodgers, occasions when the young men would go off into the mountains, not returning until the officers were gone. And a month after Goodarz deserted, two gendarmes showed up at Sayed Ayoub's shop asking questions but went away empty-handed after a young boy discreetly moved away from the gathered crowd and ran to where the bulldozers were working to warn him.

However, the approaching car didn't appear to be a military vehicle. It came roaring up to them, stopping a few yards away from the tent, and a man as tall as a tent pole got out. He took off his dark glasses and ran his hand over his sandy goatee as he looked at the old men and then at the blacksmithing tools in front of Danial. A woman with long straw-colored hair and eyes the color of the sky made every head turn as she got out of the car. They watched the bearded man turn and say something to a dark young man who got out from behind the wheel. Hearing the stranger talking in a strange tongue, many of the villagers found their thoughts going back to their youth and the days they worked at the excavation sites in the Persepolis ruins. They had seen many people like these strangers in those days and were never able to figure out what they were saying.

The woman looked around and then began taking pictures of the tent, the men, and the surroundings. She seemed to be particularly interested in the village wall and the graveyard. She walked among the dirt graves taking pictures, trying to capture the low afternoon sun over the graves.

The young man brushed the dust from his black hair and, stepping closer, spoke in Persian.

"*In dehe Sangriz-e?*"—Is this the village of Sangriz?

"*Baleh, Sangriz-e,*" someone answered.

"*Ma donbal Haydar migardim.*"—We're looking for Haydar—does anyone know where he is?

The men looked at one another. Mirza-ali spoke before anyone else. "*Haydar inja nis.*"—Haydar's not here. "What do you need him for? Can we be of any help?"

The young man gestured toward the foreigners and explained that they were looking for antiquities and in the upper village someone had said that a man named Haydar could help them.

"Haydar's been gone for a while," Mirza-ali said. "You won't find him here."

"Well, then," the man said, "*kassi chizi atigheh dare?*"—does anyone have any antiquities—"old pottery, coins, or anything old they want to sell?"

"I certainly don't have anything like that," Mirza-ali said.

"It's too bad Haydar isn't here," someone said. "He must have dug out a lot of old coins and pottery up in the hills."

Danial stood up and went inside the tent, returning with a sack whose contents he dumped out on the ground. He picked out a few marbles and a couple of worn coins from the assortment of things and handed them to the bearded man. The man looked at them, holding them up to the sun, and then called out to the woman, who was still taking pictures, and handed them to her. She tossed her hair behind her back and, after examining them in an offhanded way, put them down in front of Danial.

"*Chizi dige dari?*"—Do you have anything else?—asked the driver. "They're looking for very old things and will pay good money for them, too. I assure you that there's nothing to worry about. They're leaving the country to go back home soon. You're probably aware of the problems and the uprising in the country— all the foreigners who are visiting the country or have been here working are leaving. It's becoming dangerous for them."

"We've heard about the riots," said one of the villagers.

"And the burning down of the cinemas and the banks," someone else said. "We've heard all that on the radio." They all nodded in agreement.

"I didn't believe any of it until I saw it with my own eyes," old Najaf said. "I was in Shiraz just a week ago, and a huge angry crowd was gathered in front of the main mosque shouting, 'Death to the Shah.' I'd never seen anything like that in my life."

"That's right," the young man said. "And it looks like it's going to get worse."

Danial went back inside the tent. Old Najaf reached into his coat pocket and took out a string of ruby-colored prayer beads, a gift from Sayed Ayoub, who had brought them back from his pilgrimage to the shrine of Imam Reza in the city of Mashhad the summer before. He held out the beads to the woman, who took them, touched their fluffy green bow, and smiled, then handed them to the bearded man. "Clever old man," the man said, "he must have bought these at the city bazaar and is trying to sell them to us as an antique." They laughed, and when the young man translated, the villagers looked at old Najaf and laughed as well.

Danial reappeared from the tent carrying an old, beat-up samovar in one hand and a long, rusty sword in the other. The bearded man handed the prayer beads back to the woman, who in turn gave them to their owner, old Najaf. The man smiled at Danial, who was holding out the samovar to him, ignored the samovar, and reached for the sword. Danial gave him the sword and put the samovar down on the ground. His gaze wandered between the man and the woman. "If you would like, sir," he said, "I'll shine it for you in a second. You know, this is the sword of Jamshid-e Jam—the king of old Persia. I found it myself near Persepolis a few years ago." He pointed in the direction of Persepolis. When he realized they didn't understand him, he turned to the young man. "Tell them, sir. Tell them that this is the sword of Jamshid-e Jam—Darius the great king."

The young man smiled as he translated, and all three of them laughed again while the villagers stared.

The bearded man handed the sword back to Danial and then saw Marafi and the book with the worn leather cover that he was holding. He reached for it, but Marafi gripped the book tightly against his chest, stepping backward on his crippled leg. The man came closer and put his hand on the book. Marafi, his eyes widening, stared at him, and the sound boiling out of his half-open mouth—*la, la, la, de, de, de*—startled the strangers.

"Don't be afraid, *baba joon*," one of the older men said. "He just wants to look at it."

The man reached for the book again, and Marafi, unsure, let go of it. The man and woman both looked at the pages with their elegant intertwined lines of calligraphy and bright hand-painted miniatures depicting hunting and battle scenes of kings and fez-wearing horsemen playing polo. The man took out a magnifying glass from his coat pocket and, holding the book higher, stared at the illustrations with one eye closed. "They look fantastic," he said to the woman without looking up or paying attention to Marafi, who was reaching for the book. "I'm sure they're original. They could very well be hundreds of years old." He paged through the book and looked at a few more illustrations. Then he took a few bills out of his pocket and held them out to Marafi. Marafi, on the verge of tears, pushed aside the man's hand and reached for the book.

The young man stepped closer to Marafi. *"Ketabo mikhad azat bekhareh"*—He wants to buy your book.

Marafi didn't listen. He repeated his everlasting song—*de, de, de, la, la, la*—and struggled to get the book back. As his voice escalated, the villagers gathered closer. Mirza-ali tried to calm Marafi down, and old Najaf pleaded with the driver to tell the foreigners to give the book back. The more the driver tried to control the situation, talking in two languages, the more excited everyone became. Mirza-ali's dog started to bark. A boy ran into the village to let Marafi's mother know. Marafi, not paying attention to what the driver was saying or the bills that the foreign man was offering, made a sudden cry and grabbed the book. As he pulled it away, some pages came loose, and the man managed to grab a couple. In the midst of all the pushing and shoving, the woman, by now frightened, hurried to the car and held the door open for the man to follow. He was barely inside when the driver started the car and pulled away.

"Sir, sir . . . ," Danial called out, running after the Land Rover and shaking the rusty sword in the air. "This is the sword of Xerxes . . . the sword of Xerxes the great king."

3

It was close to sunset and the Gypsies were gathering their belongings to leave early the next day when Mirza-ali, leaning on his walking stick and holding his grandson's hand, followed by his dog, Gorgi, stopped in front of Danial's tent.

"Danial," Mirza-ali said, pulling up the boy's pants leg, "I beg you, my good man, could you see if you can figure out what's wrong with my child's leg?"

Danial had been about to tie together a pile of poles he had stacked up but threw down the rope and crouched in front of the boy. He looked at the boy's shin and reached out to touch the amber-colored skin, but the boy, whimpering, pulled his leg back. Mirza-ali squeezed the boy's hand and bent down to him. "Don't be afraid, *baba joon*," he whispered. "He only wants to look at it. He's not going to hurt you."

"That's right, son," Danial said, smiling at the tearful boy. "I'm not going to do anything, just look, okay? There's nothing to worry about." He cocked his head and examined the boy's dirty bare feet, then gently, as if he were afraid the swollen calf would burst, touched the skin with the tip of his index finger. Mirza-ali and the boy followed the movement of his hand. Danial stood up, ran his fingers through his gray hair, and thought for a moment before calling out to his wife, who was shaking the dust off an old kilim. "Hey, Zomorod, come and start the fire. And bring that kilim for Mirza-ali to sit on."

Zomorod spread out the kilim in front of the tent and added a few pieces of wood to the fire. Mirza-ali, supporting himself on his walking stick, repeated the name of God and slowly sat down. He gestured to the boy to sit next to him. A few yards away, the sunken mud graves of the old cemetery lay under the late afternoon sun, the tilted tombstones throwing long shadows across the bare soil of the graveyard. Mirza-ali was wondering why it was that the Gypsies always liked to put up their tents next to a cemetery when he was startled by the gruff voice of Danial, who had come out of the tent carrying two small bags.

"Amu, how long has the boy's leg been like this?"

"Four days. But today it seems more swollen."

Mirza-ali had been hoping that the doctor who used to travel from the city clinic to the surrounding villages once a month would show up. The doctor hadn't come around the previous month and rumor had it that it was because of the riots and the demonstrations that had escalated in the city. The schoolteachers hadn't been back for a couple of weeks, and Baraat, too, hadn't come around in more than ten days.

"It looks like you rubbed something on it."

"Yes, castor oil," Mirza-ali said and lit his pipe. "I thought it would help it. I looked closely but couldn't see any bites or stings. It's a relief that it wasn't one of the scorpions that are all over the village. I don't know what illness has gotten into my poor child."

The boy listened nervously and watched Danial, who sat down beside the fire, took a pinch of dry leaves from each bag, and crushed them into a bowl of water that was starting to boil.

Mirza-ali offered the pipe to Danial. With each puff, Danial's cheeks collapsed into his toothless mouth and a fountain of smoke whirled out of his nostrils and coiled up in front of his face. After a few puffs, he handed the pipe back to Mirza-ali. Then he took a folded piece of paper from the pocket of his threadbare waistcoat and went on talking, keeping his eyes on the boy. He unfolded the paper as inconspicuously as possible and took out a razor blade that he dropped into the boiling water, which had turned dark green. Then, using a piece of cloth, he grabbed the smoke-darkened bowl and pulled it off the tripod, putting it on the ground next to him. "Hey, Zomorod," he called out to his wife. "Where did you disappear to, woman? Come and give me a helping hand."

Zomorod came out of the tent and sat across from Danial. She glanced at the boy and then at Mirza-ali. "Our youngsters," she said, "have fallen in love with the machines. They've left everything and have gone to watch those clinking-clunking bulldozers and trucks. They haven't even come back to give us a hand gathering our things so we can go to another village and try to earn a piece of bread. Amu Mirza-ali, what's wrong with the boy?"

"I don't know," Mirza-ali said sadly, "maybe something bit him."

Danial gestured to her to get the boy ready. Zomorod held the boy's hand and gently pulled him closer, her bracelets jingling. "Come here, *aziz joon*," she said. "What a beautiful boy you are. I always see you with your grandpa—that's nice. He's a nice grandpa, isn't he?" The boy looked at her smiling face and big black eyes and let himself be pulled onto her lap. Then Zomorod turned to Mirza-ali. "Amu, here—hold his hand."

Mirza-ali put down his pipe and, moving closer, took the boy's hand. "There, there, my dear child," he said. "Don't be scared. It will be over in the blink of an eye."

The boy tried to move but Zomorod had him tight between her arms and was holding his legs below the knees. Suddenly Danial plunged his hand into the bowl of hot water. His eyes went shut for a moment and the wrinkles around them and his mouth twitched. When he pulled his hand out, the razor blade was between his fingers and steaming wet leaves were stuck to the hair on the back of his hand. With a quick, skillful motion, he ran the razor several times across the boy's swollen calf. Zomorod held the boy more tightly and whispered, "There, my dear, it's over, it was nothing." By the time the boy cried out, Danial was finished. Tears came to Mirza-ali's eyes and Gorgi, lying close by, abruptly stood up. Danial dipped his hand into the bowl again and brought out a handful of steaming leaves. After blowing on them and letting them cool, he put the leaves on the wound and wrapped the leg with a piece of cloth. Zomorod loosened her grip on the boy's legs but continued to hold him in her arms.

"There, my dear," she said again, "it's all over." She held out a bowl of water to the boy's lips, but he pushed it away, tears streaming down his cheeks. She let him go to his grandfather and went

113

inside the tent. After a few minutes she came back with a few pieces of rock candy and divided them between the boy and Mirza-ali.

"I wanted to take the boy to the clinic," Mirza-ali said, "but Baraat hasn't come by in a week or so. I hope he's all right with all the troubles in the city. I still may try to get to the city somehow."

"It may not be a bad idea," Danial said, thoughtfully. "Just to make sure." He dumped out the contents of the bowl and started to pick up his things. "It's some sort of bite, an insect bite or something. Drawing blood the way I did took the venom out. Boil some of the herb I'll give you and put it on his leg every three to four days. Don't worry, Amu, he'll be fine." He patted the boy softly on the head. "Yes, you'll be fine. You're a brave little one, aren't you?"

The boy turned his face from him and leaned against his grandfather.

Mirza-ali took out a note from his money bag, but Danial wouldn't accept his offer.

"May God keep you and your family safe," said Mirza-ali. "I'm much obliged for your kindness, my friend."

The next morning, the Gypsies picked up their tents and tied together their belongings. A sharp autumn wind was blowing and great flocks of crows circled over Sangriz. There seemed to be thousands of them, and more kept coming. Their raspy calls were deafening. They perched on rooftops, the village wall, and the graves in the cemetery, then took off and flew over the pump house and toward the fields to claw at the worms wiggling in the earth newly torn up by the bulldozers. From a distance it looked as if rows of black banners had been raised atop the village wall and a huge black tent had been spread over the graveyard. Everyone was tormented by the birds. Soon a rumor circulated that the crows had pulled out the eyes of the lambs and baby goats and that little children playing in the village square had been pecked at. Terrified mothers kept their children inside.

Danial had seen many odd things in his roaming around the country, but never anything like this. He was standing by his belongings, watching the crows clawing at the graves and feeling anxious to take his family away. He was upset that his son Hatam hadn't shown up. He and Zomorod had stayed up late the night before arguing and trying to reason with him, saying he shouldn't stay in Sangriz and work for Bahram Khan at his newly built brick factory. Who knows, they told him, they might never come back to this area and, the way things were going, might never see him again.

Hatam was nineteen or twenty—his parents didn't exactly know the year he was born. They often referenced the time of his birth as the winter of Koli Kosh. They were on their way through the pass in the Zagros Mountains known as the Koli Kosh—Gypsy Killer— and had been caught in an early snowstorm that lasted more than a week. Hatam, then a newborn, had survived, while many had died, including Danial's old parents and a few of Zomorod's relatives. Hatam had grown up to be an intelligent and restless young man. He was tall, with strong arms and shoulders, the result of pound- ing the hammer and anvil from childhood alongside his father. But he was not happy with the smithery and their nomadic life. Since the first day they arrived in Sangriz, he had been visiting the pump house, watching the bulldozers and dump trucks. Bahram Khan had seen him hanging around asking Goodarz questions. When he found out that Hatam was a blacksmith, he immediately thought he would be a good candidate to run the brick factory's furnace and was able to convince him to stay and work for him. But Hatam's heart's desire was to become a driver. The idea of having a steering wheel in his hands and driving a big truck delighted him.

"If possible, sir," he had said to Bahram Khan, "I would like to be Goodarz's helper on one of the dump trucks and learn how to drive."

"Why not?" Bahram Khan had said. "Start by running the fur- nace in the brick factory and then little by little Goodarz will teach you how to drive a dump truck. This same Goodarz," Bahram Khan had said, laughing, "didn't know driving from his mother's womb. He had to be kicked in the butt when he was in the military to learn how to drive."

Danial was sitting with Mirza-ali and a few of the older villagers on a kilim by the fire. They were smoking their pipes and drink- ing tea. Since yesterday he had been waiting for Hatam, who had

115

gone to the city with Goodarz to bring a dozen immigrant Afghan laborers to work at the brick factory. It was long past midday and the sun was shining at an angle through the dusty sky, but Hatam hadn't returned.

The roar of the digging machines rose and fell in the wind. Marafi and a few boys were sitting close by the fire absorbed in listening to the men. Gorgi, who was lying nearby with her head on her paws, seemed to be immersed in memories, perhaps seeing in the depths of her cloudy eyes the herds she used to run, trying to keep them safe from the mountain wolves.

"How's your grandson, Amu Mirza-ali?" Danial asked.

"My poor child was whimpering last night," Mirza-ali said as he emptied his pipe by the fire. "He was frightened and his mother sat beside him all night, praying to the Prophet Mohammad and the Imams. I don't know what may have happened to his leg. If he's not well in a day or two, I'll take him to the clinic. Maybe one of the dump trucks will take us to the main road and from there we can get on a bus."

"Yes, do that. I still think it's an insect bite," Danial said, scratching his head thoughtfully. "But I think he'll be fine. Just boil some of the herb I gave you yesterday and put it on his leg. It may take a few days, but it will pass. It has to take its course."

Danial drank the last sip of his tea, dumped out the tea leaves, and pushed the cup under a blanket in a corner of one of the bundles that he had put together to be loaded on a donkey.

"Any news from Haydar?" he asked.

"Yes, his wife and sister visited him a few days ago and say he's fine. But"—Mirza-ali looked into the distance beyond the graveyard—"how could he be? I know him, he couldn't be fine in a place like that."

"All we can do is hope, Amu, and pray for his safety and release. I missed him very much this year. He used to sit with me late into the night and we would talk about the old days. I remember him from when I was a young man and he was a little boy, as old as your grandson is now. He would come with his father—his dad and mine were good friends and I would make him *ferfereh* and wooden animals. He loved to listen to stories and was fascinated with the old things my dad had collected over the years—coins, broken pottery, and things like that. He wanted to know all about them and how it happened we had them. One time he wanted to come with us, but his grandfather wouldn't let him. He liked to repeat the stories he had heard from his grandfather about hidden treasure in the ruins and how the foreigners, the *farangiz*, had found many of them using some kind of listening tools." Danial stopped for a moment and then looked Mirza-ali straight in the eyes. "Maybe he found a treasure after all these years of searching. I heard that he did."

"No, Mash Danial, I doubt it. It's all people's animosity, my friend. Bahram Khan, that no-good man, wanted him out of the way, and he and some of our villagers—I'm not going to bring up names, but you may know who—made up some wild story about a treasure found in the hills."

"That's what his wife told Zomorod."

"I can tell you this, though," Mirza-ali said in a whisper, "Haydar never said anything, but I heard—you know how people talk—that he was searching for something special. A Black Globe . . . or Jaam-e Jam, King Jamshid's drinking cup. He never mentioned that, but he did say he believed there was something in the hills, because the foreigners had been looking there and had taken things out."

"Who knows, Amu," Danial said thoughtfully, "it could be true. People have found things in the old hills . . . I think I'll give Haydar a visit when we go by the city. I know where the prison is," he said with a laugh. "I've visited friends and relatives there. We Gypsies are familiar with places like that."

"I know," Mirza-ali said, nodding. "Tribal people, too. There's always one of us in that place because he stood up to defend himself. It would be nice of you to give Haydar a visit, Danial. If you do go, make sure to let him know we're thinking of him and hope that he'll be back with his family soon. If he's not out soon, I may try to visit him myself. Maybe I'll go with his wife and sister when they're going."

The crows had moved away from the village and were black points over the fields and the mountainside, but their harsh calls

117

still reached Sangriz. Mehrangiz and Golandam were sitting with Zomorod away from the men. The year before when Mehrangiz had asked the Gypsy woman to tell her fortune and say whether she would have babies—she wanted a girl first and then a boy—Zomorod had said that it would happen but she must be patient. This time Mehrangiz was there for a different reason. She was desperate to find out something about Haydar. It was the second time in a week that she had gone to have her fortune told before the Gypsies left Sangriz.

Mehrangiz and Golandam watched Zomorod's hands as she scattered the fortune-telling beans on a tray and studied them. Zomorod's hands trembled as she moved the groups of beans around. "No matter what I do," she said, "they don't want to come together. They go every which way." She closed her eyes and murmured the spells over again. Then she opened her eyes, pushed all the beans into a pile, and separated them into smaller piles with her long, tattooed fingers, pushing a few to the upper or lower part of the tray and a few to the right or to the left, dividing them into threes, fours, sevens, and nines until all the beans were divided up and only one was left in the center. Her bracelets jingled with her movements and her forehead furrowed in displeasure as she kept repeating the spell. She lowered her tattooed chin and narrowed her eyes as if trying to penetrate to the depths of life and discover Haydar's fate. "I see disorder and confusion," she said in a shaky voice. "There is some sort of commotion going on. People are running around aimlessly. Smoke and fire are pouring into the sky . . . I can't see what is going on or what all those people are after . . . See . . ." She pointed to scattered beans on the tray, then started to push them together and separate them again in the same fashion as before. She was all concentration, the movement of her hands and shoulders, the expression in her eyes, and her murmuring all rhythmic and complementary, as in some sophisticated and mysterious ritual handed down to her by her ancestors. "Ah, there. I see him," she said excitedly. "I see Haydar." She pointed to a bean in the center surrounded by groups of beans.

Mehrangiz and Golandam leaned closer, their eyes pinned on the beans, waiting to hear what the Gypsy woman would say.

Golandam looked pale and weak. She had been disheartened by her brother's being taken away, but hadn't said much. At home she tried to keep busy, cleaning, washing, and shaking the dust out of the kilims and carpets, sometimes doing the same things over and over. But every time she saw Haydar's motorcycle parked in the corner of the yard, she longed to hear it running and see Haydar riding it. She thought of her brother and the way he looked behind the prison window, a skinny figure with a shaved head and sunken, sad eyes. Seeing Jaffar and going out shopping or having ice cream were the only happy things about going to the city.

"There he is, I see him," Zomorod repeated. "I see him. He's there among a group of people. He seems well and happy. He's laughing. He's running along with the others, going somewhere . . . Oh, it's getting dark, I can't see . . . I can't see him anymore." She moved the beans and her deep voice sounded as if it were coming from another world. "Cursed be the devil, cursed be Satan. Nothing is clear, I can see no more . . . fire, smoke, chaos. People are running away from something. They all seem to be confused and not know what to do or where to run to." She pointed to the beans again. "See . . . they're all over the place."

Mehrangiz and Golandam looked at each other and then at Zomorod, who went on repeating her spells. Suddenly they were startled by the loud honk of an approaching dump truck. An orange dump truck with a mountain of dust rising behind it came and stopped a few yards away from the Gypsies' belongings.

Goodarz jumped down from behind the wheel and walked around the truck. He checked the air in each tire by kicking it with the toe of his boot.

Before Hatam was out of the passenger side of the truck, Zomorod let go of the tray, scattering the beans on the ground as she ran to him.

"You're back, my son," she called out. "We've been waiting all day."

Danial ran to Hatam as well, shouting that they needed to get going.

"I told you last night," Hatam said, "I'm not going anywhere with you. I'm tired of wandering from village to village and having nothing. I'm happy working here and I'll try to have a life here. I have a job and get paid."

He hugged his mother, who had started to cry. "It's a good job and I'll have some money in my pocket. You don't need to worry about me. It may even be better for you and Baba to stay here or stay in one of the nearby towns. We must stop moving around. Things are changing everywhere. You know it's not the way it always was. It's not even like a year ago."

But neither Danial nor Zomorod wanted to hear that. As they went on trying to persuade him, a group of Afghan men, wearing turbans and baggy pants and covered with dust from head to toe, stood in the back of the dump truck watching.

Feeling the gaze of the men, Golandam and Mehrangiz got up and left in a sober mood. Mirza-ali, Marafi, and the others said good-bye to Danial and started for the village, Marafi stopping every few steps to turn around and look back toward the truck and the group of strange newcomers.

4

On a late afternoon in the last days of winter, a man showed up at Sangriz. The villagers, including Mirza-ali, who were sitting in front of Sayed Ayoub's shop chatting and enjoying the last light of the day, at first glance didn't realize that the skinny man with shaved head and sunken eyes was Haydar. A couple of boys ran to let Mehrangiz know, and soon the news traveled to every neighborhood, and the villagers, young and old, ran to the square to welcome Haydar home. They circled him, taking turns hugging and kissing him. Then they accompanied him to his house.

For hours people kept coming to Haydar's house—everyone except for Amir Khan, his son, and the people in their circle. Some came out of curiosity to see how a man looked after months of being in jail. Some came to show their respect and support. Jamal, who heard the news while he was at the brick factory, hurried home and, without washing off the dust, went to see Haydar. Mehrangiz and Golandam, not quite recovered from the shock and the sheer happy feeling of having Haydar back, with the help of Bibigol and several other women, rushed about welcoming people and offering them sweets and tea from a big samovar. It was as if a festival were going on. Everyone wanted to find out about Haydar's days in prison and how it happened that he had gotten out. Haydar wasn't in the mood to go into great detail, but mentioned the chaotic last few days in the prison, the riots and demonstrations in the city, and how a group of demonstrators had broken down the prison doors and freed everyone—political prisoners, lawbreakers, thieves, and even murderers.

Villagers who had traveled to Shiraz or worked there had seen some of the demonstrations and witnessed the cinemas, banks, and bookstores being attacked and put ablaze by protesters demanding the end of the monarchy. Some people who had radios and had been following the situation knew that the old bazaar in Teheran and bazaars in other cities had been closed in protest, teachers and oil workers all over the country were on strike, the military had been dissolved, and the Shah had been forced out of the country. Many generals and high-level officials were fleeing or had gone into hiding or been arrested and their properties confiscated. And that any day Ayatollah Khomeini would be returning to Iran from France. The villagers listened to Haydar and talked among themselves, worried about what it all meant and what the future held.

Mehrangiz and Golandam believed that a miracle had happened that Haydar was home and kept offering tea and sweets to their visitors. It was long past midnight before everyone was gone and Haydar and his family went to bed, exhausted.

Haydar, after withstanding the humiliation of being imprisoned and seeing the joy and excitement of the people who broke into the prison, had left for Sangriz not knowing what to think about what was happening, where the roots of it lay, and whose hands were behind it, or who was likely to benefit—certainly not people like him, people who knew only how to work the land. Adding to his uncertainties were the problems of adjusting to life in Sangriz without a job and his desire to confront Amir Khan and his son for lying and taking sides with Bahram Khan.

As days went by, the more he saw the brick factories and heaps of baked and unbaked bricks on the Dashtak plain and heard the roar of dump trucks instead of the *top, top* sound of the water pump, the more withdrawn and disillusioned he became. He couldn't believe how, in less than a year, not just Sangriz and its people but also the other villages in the surrounding area had changed so much. Many people had sold their small plots of land to the brick factories that were mushrooming up everywhere. Everyone talked about making money. He could see the jealousy and ostentation in people and wondered at the root of it. Was it the paying jobs at the brick factories that put a little cash in their pockets? Sure it was hard to work the land—but to have it destroyed like that?

Amir Khan had followed the example of the junior Rahbari and started a brick factory on his land. He had bought two dump trucks. A few city people had also bought land to put up factories. There were always strangers around—Afghan laborers and people from other villages came in search of jobs. Tanker trucks were everywhere and bulldozers and loaders roared about, greedily digging and moving the dirt around. Sangriz was rumbling with noise and shrouded in dust.

Jamal had become the head foreman at Bahram Khan's brick factory. He was an important man in the village, hiring and firing workers and running the daily activities of the business. Goodarz was a truck driver. The Gypsy Hatam was a furnace man. Mirza-ali's son Kubaad had quit being a shepherd and was working as a foreman supervising the Afghan workers. Mirza-ali, lacking the energy in his old legs to drive his herds to the mountainside to graze, sold the last few of his sheep to Bahram Khan, who had them butchered for meals for the workers. Mirza-ali was heartbroken and blamed his son for not being able to hang on to his last few animals that he loved. "Shame on me that I raised you, Kubaad," he had painfully complained. "Go, get away from me. Stay out of my sight. Let me say in front of all the Sangriz people that you're not my son anymore. If it wasn't for that little boy of yours, for my dear grandchild, I would head to the desert to die alone."

"Amu," Haydar said to Mirza-ali when he was sitting with him at the village square, "if the fields of a village die, its people will eventually scatter away like dust in the wind."

"How right you are, Haydar," said Mirza-ali, nodding. "We nomadic people have a similar saying. If the herds die, no tent pole will stay up. The life of a farming community depends on its land, the life of a nomad community on its herds."

Haydar approached a few of the people he knew best, trying to convince them that they should go to the Agriculture Department in Shiraz and let them know what was happening in Sangriz. His thinking was that there was a file there from the old days that would have a record of his father's complaints about the way the senior Rahbari had cheated the villagers at the time of the White Revolution when the Shah tried to institute land and water rights, women's rights, labor laws, and education and health benefits, with the aim of having a revolution without bloodshed to modernize the country. Now, with the new changes happening and a revolutionary regime that Haydar had heard was sympathetic to the people, especially to rural people, he thought they might have a chance to get at least part of the land back. But none of the villagers would listen to him. They argued that it was too late, that the landowners still had their connections, that no one would listen to them, and they would be wasting their time. Some of them had jobs and hadn't worked the land for years, plus no one wanted to farm anymore, reasoning that it was hard work, expensive, and without much return. And above all, there was a shortage of water, and even if they got some land back, they would need to dig wells—and where would they get the money to do that? They preferred jobs and at least having some cash.

Haydar, after taking everything in, decided that the only thing left for him was to move away. He promised himself he wouldn't sink so low as to work in a brick factory as Jamal was trying to get him to do. He wasn't going to be a part of destroying the land that he loved, to work in a brick factory and suffer from sunrise till sunset in the heat and dust for the junior Rahbari, a man he despised. He'd rather leave it to those villagers who didn't gave a damn and who, after a long day's work, gathered in front of Sayed Ayoub's shop to drink Pepsi, joke, and talk behind one another's backs. They didn't open their eyes to see what was happening to the village.

"Sangriz is not a place for me anymore," he complained bitterly to Mirza-ali. "After Golandam's wedding, which we've decided will be just after the New Year, I'll take Mehrangiz and leave this place—*inshallah*. I'm not crippled and I'm not afraid of work. I'll be able to earn my daily bread somehow. And, God willing, I'll go to the Agriculture Department myself and complain. I'll go every day and never rest until I get a satisfactory answer. And as far as what Amir Khan did to me, I've decided to let it be for now. I'll tell you, Amu Mirza-ali, it's not because I am afraid of him, his son, or his men. No, not as long as there is breath in my body. It's for the sake of my wife—all of this has been too much for her. And for the sake of my little sister and the coming wedding. She has to live in this place. They've been begging me not to do anything. And I know now is not the time, but I won't forget it."

Part
Five

1

The cold winter had passed and the ground was breathing afresh. A velvet cloth of green lay over the hills and fields. Even the roofs of the village houses were covered with green grass. The scent of the blossoms of early spring wafted over Sangriz from the mountainside. It was Nowruz—the New Year. People were happy, and the wedding of Jamal and Golandam added to the joy.

For two days the sounds of the *saaz va dohol*—the horn and the drums—were heard in Sangriz. The first day was the henna ceremony. Hamaami, the bathhouse caretaker, put henna on Jamal's hands and head while Bibigol and the other women poured their hearts out singing wedding songs. In Haydar's house, Hamaami's wife, Samar, put henna on Golandam's hands, feet, and hair, while Mehrangiz and a few other women danced around the bride and sang. The young girls put henna on the palms of their hands as well in the hope that they would someday become brides.

The next afternoon, people gathered in front of the village *hamaam*—bathhouse. The old bathhouse, with its arches and dome, was as old as the village itself and stood in an open area in the lower part of the village below the main square.

First Golandam was taken to the bathhouse to be prepared for going to the groom's house. Accompanied by a group of women and young girls, she went through the old wooden door and along the narrow, low-ceilinged hall leading to the first chamber— the undressing chamber—where a shaft of sunlight fell from an opening in the center of the dome to a shallow pool with water running over its rim. Golandam undressed in one of the open-arched rooms, stepped into the pool and washed her feet, and then walked through another short, narrow hall to enter the main chamber.

The large chamber was dark and muggy and smelled of soap and rose water. Steam rose to the old arches and up to the small holes around the dome. The faint sounds of the music could be heard through the thick walls of the bath. The women and young girls circled Golandam as they sang the wedding songs. One washed her hair, another her hands, and a third her feet. As soon as a voice called out, "Water," the girls poured bowls of water over the bride and washed away the soap and henna.

Hamaami's wife, Samar, sitting in front of the bride, pulled a comb through her long hair. *Mashaallah, mashaallah*, she repeated, "what a mountain of hair. Look—so soft, so smooth, like silk. Look at how it's taken the color of the henna so nicely. What a beautiful bride we have here. *Mashaallah, mashaallah*. Tonight Jamal will go wild smelling this hair." She smiled at the bride. Throughout the forty years of her adult life, Samar, like her grandmother and mother before her, had delivered many of the village's children and prepared many brides for their wedding chamber. She particularly liked Golandam and her family and was happy to see her be married to another family that she liked. Years ago, when she delivered Golandam, she could see that she would grow up to be a beautiful woman, and now she could see how right she had been and kept admiring her beauty. "I haven't seen such a magnificent bride in all my life. You certainly are the prettiest one."

Everyone looked at Golandam. Most of them were seeing her naked for the first time. She was tall with dark eyes, fair skin, a long neck, and shapely breasts. She looked like a beautiful and perfect marble statue standing to be admired. Some of the women sighed as if remembering their younger days.

From the day before, when the musicians who were going to play at the wedding ceremony arrived in Sangriz, Golandam had had a strange feeling. She couldn't believe that the time for her to become a wife had arrived. Last night after the henna ceremony, she couldn't close her eyes and go to sleep. No matter how hard she tried, she couldn't comprehend the meaning of being a wife and going to her husband's house to live. She knew only that as long as there had been life, there had come a day when a young woman had to become someone's wife—like Mehrangiz, like Bibigol, like her mother, like the old women of the village with their wrinkled faces or the adolescent girls with soft skin and black eyes. The girls watched her in awe, wondering when their time of becoming a bride would arrive. Golandam had been thinking of her mother recently and could hear her saying, "My little one, you're going to grow up to be a beautiful woman and we'll marry you to a handsome young man." In the crowded and noisy old bath, she felt her head getting heavy and her heart beating faster.

Outside the bathhouse, Bibigol and a group of women and girls were gathered around Jamal, whose hair was covered with dried henna, as he waited to be taken into the bathhouse. Bibigol, in her raspy voice, sang *vaasoonak*, the traditional folk wedding songs:

> May you build a palace
> with forty columns and forty windows
> and live in it happily with your beautiful bride.

And then the women, all together, burst into the loud sound of the *kel*, the *kelelelelele . . . kelelelelele* that they made by clicking their tongues on the roofs of their mouths.

Another voice started up, singing, "The jingle-jangle of music is filling up Sangriz . . . Dear bridegroom, be happy, your bride is delightfully approaching."

There was another burst of *kelelelelelele* from the women and a young girl sang,

> Hey Hamaami, hey Hamaami, refresh the bathwater—
> The handsome bridegroom is ready for a bath.

The women and girls took turns making the sound of *kel* and singing, accompanied by the musicians, Delshad on the horn and his son Khoshdel on the drums, who were giving it all they had. The father and son were from Shiraz and were well known to the villagers, who liked their style and were always happy to engage them to perform at weddings.

131

Jamal sat quietly surrounded by the women. He gave no sign of joy or sadness. There was only a slight apprehension nesting in the depth of his eyes that intensified every time Marafi appeared in his view, a sense of worry that seemed to extend in an unbroken thread from the past to the present moment and perhaps into the future.

Delshad began to play the Choopy—the women's dancing music. The women and young girls, all in their best clothes, stood in a row from tallest to shortest, with long scarves of yellow, red, white, and purple in their hands. They danced in unison, whirling the scarves in the air and moving their heads and shoulders to the rhythm of the music as they slowly stepped forward to form a large circle. The men stood watching, the young ones keeping their eyes on the young girls and searching for their future bride. A group of Afghan workers from the brick factory were gathered in a corner of the square watching, perhaps thinking of their wives and children and the weddings they were missing in the faraway villages of their home country.

A huge tent had been erected on the flat roof of Amir Khan's house overlooking the bathhouse and the square where the musicians were playing. Bahram Khan and a dozen of his friends from Shiraz, tipsy and high from drinking arak and smoking opium, were taking turns standing up and walking to the edge of the roof to watch the dancing and then, with jokes and laughter, returning to their drinking and smoking. The carcass of a lamb that Goodarz had butchered that morning hung from a tripod, and he was cutting pieces of meat, running them through with a skewer, and handing them to Kubaad to put over the blazing fire that was close by. Soft blue smoke and the smell of kebab being grilled rose and floated out of the yard. Every so often, Hatam, a tray in hand, took a few skewers of kebab from the fire and put them between freshly cooked flat bread to carry up to the tent. Amir Khan's son, Sarferaaz, who was stationed beside the fire, kept his eye on the room where the bottles of beer and arak were stored under hay and blocks of ice. His father had instructed him not to let anyone know what was in the room or allow anyone to get close to it. Sarferaaz kept the key to the room in his pocket and played with it with his sweaty fingers. Once in a while he would snatch a piece of kebab from the fire and throw it between his teeth after blowing on it.

He joked with Goodarz and Hatam, ignoring their pleading for a beer or shot of arak. When something was needed in the tent, Amir Khan would come down from the roof, give the order to his son, and then go upstairs.

The women were still dancing when the bride, wearing a flowered dress, a green velvet jacket, and a yellow scarf, came out of the bath, accompanied by a group of women singing and making the joyful sound of the *kel*. Mehrangiz was on one side of the bride and Hamaami's wife, Samar, on the other. The musicians followed them past Sayed Ayoub's shop and up the alley that led to Haydar's house in the upper part of the village. All the women and girls followed behind, dancing and repeating their joyful *kel*.

Hamaami and a group of the men took Jamal to the bathhouse. The musicians returned to the front of the square and changed from the Choopy to the Choob Bazy, the men's stick dance.

As soon as Kubaad and Goodarz heard the stick-dance music, they came out of the yard where they had been cooking and were the first ones to start the dance while the rest of the villagers circled around watching and waiting for their turn. They passed the sticks between them, waving them around their heads and jumping to the rhythm of the horn and the drums, taking turns thrusting out their stick toward their opponent's legs while the other blocked the blows. At times Goodarz would pass his stick to Sarferaaz, or Kubaad would pass his to another man in the crowd. A few times they gave the sticks to the Afghans in turbans and baggy pants so they could join in and add to the fun of the dance.

Bahram Khan and a couple of his friends came down to watch the stick dance from a closer vantage point. Goodarz, Kubaad, and Sarferaaz were putting their hearts into it, chasing after one another with a confidence and eagerness that were the envy of many in the crowd. They passed the sticks back and forth and moved aggressively, trying to hit their opponents. Bahram Khan watched with interest and tipped each one, including the musicians, with crisp one hundred toman bills before going back to the tent.

Haydar and Mirza-ali were sitting against the bathhouse wall, watching the stick dance and talking. Once in a while Haydar would glance up at Bahram Khan and his friends.

133

"I can't believe that Amir Khan put up that tent and threw a party," Haydar said. "Why did I listen to Jamal? Why didn't he let me stop Amir Khan from setting up that tent? All for that no-good Bahram Khan, who has caused us so many problems. Look, Amu Mirza-ali, see how he has all the people of the village under his thumb and the way he behaves in our own home."

Mirza-ali nodded. "It's good that you listened to Jamal. It will pass and they'll go away. It's your sister's wedding, you mustn't make any trouble." He smiled. "You talk about people. People are just like sheep, including my own son. Pick up a stick and you can drive them wherever you wish."

"Amu," Haydar said, "these people have to work hard all day and put up with lots of nonsense to bring home a piece of bread. I understand that. But some of them are like dogs—if you throw them a bone, they'll wag their tails and come to you. If they would have listened to me and we could have come together as a group and gone to the Agriculture Department, we would have had a chance to get our land back. I told them that things had changed after the revolution and that country folks were listened to, but they didn't want to do it. They'd rather run behind Mr. Rahbari and Amir Khan for a job that puts a few bills in their pocket. And you know what, Amu? I've decided not to give a damn about any of them anymore. Why should I? Am I crazy to expose my head to the wind for them?"

"Right," Mirza-ali said, "why should you fight for them? Don't make it so hard for yourself, Haydar. *Bogon Khoshaloog goondur,*" he added in his Ghashghai tongue—today is the day of happiness.

Jaffar, in a brand-new suit, his long hair perfectly combed, watched the stick dance and the musicians and tried the dance for a few rounds as the crowd cheered him on to dance more since it was his brother's wedding, but he soon passed the stick to someone else. He couldn't stay in one place for long. He would go where Haydar and Mirza-ali were sitting and then go into the yard where the kebab was being cooked. Marafi, trying to get away from the boys who pulled on his satchel or coat and called him Amu Laal—Uncle Mute, the affectionate name the villagers had given him—followed close behind him. Usually the kids were kind to Marafi and would

134

leave him alone, but there were times like today when they would gang up on him.

Haydar's house was crowded with guests. The scent of perfume and rose water saturated the air of the small room where no man was allowed. Golandam was sitting on a cushion in the middle of the room and a few young girls were holding mirrors and singing. Some tried to edge their way closer to see the bride, while others left the crowded room to get some fresh air. Children cried or laughed as they snatched candies from the sweets trays and snaked through the mass of women moving in and out. Samar sat in front of the bride with the manicuring string between her fingers. She ran the string over Golandam's face with rapid motions, the threads spinning and twisting over the tender skin, grabbing and pulling every soft invisible hair and leaving reddish marks on her skin. Golandam twitched in pain, and if she tried to pull back, Samar gave her a sharp eye and worked even more enthusiastically. She paid no attention to the heat, the noise, or the crowd all around her. Drops of sweat were forming on her forehead and rolling down her round face. The girls watching the fast movements of Samar's hands over the bride's face bit their lips in astonishment. The whole scene was making Golandam's stomach turn. She wished she could get the strings out of Samar's hands and wrap them around her thick neck until her eyes popped out, then run from all these overjoyed people and everything that was happening.

After a while Samar stopped and put her hand under the bride's chin, then, moving her head from side to side, studied Golandam's face. Satisfied with the outcome, she ordered everyone out of the room so she could speak to the bride in private.

The musicians were playing and the men were still in the heat of the stick dance when Jamal was brought out of the bathhouse. Shouting happily, the men handed the stick to him and invited him to dance. Everyone was pleased to have the honor of having a round with the groom, including Haydar.

Dusk was falling over the village by the time the music stopped. The women were moving around hurriedly to prepare the celebration dinner. Huge pots of saffron rice, ten in all, were steaming slowly over a low fire in one corner of Bibigol's yard. In another corner pots of different kinds of stew were boiling—lamb and chickpeas, lamb and eggplant, and stewed beans with greens.

Golandam felt tired inside the heavy wedding dress. The smell of perfume and incense were irritating, and her face was stinging from Samar's string work. She wiped her forehead with a handkerchief and tried not to think of the things Samar had told her about what to do and how to behave when she was alone with Jamal in the wedding chamber. She couldn't believe that in a few hours she would be leaving the house where she was born and grew up. She was realizing how fast the days had gone by and couldn't understand how they had led up to a day like this. Childhood days of playing with other girls and running in the green fields were suddenly gone and she was becoming a wife and starting a new life. She was very tired. Her head was dizzy and her heart was beating hard. Her face was burning and Sangriz was spinning around her. No, she thought, she didn't want to leave her home. She didn't want to leave this small adobe house with its memories of her mother and father. What good was a husband's house? She didn't want to feel the rough touch of a man on her skin. A man with a prickly mustache. No, she wouldn't let him touch her. Even if the sky came down to the earth, she wouldn't allow it. The sound of the horn and the drums echoed in her head and the smell of rose water and makeup made it hard to breathe. Samar's words about blood and losing her virginity were on her mind. She twisted her legs tight together. Her insides were aching. She held the cushion against her stomach and stared at the yellow flame of the lantern but soon stood up and anxiously looked at herself in the mirror again—her lips red, her face covered with makeup, her eyebrows thinned, and her eyes darkened by *sormeh*. She didn't like herself this way and couldn't believe it was Golandam she was seeing in the mirror. She couldn't understand why people did these things. Everything seemed like a child's game to her. Like the games she played with the village girls and boys when she would be a bride, singing wedding songs and willingly walking to the groom's chamber that they put up using chadors. They had all played and laughed and the game had ended

136

happily and without all this fuss. She turned away from the mirror and wished she could get out of the small room and free herself from the prison of the heavy clothes, then run out to the wheat fields and feel the air on her skin. She looked at the flowers that Jaffar and Marafi had brought down from the mountain, wondering what Jaffar was thinking. Was he enjoying the ceremony, or was he confused like she was? She remembered Sizdah Bedar, the spring picnic, when they had gone to the ruins of Persepolis and she and Jaffar and the other kids had picked flowers and greens, tied them together, and threw them into the running water, a traditional Sizdah Bedar activity for girls who wished to be a bride someday. She had laughed at Jaffar. "Are you a girl," she had said, "that you tie greens and throw them into the stream? Do you want to become a bride, too?"

Had her wish come true? She wondered if Jaffar was with Jamal and what Jamal was doing. Was he anxious like her? What was in his heart? When they were alone together tonight and the door of their wedding chamber was latched, what was she going to do? She remembered Jamal's gaze that afternoon when he passed her on his horse—how his eyes had pulled her toward him.

By late evening, dinner had been served to all the guests in three different houses—one for the women, two for the men. The guests were finishing their sweets and tea and smoking water pipes and chatting when the musicians started to play again, an indication that it was time to go to Haydar's house and bring the bride.

Mehrangiz burst in on Golandam excitedly. "They're coming! They're coming for you!" But then she saw Golandam's face. "What's the matter, my dear?" she asked. "Are you all right? You've hardly touched the food I brought. You should eat something."

Golandam asked for water. Mehrangiz left the room and came back with a glass of water. She knew what sort of fear and confusion could run in the mind of a bride on her wedding night and thought about her own wedding—the noisy crowds and all the coming and going and the fuss and then being alone in the wedding chamber with Haydar. She remembered being drenched in sweat and how her heart raced when Haydar sat next to her. And how she trembled when he kissed her and put his big hand on her shoulder. It was the first time she had ever been touched by a man . . . But were all men like Haydar—rough on the outside but sweet and soft and considerate, the way he was then and had been all along, a man she had come to love so much and couldn't live without? She didn't know and didn't let her mind wander more.

"Here, have some water." She held the glass out to Golandam. "My dear, I know all sorts of thoughts are going through your mind. It's understandable. You can't believe how scared I was on my wedding night. But, I tell you, there is nothing to be afraid of. Going to a husband's house isn't a scary thing. You should be happy. Who better than Jamal? Do you know how many girls in Sangriz would love to be in your place? Jamal is a handsome young man, strong and hardworking. A woman needs a husband like that, who will work hard and provide for her. You should love your husband. He's a gentle man. Soon you'll know. There's nothing to worry about. Our menfolk are shy at first and don't say much about their feelings, but just wait, he will love you. He'll open up to you, and the same with you. You'll learn to love him. You're lucky you're not going to a husband who is much older than you, like Shamssi, who got married a year ago, or going to a husband's house in a different village, far away from here, like Nassrin. You'll be in Bibigol's house—Bibi, who loves you and is like a mother to you, and to me as well. You should listen to your husband and think about keeping a nice, clean home. Haydar and I both love you. You're special to us. My dear, you shouldn't be afraid to become a wife. Haven't I done the same? And I was only half your age. Here, have a little more water and remember when you go into the wedding chamber to put your right foot in first and pray and say the name of God and the Prophet three times."

Golandam took another drink of water. When Mehrangiz had come into the room, she had thought for a second that it was her own mother. How often she had thought of her mother in the past few days and felt her close by. A few times she even thought she saw her among the women, standing around the room smiling and glancing her way. It gave Golandam the feeling that she didn't want to leave the place she'd grown up in, where she felt the presence of her parents around her. She was afraid that after the wedding Haydar and Mehrangiz would leave this house. "I don't have any hope for Sangriz," Haydar had said. "I'll build a wall in front of the house and leave."

Haydar's words had left Golandam with an uneasy feeling. She thought that walling off the entrance of a house and abandoning it would allow the bad spirits and jinns to come in and live. She had heard that many times, and everyone knew of the abandoned and tumbling-down house behind the village bath that no one would go close to. She didn't want that for their house. She didn't want a house so full of memories of her parents to be abandoned and silent. She hated herself and the wedding. Everything, she thought, was related to the wedding—Bibigol's being hurt the day they were in Shiraz to buy wedding clothes, Haydar's fight with the landlord and going to jail, and now his wanting to leave Sangriz after she was married. My dear brother, she thought, it's not his fault. It's the fault of the people who talk behind his back. It upsets him every time he looks at the pump house and the fields and when he walks past the brick factories and hears people saying that it's lucky for him the bulldozers have made it easy by turning the hills inside out so he doesn't need to dig anymore and can just walk around and gather all the broken pottery he wants—how stupid and unkind people can be, how stonehearted, talking nonsense and telling lies. And some of those people are here at the wedding. Maybe it's better after all—better for him to go away from this place.

The music and singing could now be heard in the alley just behind the gate. "They're here," Mehrangiz said, "and, God willing, everything will go well, my dear." She kissed Golandam and, after hugging her passionately, left the room to receive Bibigol and those who were coming to take the bride away.

Golandam was pleased that Mehrangiz had come and talked to her. With all the things that Samar had told her about men and the wedding night, and all the thoughts that had made her anxious, Mehrangiz's soothing advice and hearing her talk about her own wedding night calmed her down. Knowing that she could go to her at any time and ask about anything that she needed to know or talk about anything that bothered her made her feel more relaxed.

Soon Mehrangiz returned with Haydar, Bibigol, and a few of the women. One of the women held up a mirror, the sign of light and purity. Another carried a tray with a Koran and a bowl of burning incense. Light from the lanterns flooded the room. Bibigol held Golandam's right hand and Mehrangiz her left. Golandam hesitated for a second and was about to step back, but Bibigol and Mehrangiz pulled her forward and led her underneath the tray with the Koran that was being held above her head. The woman with the mirror kept a few steps ahead so that the image of the bride and the light from the lanterns would reflect in the mirror. Haydar, his eyes moist, walked behind the bride. He felt that by sending his sister to her husband he was fulfilling his duty. Now that neither his father nor mother was alive, it was up to him, and with an open heart he would put his sister's hand into Jamal's, whom he loved like a brother.

They walked the bride three times around the fireplace in the far corner of the yard and then around the sycamore tree that Haydar's grandfather had planted years ago near the well. Golandam walked slowly. When she stepped from the yard into the alley, the first thing she saw was Abrash by the gate, her mane braided with threads of red and yellow and a long red feather fountaining above her forehead. Then she saw the alley packed with people holding up lanterns. A woman burst out singing:

> We've come for the flower,
> The white cotton flower,
> The companion of the groom,
> The light of the wedding chamber.

Soon her voice was muffled by the music and the singing of others who joined in.

Haydar, holding the bride around the waist, suddenly picked her up from the ground and put her on the back of Abrash. A shudder ran through Golandam's body and she held tightly to the saddle. Hamaami lifted up Mirza-ali's grandson and sat him on the horse behind the bride. Then he shouted out, "May her firstborn be a boy, God willing."

With the sudden burst of *kelelelelelele . . . kelelelelele* coming from the women and people starting to sing, *Inshallah mobarak baadaa, inshallah mobarak baadaa*, handfuls of candies and coins were thrown into the air over the bride's head and the children rushed over the ground to collect them.

Sayed Ayoub called out the name of the Prophet Mohammad, and they moved down the alley toward Jamal's house on the opposite side of the village. Hamaami walked in front of the horse holding up a lantern and a mirror. Jaffar pulled Abrash's bridle with Marafi limping along beside him. Samar poured a pot of water on the ground behind the bride as a sign of purity and clarity. The musicians played, the men sang *mobrak baadaa*, and the women went on with making the sound *kel* all the way to Jamal's house. Golandam watched people dancing around her, their thick shadows intermingling on the walls of the alley. Dear God, she prayed, don't give me a son who, when he grows up, will have to go to prison like Haydar or a daughter whose destiny is like mine.

In front of Bibigol's house, the crowd stopped, singing louder and waiting for Jamal, who came out holding a pomegranate—the symbol of elegance and fertility. He threw it in the air, and it split open in front of the bride, scattering hundreds of bright-red seeds. Jamal stepped to the bride, put his arms around her, and picked her up from the saddle, his face disappearing in her fluffy flowered dress. Golandam had to throw her arms around his neck to keep from falling. The sweet scent of his perfume made her dizzy and she swooned as people cheered and Jamal carried her inside the yard to the room where the wedding chamber had been set up. Bibigol, standing by the door, welcomed the bride with tears running down her cheeks, her heart filled with the wish for a grandchild.

2

The morning after the wedding, Bibigol happily tucked away the white handkerchief, stained pink in a few spots, that Jamal had handed to her just before dawn. For years she had anticipated this morning and was pleased and grateful that everything had gone well. She had wanted a big wedding for her firstborn son, with many guests and good food, music, and dancing. Most of all she was overjoyed and thankful that fate had it that Golandam became her daughter-in-law. The only regret she had was that neither her husband nor Golandam's parents were alive to see it.

She let the newlyweds sleep late and around midmorning made a big omelet—using eggs from her own hens—and strong tea and took them to the chamber. She kissed Golandam and, stepping back, looked at her as if she were seeing her for the first time.

"Look at you," she said, smiling. "My, my . . . look how beautiful you are, my dear. Welcome—welcome to your new home." Golandam shyly kept her head down. "You have a wonderful husband and, *inshallah*, will be happy in this house. You'll take care of each other and Jamal will be a kind and a caring husband. Isn't that so, Jamal?"

"Of course, Mother," Jamal said.

"Now enjoy your breakfast," Bibi said, "and call me if you need anything. Later I'll bring you some sweets and more tea. You don't need to come out at all, either of you."

By afternoon, with the help of Mehrangiz, Samar, and a few other women, everything borrowed from neighbors and relatives—dishes, pots, silverware, samovars, teapots, and water pipes—had been washed, dried, and given to Jaffar, who went up and down the alleys with Marafi lagging behind him and returned everything to their owners. The borrowed carpets, cushions, and kilims were swept and shaken clean and returned as well. Bibigol remembered exactly what belonged to whom and was grateful that nothing had been damaged, broken, or lost except for a teapot and a couple of glasses. "Thank God they were my own," she sighed with relief.

For the next three days, Bibigol did all she could to make Jamal and Golandam comfortable. She had bought a small lamb, which Mirza-ali's son Kubaad butchered for her, and with the help of Mehrangiz made kebab, lamb stew with saffron rice, and then chicken kebab with sour cherry rice for the newlyweds.

On the fourth morning, a warm spring day, Golandam ran back to her house. Mehrangiz was alarmed but received her with open arms. "Is anything wrong?" she asked. "Have you forgotten about the *pagoshah*? You know you shouldn't leave until you're released and can come and go."

"I know," Golandam said, looking around the house as if she had been away for years. "Nothing's wrong, I was just missing everything and needed to get out of that small room and the rose water that Bibi sprinkles around morning and evening. I just missed this place."

"I was the same way," Mehrangiz said. "I was homesick from the first moments, but then I told myself, 'You better get over it and get used to your new home,' and soon I did, because your mother was very kind and supportive. So is Bibi—she loves you and you'll be surprised how quickly you'll get used to everything."

She wanted to ask how things had gone between her and Jamal but didn't know what to say. She had never talked about such intimate things, but tried the best she could. "I remember when I got married," she said, smiling. "Haydar was calm and gentle. I don't know how, but all the fear I had about being alone with a man, all that went away."

"You can't believe how I was shaking when Jamal took me off the horse," Golandam said. "We just sat quietly for a long time. Then he started to talk about our engagement and how much he liked

144

bringing me gifts and staying for dinner. Then . . . I don't know . . .
we were so tired we fell asleep . . ."

Mehrangiz smiled and asked if she would like a cup of tea. "No,
thank you," Golandam said. "Maybe a glass of water. I'd better go
back before Jamal or Bibi gets nervous."

"Okay. I'll be there later to help you and Bibi take down the
chamber. Then you're all invited here for dinner."

In the afternoon Haydar went with Jamal and Jaffar to Sayed
Ayoub's shop, which he had expanded so people could sit down to
drink tea and smoke the water pipe. They left the house in order to
let the women take down the chamber that had been set up in the
tiny room at the end of the yard. First Mehrangiz and Golandam
removed the mirrors, then the curtains and the rows of tassels—
gold, red, yellow, and turquoise—hung across the room, and finally
the pieces of flower-patterned fabrics decorating the walls. Bibigol
sat on the floor and folded the pieces of cloth as they were handed
to her. Some she had bought through the years by saving a little money here and there, all in anticipation of the wedding day.
Others were borrowed from Mehrangiz or other relatives or were
gifts to the bride and groom to be made into clothes for them and
their firstborn child. Once in a while Bibigol held one up, saying
to Golandam and Mehrangiz that it would make a nice blouse or
dress or shirt.

They put things away, setting aside the borrowed ones to be
returned. Golandam tidied the bed, and Mehrangiz took the small
carpet and cushions out to the yard, shook them, and laid them
in the sun to air. Bibigol praised God and sprinkled the room one
more time with rose water before taking the jar away.

That evening during the course of supper with Haydar and
Mehrangiz, they chatted about the wedding—how big it was, how
well the musicians played, and how many people turned out. They
heard that people were saying it had been one of the best weddings
in the village for as long as anyone could remember and that some
even said it would be a long time before anything would top it.
Haydar stopped himself from bringing up anything about Amir
Khan and the tent he'd set up on his roof. Instead he turned and
spoke to Jaffar. "I saw you doing the stick dance."

145

"I can't believe I missed it," Jamal said. "You always shied away from doing anything like that."

"Yes, but I wanted to dance the stick dance at my brother's wedding."

"I wish I'd been there," Jamal said with an admiring smile. "I would have done a round with you."

"He seemed pretty good," Haydar said and, laughing, added, "maybe he was trying to impress some of the young girls."

"No, I wasn't."

"You weren't hit, were you?" Jamal asked.

"No. It was close a few times, though. Sarferaaz was after me. I think he may have had a beer or two. But do you know who got hit?" Jaffar said, laughing. "Goodarz and Kubaad were after each other. I think they may still be licking their wounds."

"That's good to know," Jamal said. "It's something I can tease them about for a while."

"Yes, that was a nice thing to do," Bibigol said smiling at Jaffar, "to honor your brother, but I don't want you to do it again. You could get hurt. Someone always gets carried away."

When they were having tea and sweets, Jamal said that Bahram Khan had promised to give him the responsibility of going to the city once a month to arrange for the fuel oil for the brick factory and that he would be making more money and, God willing, was planning to build a bigger house by next year, possibly a two-story house, maybe even bigger than Amir Khan's house. Everyone was pleased to hear that. "It's time that young man did something good," Bibigol said, "you've been working hard for him."

Jamal turned to Haydar. "I could put in a good word for you. The past is past and things are changing for the better. You could have a job here."

Haydar was quiet and everyone looked at him with anticipation. "No, Jamal," he said finally. "Thanks, but let's not talk about it. Right now we're enjoying your and Golandam's happiness."

Haydar got up, went to the next room, and came back with a new deck of cards and something he had gotten in prison and hadn't shown to anyone. They were all fascinated when he took out a switchblade, especially Jaffar, who kept releasing the blade,

146

watching it fly open with a click, until Bibigol asked Haydar to take it away, saying, "Wasn't there anything better to bring from that place?"

"Yes, Bibi," Haydar answered and spread out the set of cards on the floor in front of him as everyone watched in surprise. "I have a deck of cards for Jamal as well."

"Good, at least no harm comes from these."

As he gathered the cards, Haydar talked about his days in prison and the men he'd known who weren't just good at cards but clever in tricks and cheating. He picked out three cards from the set, a king, a queen, and a jack, and, putting them down faceup on the carpet, asked Bibigol to chose one. Bibi pointed to the queen. Haydar turned the cards facedown and rubbed his palms above them. "Look very carefully now, Bibi," he said enthusiastically as both his hands went to work shuffling the three cards, all eyes watching his movements and the progress of the queen.

"Now." Haydar looked up at Bibigol. "Tap the one you think you picked."

Bibigol studied the cards for a moment, even though she thought she knew which one was the queen, and then pointed to the one in the middle.

"Are you sure?" Haydar asked.

Bibigol nodded without taking her eyes off the card, then sighed, bringing her hand to her mouth, when Haydar tuned over the card and it wasn't the queen but the jack. Everyone laughed in amazement and Haydar repeated the sequence, this time much more slowly. Now Bibigol watched more intently, but again she didn't pick out the correct card.

"My goodness, Haydar," she exclaimed. "How do you do it? I thought for sure I knew the right one this time."

The game went on with everyone taking their turn, each time sure that they had outsmarted Haydar and being surprised to find out otherwise. Then Haydar, Jamal, and Jaffar asked Golandam to join them in a game of hearts, saying they would show her how to play.

As they were getting ready to leave, Jamal said that in a day or so, before he went back to work, Golandam and he were planning to go to the city. He had asked for an advance on his salary from Bahram Khan. They were going to buy a set of china, water glasses, and silverware, also a half dozen bracelets and a watch for Golandam and maybe a watch for himself as well—he wasn't sure. It would depend on how much they could spend. They were also going to buy a table and four chairs, something no one else in the village had.

"We're going to go to a photography shop," Golandam said, "and have our picture taken sitting next to each other."

"That's an excellent idea, my dears," Bibigol said. "You go on and do that, then on another trip we'll all go—Mehrangiz and Haydar, too—and have our picture taken as a family. I wish we'd done it when Mash Safdar was alive. All the times we went to the city it never occurred to me."

When Jamal said he was thinking about buying a radio, everyone liked the idea. Jaffar broke in, saying that he knew an electronics shop called Light and Sound only a few streets from his school that sold radios, watches, and gramophones. Haydar said that just before he ended up in jail, he had been thinking about buying a radio and had been in the store Jaffar mentioned, but he thought the radios were too expensive, and that, according to the shop owner, the best ones were either the American GE or the German Philips radios, not the new Japanese ones that were coming onto the market.

"Bibi," Golandam said when they were at the door, "and you, too, Mehrangiz—what would you like us to get you from the city?"

Both Bibi and Mehrangiz said that they didn't need anything. They just wished them a good trip. But then Bibigol told Golandam about a shop in the bazaar where they had bought henna, saying that they had all sorts of flower seeds. "You can get me some seeds. I'd like to plant flowers now that it's springtime."

Part
Six

1

Late in the afternoon one Friday, a crowd had gathered in front of Sayed Ayoub's shop. They were drinking Pepsi, joking, and laughing. A group of boys were playing soccer, running after a deflated plastic ball and yelling for their team members to pass the ball. A few women were shopping at the store. No one noticed the two military vehicles approaching the village until they roared into the square in a cloud of dust. A moment later, a short, well-nourished mullah in a white turban and black mantle stepped out of one of the jeeps, followed by six militiamen who looked like young boys not yet out of high school trying hard to grow a full beard. They were carrying submachine guns and stayed vigilant. The mullah rearranged his mantle over his shoulders and surveyed the square. Then he slowly walked toward the crowd. Only two of the militia, one on each side, followed him. The rest stayed beside the jeeps.

Jamal, Goodarz, and Hatam the Gypsy had been bending over a used bicycle that Kubaad, Mirza-ali's son, had bought a few days earlier, trying to fix its broken chain. When they saw the jeeps, they stood up and Goodarz disappeared into the upper alley before anyone noticed. Sayed Ayoub paused in the middle of attending to Golandam and the other women who had come to buy rice, beans, onions, and whatever else they needed for dinner. The elders Mirza-ali, Amu Najaf, Mash Rahim, and a few others sitting against the wall of the shop stopped talking and put down their pipes. Amir Khan's son, Sarferaaz, was slow to notice the silence that fell over the square since, as usual, he was engaged in a heated debate and

151

had been challenging a couple of his friends to wrestle with him. The boys playing soccer were the last to stop and turn their attention toward the approaching mullah.

It wasn't the first time that the mullah had come to Sangriz. A few months earlier, after the Iraqi military had attacked the country, capturing several border towns and bombing the large Abadan oil refinery on the Persian Gulf, the mullah had come out to this rural area and gone from village to village to recruit the men of the villages, young and old, even the teenagers, to join the Basij, a newly established group drawn mostly from the cities that was to be deployed to the front even though most of its members lacked military training.

The mullah, holding himself erect and walking with deliberate steps, put his hand over his chest, bowed his head slightly, and said, *A salaam-o alekom* as he approached the crowd. He shook hands with the village elders, then looked at the crowd, who hadn't moved from where they were standing, and launched into his preaching. He showed more enthusiasm than on his first visit, when he'd had only the women and children and a few elderly people in his audience since most of the men had been out of the village, either cultivating their strips of farmland, gone to Shiraz in search of employment, or working at the brick factories. This time the mullah had come on a Friday to take advantage of the day of the week when the men would be off work and the children home from school. In a slow, sermonic way, brushing his gray beard with his long fingers, he talked about the revolution and how the brave Islamic nation under the advice and leadership of Imam Khomeini had struggled and shed blood to bring down the brutal dictatorship of the Shah and establish the Islamic Republic to bring equality and justice to the people. His voice kept climbing steadily and was booming by the time he got to the part about Islam and the revolution being under attack, not just by the homegrown enemies of God and the revolution who received help from Western countries but also, and most dangerously, by the infidel Saddam Hussein and his Western supporters like America and England, who were nothing but sworn enemies of Islam and the people of Iran and thought that the country was in a weak position because of the revolution,

152

not knowing that a nation of martyrs would be a thorn in the eye of those who couldn't see its progress.

Every so often, he would pause, fix his eyes on the boys who had come to the front of the crowd or on the women who were in the back standing on the shop's step, or pull on his mantle and rearrange it.

He emphasized that it was the duty of all Moslem men, young and old, as Imam Khomeini had declared, to join the fight to defend Islam and the country and defeat the enemy. He promised that the country's brave forces would take over Karbala and other cities in Iraq where the shrines of the Imams were located, and then, after Baghdad was conquered, Allah willing, the march would continue all the way to occupied Palestine to free it from the Zionists and gain control over the great mosque of Al-Aqsa, where the Prophet Mohammad ascended to the sky on a winged horse and toured the rings of heaven before returning to earth. He recited a few verses from the Koran and assured them that anyone martyred in this "Holy Defense," especially the young, would be granted a place in heaven where they would be in the company of the Prophet and the Imams. He said that all over the country, in the cities as well as in the villages, universities, schools, and factories, people were pouring into the mosques to register to enlist to go to the front and that they should, too, and should be ready to give help in whatever way they can.

The women who were present looked at one another. They had heard all this in his earlier visit, when he told them that it was their duty to encourage their draft-dodger sons and husbands to join the Basij. He had cited examples of villages where people had joined and had already been deployed to the front. But the mothers who had seen the Shah's gendarmes coming after draft dodgers and sent their sons out of the village into the mountains were not ready to give them away now. As the mullah went on talking, they moved through the crowd and slowly took hold of their young boys, who seemed captivated by what they were hearing, and quietly pulled them away and headed for home. Golandam ran to their house to let Bibigol know, and Bibi hurried to the square, pushed through the crowd, and asked Jamal to come home because she needed his help with something. Next came Sarferaaz's mother, then Faried's, then Karim's grandmother, and several other mothers, wives, and grandmothers, who, pretending to be listening, edged closer to their sons, grandsons, or husbands and slowly pulled them away. Even Mirza-ali, who hadn't talked to his son Kubaad since he took the job at Bahram Khan's brick factory, drew him aside and was talking to him when Kubaad's wife showed up.

The mullah finished by praising the Allah and the Imams. His militiamen pumped their fists and chanted, *Allah-o Akbar, Khomeini rahbar* three times. Then the mullah prayed for everyone's safety and said he was in a hurry to get to the next village before the sun went down but that he would be back. As they were about to leave, Sayed Ayoub brought a few bottles of Pepsi for them.

"Don't you know that this drink is religiously forbidden?" said the mullah with scorn. "Don't you know you shouldn't be selling it? This industry is in the hands of Baha'is and Israelis. With the help of Allah, soon we'll be closing all their factories."

"My good mullah"—Sayed Ayoub put on an apologetic face—"I didn't know that. We're far away in this village and news doesn't get to us fast."

Before heading for the jeeps, the mullah took Sayed Ayoub aside, as he had on the previous visit, saying that since he was a Sayed, a descendant of the Prophet Mohammad and Imam Hosseini, he should talk to the villagers and encourage them to sign up. He also promised, as he had done before, that as soon as the war was over, which he believed would be soon, he would see to it that Sangriz had a mosque and hopefully a young mullah, because the Islamic Republic was not like the old regime that never helped the villagers and, rather than building mosques and roads, wasted the wealth of the country on importing unnecessary things, building luxurious resorts on the Caspian Sea, and taking fancy trips to Western countries. Again he promised he would be back, put his hand on his chest, bowed slightly, saying, "May Allah be always with you," and walked back to the jeeps.

By this time the dark shadow of the mountain was crawling closer toward Sangriz and only Mirza-ali, Sayed Ayoub, and a few others stayed in the square to talk among themselves. Sayed Ayoub said that Islam and the country were in danger and it was their duty to defend it. Some of the others argued that they should wait and that the war would be over before too long since a powerful country like Iran wasn't going to have any difficulties defending its borders and defeating a small country like Iraq.

2

An early winter wind, sharp and eager, whipped against the village wall and the three dump trucks parked by the graveyard. One of the trucks belonged to Amir Khan and the other two to Bahram Khan. Green military camouflage tarps covered their loads. The day before they had been loaded up with food, blankets, tents, and other materials donated by people and brought to a mosque in Shiraz to be taken to the southwest of the country where the war was raging.

A group of villagers waited beside the trucks. They had their hats pulled down over their ears and their scarves wrapped around their necks and were trying to get some warmth from the faint morning sun that occasionally showed itself from behind scattered clouds. Sayed Ayoub, turning his prayer beads, was talking to Amir Khan and his son, Sarferaaz.

"God's curse upon Saddam Hussein and his war on our country," said Amir Khan. "It's changed everything for us. The price of fuel has tripled. And now the government is requiring us to take food and materials to the front before we are given permission to buy fuel—one trip to the front for one tanker truck of fuel. It takes at least ten days, and at least five thousand toman in damage is done to a truck each time it goes and comes back." He touched the fender of one of the trucks. "If an enemy shell comes down on us, what can we do, dear Sayed? We'll be doomed."

"Whatever the Almighty wills, will be," Sayed Ayoub replied, stroking his henna-colored beard. "With the help of the great Imams, they'll come back safe."

Amir Khan shook his head. "In ten days, they could have taken ten loads of bricks to the city."

"But Khan," Sayed Ayoub protested, "it's our duty to defend our homeland and our religion against the infidel Saddam Hussein. We have to be ready to do what we can, in any way we can. All over the country people are volunteering to go and fight. Young and old. The mullah who's been coming around has been able to organize a group from the neighboring villages, and any day they'll be deployed. Now people from Sangriz have signed up—Habib, the son of Mash Abdoleh, and Askar, the son of Mostagha. You may know them."

"What a disaster this whole thing is turning out to be."

"We're still the lucky ones," Sayed Ayoub went on. "The city of Abadan and the big refinery have been hit. Towns at the border have been taken and homes destroyed. I heard on the radio that thousands of people are fleeing the war zone and many have already come all the way to Shiraz. We should be thankful, Khan, and pray that the war will be over soon."

"Yes, Sayed, you're right. Thanks be to Allah we're far away from all that misfortune."

Hatam and Kubaad were standing beside another truck. Kubaad held the end of a rope that was tied around the horns of a ram. The ram stood alongside him, calmly chewing its cud and occasionally rubbing up against the tire of the truck with its head, which had been reddened with henna.

"What are you waiting for?" Amir Khan called out to Kubaad. "Why are you fussing around? Hurry up. Don't you see the sun? It's almost noontime."

Kubaad pulled the ram closer, held its horns, and, rolling the animal over on the ground, quickly tied its four legs together with the end of the rope. He grabbed one of the horns and pulled the animal to face Mecca. Then he took the pitcher of water that Hamaami held out to him and tried to pour water in the ram's mouth. The ram's teeth clunked against the copper pitcher and it bleated and jerked its head, the water dripping from its mouth. Kubaad put down the pitcher and, taking the knife from Hamaami, asked him to hold the animal by the legs. Still gripping the ram by the horn, he put the knife between his teeth and used his free hand to find the ram's Adam's apple. Chanting, *Besme Allah-o rahman-o rahim*, he put the knife to the ram's throat.

A sudden movement of the animal pushed Hamaami backward and he lost his grip on the ram, falling down on the ground on his back. A group of boys who were watching stepped aside and laughed.

"What's the matter with you?" Kubaad snarled at Hamaami. "Do you call this helping? Grab his legs, you good-for-nothing."

Hamaami straightened up and made a move toward the boys, who had gathered closer and were still laughing at him. He spat from between his missing teeth, crouched down again beside the ram, and gripped its legs. This time Kubaad didn't take any risks and, with a slick movement of the knife, slit the ram's throat. Blood gushed out and the boys stepped back. The rising steam from the blood slowly dissipated in the air. Hamaami's body shook with the ram's kicking, which continued for a minute or so before the animal went limp. Then Kubaad let go of the horn and, still bending down, wiped the blood of the knife blade by rubbing it over the white wool.

Hamaami put his hand in the warm blood and touched the fender and tires of each truck, repeating the name of God and the martyr Imam Hossein. Sayed Ayoub walked alongside and prayed beside the trucks, raising his hands to the sky. "Allah, you are the greatest. We sacrifice this ram for the safe return of our young men. Take care of them and take care of these trucks. Take them safely to the front and bring them back safely. Allah, end this war that has been waged on us so unjustly by the infidels and make us victorious. We're at your mercy."

The crowd followed behind Sayed Ayoub as he repeated the prayer. Marafi, murmuring his usual mute song, stood by the ram. He looked at its open mouth and glassy eyes and was shaking the carcass as if to awaken the ram from sleep when he was startled by Kubaad, who called out to him, "Leave it alone, Amu Laal."

Golandam came out of the village with a pot of water. Behind her was Bibigol, carrying a tray of burning incense, and Amir Khan's wife, who held a volume of the Holy Koran. Sayed Ayoub, seeing

159

them approach, recited the prayer more loudly—"Praise be to the Prophet Mohammad and the Imams." And the crowd repeated the verses.

Bibigol located Jamal and put down the tray. She took a pinch of incense from the bowl and moved her hand in a circle above his head, praying under her breath for a safe trip, then let the incense fall from her hand on the charcoal. She held Jamal in her arms and kissed him. "My dear son," she said in her sad, dry voice, "be careful. Take care of yourself and come safely back to me."

She went over to Hatam the Gypsy, who was standing alone leaning against one of the trucks. When she stretched up to kiss his forehead, he bent down so she could reach. She repeated the same ritual with incense, moving her hand above Hatam's head. "Hatam," she said, "please take care of yourself and Jamal. You're a stranger in our village but you're as dear to me as my Jamal. You two are like brothers. I place both of you in Allah's hands and will pray for your return."

"Don't worry yourself a bit, dear Bibi. It should take only a few days. We'll mind our own business and hurry back as soon as we can."

Hatam's pleasing, optimistic smile soothed Bibigol. She left him and went to find Goodarz and Sarferaaz to repeat the blessing for them as well. Sarferaaz's mother was crying and talking to her son. "My dear, God be with you. There's going to be danger out there, promise me you won't do anything crazy and will take care of yourself. I want you back just the way you are going there. I want to find you a beautiful bride when you come back."

Golandam stood away from the crowd. She loved to see Jamal with people and watch his friends hover around him, talking and laughing. She hadn't known that side of him until they were married and he started to invite his friends over. They would play cards, tell stories, and tease one another. He would smile and show how happy he was being married to her. *Azizam*, he would say, "come here, come sit beside me and watch the game," or "My beautiful wife, could you make more tea?"

In private he was even more appreciative and would praise her beauty, telling her how calming her black eyes were and how elegant the turquoise necklace looked on her. He would promise that next month after he got paid they would go to town again and they would buy another necklace and set of earrings. No one had ever told her how beautiful she was. She had hardly ever heard Haydar say anything like that to Mehrangiz, whom she considered a beautiful woman.

After the villagers finished praying for the travelers and said their good-byes, she walked over to Jamal. "God be with you," she said, her voice shaking. "I won't sleep until you're back." She kissed him. "I have nothing except you. You're everything to me. Be careful and come back to me safely."

"Everything will be fine." Jamal held her hand. "You look so pale. Are you all right?"

"I couldn't sleep last night. I kept thinking about the trip."

Jamal shivered and for the first time had doubts about the trip. "I'd rather not take this trip," he said, looking at Golandam. "I hate to leave you alone and wish I had a way out, but I have no choice. A job has been given to me, and I need to finish it." He squeezed her hand. "Promise me you won't worry. Go home and make yourself some *golgavzavan* tea and rest. It will be only a few days. I'll be back soon—in the blink of an eye. As soon as we deliver the materials, God willing, we'll turn around for Sangriz. You're my everything, too. I love you more than you can imagine. I'll be thinking of you every moment." He put his hand over her stomach and she put her hand on his. "The baby is the most important thing for us now," he said. "I'll be thinking of you both every minute."

Golandam held his hand and closed her eyes for a moment.

"When I'm back," he continued, "we'll go to Shiraz for a couple of days and visit Haydar and Mehrangiz . . . It's cold—don't stay out here, go home. We'll be leaving soon . . . And take care of Abrash. Don't forget to give her barley and remember to comb her mane—you know she likes that."

Golandam relaxed with his words. She smiled and kissed him again. "God be with you, *azizam*. Come back soon."

Sayed Ayoub was still turning his beads and praying. Hamaami had washed his hands and was walking with a Koran and blessing the trucks.

"Hurry up, man," Amir Khan called out. "Let them drive away. It's already late."

Goodarz was the first to get behind the wheel. He was followed by Sarferaaz, and lastly Hatam. As the trucks slowly roared away, Jamal ran after Hatam's truck, grabbed the bar, and hopped on the running board. From behind her tears, Golandam saw him wave before opening the door and getting in. She didn't want him to go. She wanted him to come home for lunch the way he always did, giving her the feeling he couldn't stay away from her even for a day. He would take his lunch with him like all the workers at the brick factories, but then she would see him at the door just as she was making tea.

Hamaami poured the pot of water behind the trucks to ensure a safe trip. Sayed Ayoub raised his hands to the sky, his prayer beads hanging from his hand. The sun disappeared behind a patch of clouds. After the trucks passed the graveyard and sped away, leaving a cloud of dust in the air, people headed back into the village. Kubaad and Hamaami hauled away the ram's carcass to skin and divide the meat among the village poor. And the dogs, which had stayed away until the crowd left, ran to the spot where the ram's blood had been spilled.

Part
Seven

1

Golandam kept herself busy doing the day's chores and checking on Bibigol to see whether she needed anything. She swept and washed the same places she had swept and washed a few hours earlier and went several times to the stable to see Abrash and add to her feed and water or brush her coat. Ten days had passed since Jamal and the others had left for the front. At the sound of a truck she would run up the stairs to the roof of the house and look toward the road. Bibigol would call out from the yard, asking if it was them, but then, seeing Golandam come down with sadness all over her face, would go back inside and sit by the fire in the corner of the room or busy herself with the housework.

As days went by, they grew more impatient. Bibigol would talk to herself and blame herself for letting Jamal go.

"I begged him. I told him a thousand times, 'Son, don't go. I don't care about their brick factories. What's in it for us?' But would he listen? Now he's gone and I have no idea what's become of my dear son."

Golandam would try to comfort her. "It's not his fault, Bibi. It's his job. If they say go here or go there, he has to do it. Bahram Khan didn't trust his trucks being sent so far away without Jamal going. The same with Amir Khan—he sent his only son with his truck."

"Amir Khan, Amir Khan . . . What sort of man is he? A man who loves only money."

Most afternoons Mirza-ali would come for a visit. He would sit by the fire opposite Bibigol, and his dog, Gorgi, would lie by the door. He would fill his pipe and, as he puffed on it, sending up a fountain of smoke, tell stories of his younger days. Often these stories were about the difficulties the tribes had when the government was trying to disarm them and was pushing hundreds of families with herds, horses, and camels numbering in the thousands to settle in the villages scattered across their migration route.

One whole afternoon all he did was talk about a famous battle between tribal gunmen and Reza Shah's gendarmes in the valley of Taamoradi in the southern mountains of the province.

"*Hay jahalog! Hardayung, yadung khir olsoon?*" he said in his Ghashghai tongue. Then he translated into Persian for Bibigol to understand: "Where are you, youth, that your memory is so sweet?"

"*Martini tofngak godagin dushmeh yaposhed vervirdoom*—With these hands I wore a Martini rifle against my shoulder. I swear on my grandchild's life if I lie. I would wear two bandolier belts full of cartridges like this"—he marked an X across his chest—"and was ready to defend our honor. How many gendarmes were killed in those battles? One? Two? No—the valley was filled with the dead bodies of gendarmes . . . The tribe had its casualties, too—many young people were killed. Do you know why all that was happening, Bibi?"

Bibigol shook her head.

"They wanted to push the tribal people off the lands because there was oil underneath. And eventually they succeeded. Most of the land of the oil fields in Khuzistan Province used to belong to the tribal people."

When Mirza-ali stopped talking, Bibigol noticed the sadness in his eyes. She was familiar with that look, especially when he opened his heart and talked about the past. Mirza-ali emptied the ash from his pipe onto the fire. He asked Bibigol if he had ever told her about his brother and the way he had been shot. Even after so many years, he said, that late afternoon was still clear in his mind, as clear as the slash of sunlight coming in at an angle through the crack of the door. His brother was four years older than he, tall and slim, an excellent horse trainer who taught him how to ride, how to shoot a gun, and how to be alert and protect the family and herds against danger. That day they were overlooking the enemy

166

from a hill, lying low to the ground. Bullets were coming down around them, ricocheting against the boulders and scattering dust. His brother was crawling ahead of him and suddenly called out, "I'm hit." All Mirza-ali could do was to reach forward, grab his brother's ankle, and pull him behind a boulder. The bullet had hit him across the lower back, going in one side and out the other . . . Mirza-ali remembered how the bonesetter of the tribe worked on his brother for months. He would twist a piece of cotton into a long string, soak it in urine, and then push it all the way into the wound, repeating the procedure every twenty-four hours. He survived because he was young and strong. But he died a few years later. The year that became known as the deadly year, the year that illness—some say it was the plague—struck the country and many people died. His brother left behind a beautiful young wife, two years older than Mirza-ali. As was the custom of the tribe, Mirza-ali married her and never regretted it. They learned to love each other, and she gave birth to their daughter and then a few years later to their son Kubaad.

Mirza-ali filled his pipe again. "Yes," he went on, shaking his head, "if that day, the day my brother was shot, if we had been only a stone's throw higher on the hill, we would have been safe. Many of our people were killed by Reza Shah's soldiers. Reza Shah—you know, the father of the current Shah who was forced to leave the country. Neither father nor son was good with the tribal people, and not just our tribe, tribes all over the country. Anyway, Bibi, they say nothing set on brutality will last. I can't see that these ayatollahs will do any better for the country and the people. It's on the radio day and night that so-and-so was put to death as antirevolutionary. After all the young blood spilled and the damage done to bring about the revolution, now they're executing the military officers of the old regime and even the tribal leaders. Just a few days ago, Baraat gave me news from Shiraz. There's rumor that they are after Khosrow Khan, the younger brother of our tribal leader, Nasar Khan, whom they've accused of being an antirevolutionary trying to unite the tribal people against the regime." Mirza-ali talked bitterly. "How he could be antirevolutionary is beyond me. It's nothing but a lie to weaken our tribe even more, if you ask me.

A man so nationalistic, a man who was on the side of Prime Minister Mohammad Mossadeqh and whose brother was a representative in the Majles during those years of trouble when Mossadeqh was fighting to nationalize the oil company—such a man can't be an enemy, I assure you, Bibi."

"I didn't know that," Bibi said, shaking her head. She looked at Mirza-ali's hands and found it hard to believe that these same hands that trembled when he held a cup of tea had pulled the trigger of a rifle and that this kind, soft-spoken man had shot people. She had a hard time imagining it, but then she was starting to believe anything was possible. Many people had been killed in the revolution, and now with war more people were being killed. People from nearby villages had gone to the war and come back dead, thank God no one from Sangriz.

Mirza-ali took the cup of strong tea that Golandam offered him, dropped two small pieces of sugar in, and stirred the tea as he went on talking. "As long as there have been humans on this, God's earth, on this same ground that we walk on, there have been quarreling and bloodshed. The sons of Adam have no rest. They're always at one another like dogs and cats."

Another day Golandam was washing the teapot to make some tea when Mirza-ali came in and sat down beside the fire. "Salaam, Bibi. *Halong niche dour?*"—How are you doing? he greeted Bibigol.

"Aye," Bibigol answered, "there's still a little breath left, *shokr-e Khoda*—praise be to God. Another day is about to be gone and our young men aren't back yet."

"They will be, Bibi," said Mirza-ali, taking out his pipe. "Don't worry yourself. They'll be home soon—God willing, they'll be home soon. I heard that the brick factories have fuel for a year and maybe more, but Rahbari and Amir Khan are greedy. The war, God willing, won't be going on much longer. Couldn't they have waited until it was over? They only want to get more fuel so they can bake more bricks and make more money."

Bibigol took the pipe from Mirza-ali's offering hand and began to smoke. She wished he wouldn't talk so much of war and fighting. She was afraid for her pregnant daughter-in-law, and his talk made

168

her worry more. She puffed on the pipe a few times and handed it back to Mirza-ali. "From the day they put fire to the field," she said, "everything changed for Sangriz."

"Yes, they brought misfortune down upon us. They're greedy people, Bibi. Yesterday evening at the village square, I heard some of the brick factory workers talking. They were saying that Amir Khan and the junior Rahbari have more than a hundred barrels of fuel hidden underground. A hundred! Can you believe that? They have connections in the city. They know how to do this sort of thing." He looked at Bibigol, a mass of smoke rushing out his nostrils. "They're sneaky people. And here we are in need of a few drops of kerosene on a cold winter day. What can I say, Bibi?"

Bibigol nodded absentmindedly.

"They're the sort of people, you know," he went on, "that took away Haydar's job, accused him of a crime, and put him in jail. Now he's taken his wife and left his home to wander in a crowded city looking for a job. *Allah blesin gechemsin*—May God not forgive those who caused him harm. Haydar said he would have his revenge, but I advised him against it. I told him how things like that could get out of hand and cause unforgettable suffering. I saw it happen in my own tribe with two families who were even related. It was just a small incident—two boys had a fight and the families got involved—but the hardship went on for months, and finally there was a big clash and people from both sides were killed. I told Haydar to be smart, because both Amir Khan and his son are arrogant people and have bad men around them, and that he shouldn't do anything that would lead to more trouble, especially nowadays with this new government of the mullahs and a war going on, a time when a dog doesn't recognize his owner, as we nomads would say."

"You did well, Amu," Bibigol said. "We all have been worried about this. We have been telling him the same thing. We don't need more trouble."

"He's a good man and I believe he won't do anything foolish. He wouldn't want to end up in jail again, would he?"

Golandam sat listening. Sometimes the conversation upset her, but she was happy that Mirza-ali was there to keep Bibigol company. She refilled their teacups and let them go on talking. She hadn't been separated from Jamal since their wedding and in the past few days had realized how close they'd become and how much she loved him. She'd gotten accustomed to having him around and she was missing him terribly. She thought about how shy they had been with each other at first and how things slowly changed and took their natural course. She often looked at the framed pictures they'd had taken a week after their wedding. She would study Jamal's face and thought she could see a lost look in his eyes and had the feeling he was thinking about something the way he seemed to be looking somewhere far in the distance. She would look at the picture and think about the nights when she lay in bed beside him and they would talk. "My dear," he would say, "you must be careful and take care of yourself. You shouldn't pick up heavy things. It's not good for the baby. Don't fuss so much with the cleaning of the house, washing, and cooking. I can help you."

She smiled, remembering how she had responded. "You're a crazy man," she had said. "It's only two months and I don't feel any different. But maybe you could put a pot on your head and fetch water." They had both laughed.

"We'll name him Jalal"—Glory—Jamal had said. "He'll be our glory. God willing, we'll send him to the city to go to school."

"And how do you know it's not going to be a girl?" she had said, laughing.

"Even if it's a girl," Jamal had said, "she must go to school. We'll name her Golnaz—Pretty Flower."

The days were much easier for Golandam than the nights. As soon as she put her head on the pillow, she tried to imagine where Jamal was at that moment, where he was sleeping, what he'd had to eat, and whether he was close to the war and all the shelling, explosions, and killings. She couldn't picture it at all. Her mind was blank about anything like that. She'd never been close to war and had never known or talked to anyone who had been. She'd never even seen any pictures of the war and didn't want to see any.

2

For a time Bibigol and Golandam busied themselves with Mirza-ali's visits and sewing baby clothes. Then they decided to go to Shiraz to see Haydar and Mehrangiz, who had rented a place and had Jaffar living with them. Bibigol also wanted to go to the shrine of Shah-e Cheragh and light candles and pray for the safe return of Jamal and the others.

The city was filled with war refugees and talk of war, casualties, and martyrdom. When Jaffar told them about the military training the students were receiving at school and said some of his classmates had volunteered and gone to the front, Bibigol would get upset. "Dear son," she would say, "don't talk so much of war and don't be excited by it. You're just a kid. You're here to go to school. Have they lost their minds sending young boys like you to war? Don't even think of doing anything crazy like that or I'll take you back to San-griz right this minute. Just pay attention to your schooling."

Bibigol couldn't abide more than a few days in the city where religious ceremonies were going on day and night, shrines with candles and green-and-black flags were in every square and neighborhood, and bouquets of red tulips—the sign of martyrdom and mourning—had been put in the middle of every rotary and alongside the boulevards. She told Mehrangiz and Haydar that she was afraid for Golandam, that it wasn't good for a pregnant woman to see all these upsetting things. Sangriz was more peaceful, she insisted, and, God willing, by the time they got back, Jamal would have returned.

Before leaving for Sangriz, they visited the shrine of Shah-e Cheragh. The courtyard was full of remembrances of the war dead. Wives and mothers of those who had been killed, dressed in black, were coming to mourn their loss. Banners were everywhere. Loudspeakers broadcast words from the Koran. With the help of Mehrangiz, Bibigol and Golandam found their way through the crowd and went inside the shrine. They lit candles, kissed the tomb, and left hurriedly. Then Mehrangiz took them to the square where they could get Baraat's minibus. She had never seen Bibigol so worried and agitated. Golandam, on the other hand, was quiet, although there was anxiety in her eyes.

The day was cold and it had began to drizzle by the time they left the city. Golandam felt tired and had a headache from all she'd seen. The scene in the courtyard of the shrine especially weighed on her heart. It was so different from the last time she had been there, when they came to buy things for her wedding. She leaned her head against the window and watched the raindrops falling. When we get to Sangriz, she told herself, Jamal will be back. God willing.

The minibus had turned off the main road toward Sangriz when the passengers were startled by the shriek of a car horn and then two military jeeps speeding toward them. Baraat slowed down and pulled to the shoulder of the road. He had faced similar scenes every day—the military and militia groups riding around as if they were on a mission. Not giving it any thought, went on humming and whistling. As they got closer to Sangriz and Amir Khan's two-story house became visible, the same two military jeeps came toward them, this time going by without blowing their horns.

It didn't take long for the minibus to reach Sangriz and stop at the village square. The passengers got off in a hurry, carrying their bundles. Bibigol and Golandam, tired from the trip and the movement of the bus, were anxious to get home to have some tea and rest. In front of Sayed Ayoub's shop on the opposite side of the square a group of people were gathered. As soon as they saw the returning travelers, they grew quiet.

Mirza-ali, leaning on his walking stick, left the crowd and walked as quickly as he could toward Bibigol and Golandam. "Bibi," he

172

called out before reaching them, "why don't you and Golandam come over to my place?"

Bibigol looked toward Mirza-ali and the people who were watching quietly. Everything seemed unnatural. She felt her knees going weak and was about to fall when Golandam took her arm.

"What's happening, Mash Mirza-ali?" Bibigol pleaded.

No words came out of him. She took a step closer and called out to the crowd. "Would someone tell me what's going on?"

There was a heavy silence. People stared back at her, not knowing what to do. Three military blankets, crumpled and dust covered, lay in a row in front of Sayed Ayoub's shop. Golandam saw them and a loud cry escaped from her.

Bibigol tried to go over to the blankets, but Sayed Ayoub stepped in front of her and held her arm. The women, seeing Golandam and Bibigol so shaken and confused, couldn't hold back any longer and began to wail. It wasn't long before their cries traveled through the village and across the fields and echoed against the mountain. More people rushed to the square. Sarferaaz's mother came running and, when she saw the blankets, knelt on the ground crying.

Hamaami's wife, Samar, held Golandam in her arms. She had fainted and her face was as white as milk. Samar struck a match and moved it back and forth under Golandam's nose, trying to bring her around. A woman came running with a bowl of water. Children stood here and there watching silently. The smaller ones were holding on to their mother's skirts and crying softly without exactly knowing what was happening.

Bibigol pulled off her scarf and her gray hair flew out. She tried to free herself from the women holding her back.

"Let me see my Jamal." She looked around with wild eyes as if she didn't know where she was or who the people were. "Let me go," she demanded. "Let me see my Jamal."

Amir Khan, sitting on the ground next to the blankets, kept repeating his son's name. "Sarferaaz, my dear son . . . my dear son, Sarferaaz . . ." Hamaami was sitting beside him, trying to console him. Kubaad had picked up Amir Khan's hat from the ground and stood beside them holding it.

Sayed Ayoub turned to speak to several villagers who had left their work at the brick factories and run to the square after hearing the cries. "Two military jeeps came, put them there, and left." He pointed toward the blankets, then turned his eyes to the gray sky. "They said, 'Accept our congratulations and condolences. Now your village is blessed by the blood of the martyrs you have offered to Islam and the revolution.'" He took out his handkerchief and wiped his tears. "They said the trucks had been shelled by the enemy and burned to ashes. Nothing was left of them except this." He turned and looked at the blankets. "Nothing of Goodarz was found that they could bring back. Thank God his old mother died six months ago. She wouldn't have been able to bear this—he was her only son. No one should say anything to his father until later. The poor old man can't even come out to see what has happened. And keep the womenfolk away from the dead."

Baraat took Sayed Ayoub aside and told him that the rumor he'd heard must be true—that the Basijis and other volunteer groups that the government had organized and sent to fight the war had loaded the trucks not just with food and tents but with ammunition as well. It was possible that the trucks exploded even without being hit by the enemy. There had been incidents like that before. Sayed Ayoub stood silent, not wanting to believe it, and then asked Baraat not to repeat it to anyone else for now, saying that these poor families didn't need to hear something like that at this moment, if ever. It was best not even to mention it.

"What are you waiting for?" Sayed Ayoub suddenly called out to the men. "Come on. Get going before it gets dark. These poor souls need to be buried before the day ends. Go—go and dig the graves as fast as you can."

Baraat looked at the blankets, unable to believe that Jamal was wrapped in one of them. Mirza-ali sat against the wall, his head down, repeatedly hitting the ground with his walking stick. "Saddam Hussein," he said as if the man were nearby and could hear him, "you, the horrible man, see what you returned to us of our young men. See what disaster you've brought upon this village."

Marafi sat beside Mirza-ali. He had pulled off his shoes and was lullabying his lonely song—*la, la, la . . . de, de, de*—his eyes going back and forth between Golandam, who was moaning quietly, and Bibigol, who was reciting mourning verses.

Suddenly Bibigol freed herself from the women and went to the blankets. "Let me see my flower," she wailed as she pulled open a corner of one of them. Part of a charred body came into view. Startled, she pulled back. Golandam, trembling, closed her eyes and again fainted into Samar's arms.

Bibigol sang in a moaning voice,

> My flower had a headful of hair—
> *(no head was left to caress the hair)*
> My flower had a birthmark on his chest—
> *(no chest was left to carry a birthmark)*
> My flower had a scar on his leg—
> *(no leg was left to find the scar)*

She was about to pull back another blanket, but the women held her back. Her broken voice trembled in her throat.

> O Moslems, my heart is wandering tonight,
> My heart is gone and cannot be found tonight.
> Sow wheat under my tears,
> My tears are a sea tonight.

"There was a sign," she said, stretching her hands toward the heavens, "there was a sign, and I was blind, I didn't see it. The piece of brick that came from the sky and hit me on the head was a sign. It was telling me that the brick factories were going to bring us misfortune. Now my dear son is taken away from me. What will be next? What more awaits what's left of my family?"

The sky grew darker and drops of rain sent the dust from the square into the air. Baraat came back from the cemetery and told Sayed Ayoub that the graves were ready. The men, repeating *Allah-o Akbar*, picked up the bodies and walked toward the graveyard along the dirt road, which was quickly turning to mud. The women helped Bibigol, Golandam, and Sarferaaz's mother get up, trying to take them home, but they wouldn't give in and insisted on going to the cemetery and being with their loved ones until the last moment. Marafi, barefoot, limped behind the crowd, followed by some of the older children who couldn't be made to stay away.

"Oh, villagers," Sarferaaz's mother cried out as they entered the cemetery, "gather around—gather around and mourn our sons."

Bonds of sisterhood had emerged among the women and they began to communicate with one another using the traditional words of mourning. It was as if a wailing as old as history were falling over Sangriz.

"With pain you raise a child, a flower . . . ," began Bibigol.

"Then a war makes a martyr of him . . . ," Sarferaaz's mother added.

"Dear God," continued another, "we didn't want a war with anyone."

The men put the dead by the graves and stood behind Sayed Ayoub to pray. The women gathered together and sat a few yards away. Their crying died out as the praying started.

Golandam, exhausted, looked at Bibigol and at the blankets and then began in a weak voice,

> You, who went away, did you think what I should do?
> In this strange place whom should I look up to?
> You were my beautiful and fragrant flower,
> And now your petals are lost in the wind.

She moaned and thought about Jamal, not believing that his body was under one of those blankets and that she wouldn't see him again. Then she thought about Jaffar and Haydar. She pictured Jaffar hearing about his brother's death. She saw Haydar by the new grave, crying. It was impossible for her to imagine Jaffar without a big brother or Haydar without a friend. She thought of Bibigol, whom she couldn't stand to see heartbroken.

"There's no Golandam anymore," she cried softly. "Everything is finished. What good is this life now? Good-bye, my Jamal. Good-bye, my hope and my life. I'll repeat your name every day and dream about you every night. Sorrow will be in my heart until the judgment day. God be with you. Good-bye, my Jamal."

Just at the moment the men were about to lower the dead into the graves, three figures emerged from the fields like shadows in the rainy gray afternoon. As they approached, the villagers could recognize a woman, a man, and a donkey and soon realized it was Hatam's mother, Zomorod, leading the donkey and Danial the Gypsy following. They came past the group of women and men and stood by the blankets next to the graves. Everything was still. There was no sound from the women or the men praying, nothing except the muffled sound of the rain over the graveyard. Zomorod looked at the blankets for a moment and then turned and looked at the villagers. Her gray hair hung down, wet and dripping. It was as if she had stepped into the graveyard from an unknown world. She pinned her gaze on the villagers, a look no one had the will to withstand, which seemed capable of putting everything ablaze— the villagers, the graveyard, the world. Then she looked away and, bending down, picked up one of the blankets as if she knew exactly which one contained the remains of her son Hatam. Danial, who had been standing with his head down, pulled the donkey closer. They put the blanket on the donkey and Zomorod started ahead, the donkey and Danial following. They headed away toward the stone columns of the ruined Persepolis and soon were barely visible through the threads of rain.

Part
Eight

1

The overcast sky of early morning showed no desire to rain or to let the sun come out and warm up the sleeping town. The end of winter was near, but chill persisted and the days were passing slowly. Jaffar paid no attention to the wind and cold as he ran toward the Plasco factory at the outskirts of town. At the gate, he asked the gatekeeper for Haydar.

"Haydar?" the old man said, holding his sleepy gaze on Jaffar, who stood outside the gate, his chest heaving. "Oh, Haydar from Sangriz?"

Jaffar nodded.

"Okay, I think he works on the loading dock. Stay there and I'll call the dock." The gatekeeper disappeared into an old shack weathered to a faded green that stood a few yards away from the gate.

Jaffar rubbed his hands and pushed them deep into his coat pockets. His hair was uncombed and his face pale. He was feeling uneasy about how to break the news to Haydar and walked back and forth alongside the fence, looking at the factory yard from between the fence rails.

What happened? he asked himself. Where is he? He thought maybe the old man had fallen asleep without telephoning Haydar and was about to call out to him again. Then he saw Haydar at the end of the yard coming toward the gate. He was covered with dust and looked tired.

"Oh, it's you," he said. "I was wondering who was asking for me so early in the morning. What's the matter? I thought you went to Sangriz."

181

"I did. It's Golandam . . . ," Jaffar said hurriedly. "She's not well and we took her to the clinic."

"What's happened?" Haydar asked, his eyes pinned on Jaffar.

"I don't know. No one told me . . . but I think she lost her baby. She started to have pain in the middle of the night. It was good that Baraat was in Sangriz. We took her to the city clinic right away. Mother sent me to let you know."

Haydar stiffened, his fingers clenching the cold iron rail of the gate, and stared into the distance. It was as if the life had suddenly rushed out of his body. He was lost for a moment, not aware of himself or where he was, the words "lost her baby" alive in his ears, until he was startled by a truck's horn and stepped aside. The gate-keeper ran out of the shack to open the gate.

"Go back to the clinic, Jaffar. I'll be there as soon as I can."

Haydar watched Jaffar walk away with his head bent down. It was as if he had seen him in a dream, coming like a shadow and going away like a shadow. He always seemed to see Jaffar walking away, his narrow shoulders moving slightly and his light steps taking him to some unknown place. I don't know where we're all headed, he said to himself. Where is this tired family heading? My poor baby sister lost her husband. Wasn't that enough? Now her baby? How much must she suffer? It's just not fair . . . It's not fair.

Haydar hated to face his foreman to ask for a leave. If it was going to go this way, he might lose this job, too. Since he'd started to work at the factory four months ago, he'd had to ask for time off a few times. First he had to go to Sangriz for Jamal's funeral. Then, just last month, he had to go back twice to Sangriz. Bibigol had sent for him to come and talk to Golandam, who had started to wander outside the village and through the brick factories. He'd tried to discourage her from what she was doing, telling her that it wasn't good for a woman, especially a woman who was pregnant and a widow, to go where strange men were working, all sorts of men—Afghans and truck drivers from all over the province. He told her that people would talk behind their backs. He had pleaded with her, saying that noisy and dusty places with earth-digging machines and trucks roaring around weren't safe places for her or the baby. And if not for all that, then for the sake of old Bibigol, who followed her around and watched out for her, she should stay at home.

Golandam had sworn that it wasn't her fault, that somehow she had no control over what she was doing and felt the need to walk. She would have preferred to sit at home and mourn or to go to the graveyard, but her heart felt heavy and she couldn't sit still. She had to get out of the house and felt drawn to the brick factories and the places where Jamal used to work.

Haydar had proposed taking her and Bibigol to the city to live with them. They could manage until her baby was born and then they would see what options they had. But Golandam wouldn't accept. She didn't want to go anywhere else, not after what had happened to Jamal.

He could understand her feelings, he thought, as he walked across the factory yard. That Golandam had been shocked by the whole event there was no doubt, and he hoped she would slowly recover and grow out of it, but what was he supposed to do now, and how could he help her? In the city, pictures of the martyrs had been put up all over, and their families received medical help, food, and household goods—refrigerators, TVs, and all sorts of other things—from the government in compensation. But what about the villagers who had lost someone, what did they get? He tilted his head to the sky and wondered how he could help his little sister, telling himself that maybe all Adam's children are doomed for what they do to one another.

He hated himself for thinking that sort of thing at a time when Golandam was in need of help. If he'd stayed in Sangriz, maybe everything would have turned out better. After Golandam's wedding, he had tied his few belongings on his motorcycle and had left for Shiraz with Mehrangiz sitting behind him. No matter how Bibigol and Jamal had tried to talk him out of it, he hadn't listened. Even Golandam's crying and pleading hadn't stopped him. He sold his motorcycle and rented a room in the city, working odd jobs—in construction and as a street vendor, selling fruits and nuts in the summer and hot beets and turnips in the winter—to earn enough to get by. Then he was hired by the Plasco factory. But after more than a year in the city, he still wasn't used to it. Sometimes he thought he would never get used to city life. He had gone to the Agriculture Department and filed a complaint about Bahram Khan, but with war going on and the chaotic situation in all the government offices, it was doubtful anyone would pay any attention to such a request. But he wasn't going to give up. How could he after struggling on the land all his life, like his father and his father's father before him, and now being cut off from it—cut off from the place he was born? Where his parents were buried. God, he said bitterly, you haven't been good to me or my family. In this godforsaken town, every person is out for himself. Everyone holds on to their own hat. From morning to night, you have to run like a dog and be kicked around like an old bone. And now, with this stupid war, day by day there are more and more shortages and prices keep increasing. And you can't find anything except at the black market if you are lucky. How can a family like mine with no connections or decent source of income survive? How can a man get a chance?

The supervisor was sympathetic when Haydar explained the reason for his leave and told him to take the day off and the next if he needed it. Haydar, without wasting a moment, hopped on his bicycle and rode across the factory yard. He had to wait at the gate for a couple of trucks to go through. Then he rode down the street toward the clinic, which was located in a neighborhood not too far from the factory, pedaling as fast as he could. Passing the old Aria primary school, which had been renamed Martyr Razavi School, he slowed down for a group of children and old men and women coming out of the school carrying their blankets and belongings in bundles. With the start of the war, the thousands of people from the war zone who had taken refuge in Shiraz had been given permission to stay in the schools at night. In the morning when school started, they had to pick up their belongings and wander the streets and parks until nighttime. In front of the school, children were running around, laughing and shouting, "Death to Saddam," "Death to America," as if they were competing to see who was the loudest.

Haydar entered the clinic grounds across the street from the school and propped his bicycle against the fence. The clinic yard, which used to be a pleasant place, with tall sycamore and maple trees, flowers and grass, and a shallow pool, had been neglected after the revolution. An old couple were sitting on the edge of the empty pool. In front of them was an open handkerchief with a few scraps of dry bread, and the woman was pouring tea into clear glass cups from a thermos. A few tired-looking women were gathered by the wide stone stairs leading to the building. One of them was holding an infant in her arms. The sudden smell of alcohol and drugs hit Haydar, making him sneeze, as he went into the hall.

Halfway down the hallway, Bibigol, dressed in her mourning clothes, was sitting in front of the doctor's office like a black crow, her belongings in a bundle beside her. When she saw Haydar, she stood up, put her long bony fingers on each side of his face, and kissed his forehead. "Haydar *joon*. I'm glad you're here." She spoke as if she had no energy to push the words out of her mouth. "She lost her baby last night . . . I'm afraid . . . and I'm afraid for her . . . May God help us. She's been in the doctor's office since we came, and they won't let me see her." She wiped her tears with her scarf. "I don't know what to do. She has no blood left in her. I don't know what sin we've committed to receive such a punishment."

Haydar looked at the closed door of the doctor's office. Bibigol sniffled. "My dear girl was shocked by the death of her husband. May Allah destroy the house of those who started the war."

Haydar took his hat off and hit it on the palm of his hand, causing the dust to fly, then put it back on. "Bibi, don't upset yourself now. Don't cry. Try to be calm." He could see years of agony and hardship in her eyes. "Sit down, Bibi. Don't make it harder on yourself. It won't do you or Golandam any good." That was all he could say.

"Where's Jaffar?" Haydar asked after a while.

"He took the prescription to the drugstore," Bibigol said. "Maybe with God's help he'll find the medicine."

A few mothers holding waiting cards came in with their children. A child's cry echoed in the hallway. Haydar thought about his mother and how, when Golandam was a baby, she had held her, trying to calm her down and give her medicine with a teaspoon, and how she had prayed for her health to come back.

The doctor's door opened and a nurse pushed a bed out with Golandam lying on it. An IV tube ran down to a needle in her arm. Some blood had dried around the needle. The nurse pushed her to a room at the end of the hallway. Bibigol picked up her bundle and, with Haydar, followed her down the hall. After securing the bed, the nurse turned to Bibigol. "She went to sleep right after we gave her some pain reliever. She'll be fine, but she's lost a lot of blood. When the IV is finished, we'll have to give her blood."

Bibigol stared at Golandam's pale face. "Let all your ills come to me," she pleaded silently. Then she turned to the nurse, holding out her skinny arm and pulling up her sleeve. "Here, take my blood, as much as is needed."

"It's okay, dear lady," the nurse said. "Don't worry yourself—we'll see."

Haydar wanted to know if Golandam should be taken to the hospital, and the nurse advised against it. "The hospitals are crowded with the war injured," she said. "And there are shortages of everything. She'll be better off here for the time being, and hopefully she won't need to go to the hospital."

Bibigol rearranged the blanket over Golandam's small body and spread her chador over her as well. Haydar stood beside the bed, his eyes filled with tears. Golandam's head was tilted to one side and her hair covered part of her face. Bibigol gently brushed aside the strands of black hair and put the back of her hand on Golandam's forehead. "She's burning up with fever."

Golandam half opened her eyes. She saw the figure of a man standing over her and thought it was Jamal. She wanted to straighten up and put her arms around him but had no energy. "Jamal you're back . . . ," she wanted to say, "why did you take so long?" but her tongue was stuck to the roof of her mouth and a moment later the figure faded away and she was at home and a lantern was spreading honey-colored light around the room. She heard the door. Is it you, Jamal? Are you back? . . . Oh, no, it's Mirza-ali . . . he's here again with his dog, Gorgi, he's come to visit Bibi. She thought she should prepare tea for him. Mirza-ali is sitting by the fire and leaning with his lips to Bibi's ear . . . What is he telling her that he doesn't want me to hear? It must be bad news . . .

He sucks on his pipe . . . there's smoke, so much smoke . . . Please, Amu Mirza-ali, please stop smoking. There's too much smoke. It's choking me—I can't breathe . . .

Poor Gorgi, there by the door as always. That helpless creature is getting to be too old to follow you around, Amu. Maybe she's taking her last breath, too . . . Ah, Abrash. I forgot all about you, poor animal. You must be hungry and thirsty. Come here, my dear friend. Here, I'll get you some water and then get you some hay . . . I know it's very hot and you're thirsty, too. I'm glad Haydar didn't sell you the way he sold his motorcycle when he moved to town. Jamal loved you, how could we sell you to some unknown person and let him take you away? When Jaffar comes back from school, I'll have him take you to the fields and let you run around. It's hot in here. Aren't you hot, Abrash? Come, put your head on my lap. Oh, you must have a fever. Let me go and get you a pail of water. Do you remember how Jamal used to ride you? I'm sure you remember. Do you remember the afternoon I was bringing water from the pump house with the girls and you and Jamal came galloping past us? It was spring then, do you remember? I can smell Jamal's perfume. Do you smell it, Abrash? I do . . . Why are you breathing so slowly, are you ill? . . . Abrash, I can't believe that scorched body was Jamal. They buried him and then lit straw fires by his grave, one at the head and one at the foot, every night for three nights. I watched from the roof. I can still see the flames in the pitch-darkness. Sayed Ayoub said they light fires so that the soul won't be afraid to leave the body and go to heaven and that sometimes it takes three days. But I don't believe that scorched body was Jamal. I know you don't believe it, either. It was all a lie. He's somewhere on the front and he'll come back. He'll take you out to the fields. I'll come, too . . . There, I hear the door. It must be him—no, it's Mirza-ali again . . . that poor man has no one to talk to. He comes and talks to Bibi, comes and opens his heart to her . . . Why isn't Jamal back? He's been out there working all day in this heat. I'll go out to the brick factories after him . . . I don't care what people say. To hell with them. I'm going to go look for my husband. I don't care if Haydar doesn't like it, if Bibi doesn't like it . . . My God, look at all the dust out here. It's choking me. Look at all the bricks piled up on top of one another. If they come down on the poor workers, they'll all die. Hey, Amu, have you seen Jamal? . . . Did you hear that, Abrash? He said Jamal has taken a truckload of bricks to the front. He's gone with Goodarz and Hatam. Why didn't he tell me where he was going, Abrash? Don't you think he should come and visit his pregnant wife? He's left me and you and gone to the front. At least he should send a letter or some news so we won't be worried, so his mother won't be worried. Who is this Saddam, anyway, and where did he come from? We never heard of him in our small village. What harm did we do him that he started a war with us? Our little village didn't want a war. We didn't want a war with anybody. Now Jamal is gone to the front. God be with him. God punish those who start wars.

She opened her eyes and saw bright lights and moving shadows, then her eyes went shut again . . . Ah, Marafi, it's you, you're here, too. Did you hear that? Come, let's go home, Marafi. These people don't know what they're talking about, saying that Jamal took a truckload of bricks to the front. Who would need bricks at the front? Come, they don't know what they're talking about. Come, let's go to our house, I'll make tea and fix something to eat. We'll wait for Jamal . . . I'm very thirsty . . . Marafi, did you hear what they said about Goodarz? They said he wasn't burned in the truck's explosion. First they said he had taken the dump truck somewhere and was working for himself without Bahram Khan's knowledge, then they said he'd been captured by the Iraqis. They took him to the tomb of Imam Hussein in Karbala and chained him to the shrine. Maybe Jamal is there, too. I don't believe that scorched body in the blanket was Jamal. What do you think, Marafi? . . . Do you have things you keep in your heart? . . . Why don't you talk? For as long as I've known you, you've never talked. I know you have seen a lot in this forsaken place. You only read the Koran, without uttering a sound. You read the tragedies in *The Epic of Kings* and don't say a word . . . Well, say something—you can talk to me. I talk to you, I tell you what's on my mind. You can talk to me, too. I would love to know what's going on in your heart, what pains you've collected there over the years. You can tell me what happened to you when you fell in the well and what you saw down there. Marafi, I'm very afraid. I am drenched in sweat. I think I'm ill. Oh God, what's happening to me? I never did anything bad in my life. I never caused any problems for anybody. Why are all these things happening to me? As you're my witness, Marafi. Tell Bibigol, tell Haydar not to be upset with me . . . Oh, who's that coming this way? It's Jamal. It's him, I see him, he's waving . . . Over there—look Marafi, that's him. He has our baby in his arms and is coming this way . . . he's bringing my baby . . . Hello . . . Jamal . . . Jamal . . . here . . . I'm here, come this way . . .

Bibigol, seeing Golandam trembling and breathing rapidly, was terrified and ran to the doctor's office to find the nurse. "Please," she said, pulling her by the arm, "please come— hurry."

Haydar stood in silence above the bed. He couldn't stand to see his little sister or Bibigol so tormented. The nurse flicked the IV with her finger.

"Did you get the medicine?" she asked Haydar.

Haydar shook his head.

"What are you waiting for? Go—hurry."

Haydar rushed out of the room, wondering what had happened to Jaffar. Was he going from drugstore to drugstore looking for the medicine? He had a feeling that was the case and didn't know how they would be able to find the medicine in this time of shortages. He passed the patients waiting in the hallway and ran down the steps and into the yard to get his bike. It was high noon and the muezzin was calling people to midday prayer.

2

The Square of Darvazeh Isfahan was crowded. Taxis, buses, and trucks, horns blowing, roared around the rotary and turned up side streets, leaving clouds of exhaust fumes. Minibus drivers stood beside their vehicles or drove by yelling out their destinations— "Zarghoon . . . Marvdasht . . . Takht-e Jamshid . . . Hurry up, we're leaving. Come on, we're getting full . . . hurry." Vendors shouted out their offerings of fruits and nuts, tools and batteries, shoes and clothing. Sellers of music tapes carried portable tape players and advertised their products at full blast. Kebab vendors invited passersby to eat, *"Khoshmazeh, khoshmazeh, yeh sikh bebar"*— Delicious, delicious, take a skewer—the smells of cooking meat, spices, and smoke wafted lazily into the air. Beggars—men, women, children—mingled in the crowd pleading for money or food. Religious verses broadcast from the minaret of a nearby mosque added to the noise and commotion.

Bibigol, Golandam, and a few other passengers going to Sangriz or nearby villages sat in the shade of a tree at the corner of the square waiting for Baraat to leave. Golandam was feeling better, even though her complexion was pale and she was still weak. After a week at the clinic and a week at Haydar's, she and Bibigol had decided to go back home. They couldn't take any more of the crowded, noisy city full of war refugees and pictures of martyrs everywhere.

During the two weeks they'd been in Shiraz, Jaffar had been very attentive. He ran to the clinic every afternoon after school, taking fruit juice or saffron ice cream, one thing Golandam particularly liked. Later when they were at Haydar's, he slept in the hallway in front of Golandam's room and at the slightest sound would jump to get a glass of water or whatever she needed. He would have taken her to see a movie, but the cinemas that had been burned down during the revolution hadn't been rebuilt and might never be with the war still going on and requiring more people, even teenagers like himself, to be drafted to go to the front.

In spite of the sadness Jaffar felt, he tried to be positive and encouraging, and one day when Golandam was feeling better, he took her, his mother, and Mehrangiz to the ice cream shop and he bought them saffron ice cream and *falodeh*, his mother's favorite.

As the passengers sat waiting for Baraat to finish loading the minibus, Golandam watched a little boy and girl sitting beside their mother eating sweet bread and another mother nursing her infant.

An old beggar woman in a shabby chador stopped by. "May God keep illness from you and your families. Please help me," she pleaded. "I'm hungry."

Bibigol untied a wing of her scarf and put a small coin in the woman's outstretched hand. "Here, dear woman," she said, "pray for us."

"God bless," the woman said and moved away.

Baraat, a cigarette hanging from his lips, was on top of the minibus tying up sacks of rice, flour, and sugar, crates of cooking oil and Coca-Cola, and containers of kerosene that Haydar and Jaffar handed him. After he secured the load, he jumped down from the minibus, took one last drag on his cigarette, and threw the butt on the pile of trash in the gutter by the sidewalk.

"Haydar," Baraat said, lighting a cigarette and handing it to him, "did you ever imagine it would be like this?"

"What do you mean? Like what?"

"Everything is backward. For years I used to bring flour, rice, and fruit—you name it—from the countryside to the city. Nowadays I do the reverse."

"I see," Haydar replied, shaking his head in dismay. "And things aren't just getting more expensive, they're getting harder to find as well."

"It puzzles me," Baraat said. He opened the door for the passengers. The little boy and girl eating pieces of sweet bread ran up ahead of everyone else. Behind them Golandam and Bibigol climbed into their seats. When all the passengers were inside, Jaffar got in and sat beside Golandam. He didn't yet comprehend his brother's death, and Golandam's situation had shaken him further. He had been happy coming back to the city and starting school, never imagining that something could happen to Jamal or Golandam. He was growing more quiet as the days went on.

The bookstore where he liked to go had been closed and the cinema houses burned down. He didn't feel interested in anything—not his school or hanging out in the parks or playing soccer with his classmates—but he never mentioned his feelings to anyone, especially not his mother or Golandam since he didn't want to add to their pain and worry.

Haydar sat in the front passenger seat beside the driver. Baraat drove through the crowded square slowly, watching for potential passengers. Several times he stopped alongside the curb to pick up a few Afghans who were going back to their work at the brick factories after spending a day in the city.

"How's it going, Karamyar?" Baraat asked one of the Afghans. "Did you have a good time in the city?"

A smile covered the man's sun-scorched face. He was middle-aged with shiny eyes and a bushy mustache. "Yes, it was very nice," he said. "*Chakar zadim*—we strolled around—and had *shiryakh*—ice cream. We came to take Hekmat to the hospital. Yesterday a pile of bricks came down on his leg." He pointed toward a young man at the back of the minibus.

"Is he okay?" asked Baraat, taking a quick look at the man. "He didn't break any bones, I hope."

"No, he didn't. God's eyes must have been with him. He was very lucky and managed to get out of the way. We took him to the *shafa-khaneh*. The doctor said his leg wasn't broken, only badly bruised."

193

He took a handful of walnuts and raisins from a plastic bag and offered some to Baraat and Haydar. "*Char maghz befermaieed*"— Have some walnuts. Then he went to the back of the minibus and sat down beside his countrymen.

"These poor men," Baraat said as he turned up the street to drive out of town. "They love to get away from the brick factories on Fridays and come to the city. They love ice cream. They all go into an ice cream shop and eat three or four bowls of ice cream apiece." He smiled and went on. "You know, they speak the same tongue we do, but they have more interesting words for certain things. You heard him call ice cream *shir yakh*—frozen milk. Not like us, who say *basstani*—frozen. He calls the hospital *shafa-khaneh*—the house for getting well. It's much better and nicer than calling it *bimaresatn*—the house of illness—the way we do."

Haydar nodded.

"I don't know if I ever told you this," Baraat went on, keeping his eyes on the road. "One time, years ago, when I was young and adventuresome, I went all the way to Kabul. I took a group of Afghans who were going back home. I'll tell you, it was a very long trip, but I liked it. The people were friendly and kind. The country is very poor and has always been attacked by other countries. As you know, the Russians have occupied their country. There's a war going on there as well."

"I know," Haydar said. "And they're running away and coming here for safety and jobs. May God help them. Our own situation isn't any better with the war we're having."

An hour later, Baraat turned onto the dirt road that led to Sangriz. The minibus roared around the bend, and every time it slowed down to go over the bumps and rough spots, dust overcame the bus. Occasionally Haydar turned and looked toward Golandam and Bibigol, whose heads were shaking with the movement of the minibus. He was worried about them and not happy he hadn't been able to convince them to move to the city.

In the distance, Sangriz lolled on the foothills of the Zagros Mountains like an old and fatigued camel. Farther down the hillside, the Kor River snaked away to disappear in the water of a small salt lake more than a day's travel away. Baraat went on talking about the war, the number of casualties, and the shortages of gas and food. Haydar, listening and not listening, looked out at the arid land, but he didn't have the heart to look for long. A few small dust-covered trees here and there alongside the dirt road reminded him of the time years ago when the villagers had planted them with the hope that someday the road would be paved. It was when the Agriculture Department had come to Sangriz. One autumn afternoon he and the other children at the madrese, after being released from the mullah's teaching and rushing out to go home, saw a white minibus parked beside the village entrance.

A group of women and children had gathered, thinking that it was Dr. Kohlmann, the foreign doctor. The rare times he came to the village, everyone, especially the mothers, would flock around eager to have him take a look at them and their children. That day, though, it wasn't Dr. Kohlmann and his nurse in a white apron but a couple of strange men wearing dark glasses. They asked everyone to sit close to where the minibus was parked. Haydar sat in the front with Jamal and Marafi next to him. The villagers returning from the fields stood leaning on their shovels. And the women, who had hurried to finish preparations for the evening meal, joined in, coming one by one with their children. Everyone was anxious to know what the strangers were up to.

It wasn't long before darkness fell. One of the strangers turned on the machine that had been placed on the roof of the minibus. A bright square of light appeared on the village wall, and they could see people walking in the parks and streets of a noisy city with tall buildings and cars going by. Then the scene shifted to a field where a group of men, shovels in hand, were digging. A truck drove up full of small trees and bushes. Men unloaded the trees and dragged them to the holes and planted them—first the trees, and then the bushes—as someone talked about the benefits of planting trees. The villagers watched in silence, no one saying a word and no sound of a dog, cow, or rooster coming from the village—or, if it did, no one heard it. As soon as the bright square disappeared and the noise of the machine died out, the children and some of the adults ran over to the wall to examine it.

195

Haydar smiled and looked at the few surviving trees alongside the road, all that was left of the ones the Agriculture Department had brought to Sangriz and the villagers had planted.

Baraat stopped and the Afghans got off and cut through the ditches and unplanted fields toward the brick factories. Seeing the piles of baked and unbaked bricks in the middle of the field, the smile died on Haydar's face. Look what they've done to God's land, he thought—they've silenced the *top, top* of the water pumps and replaced it with the roar of trucks and bulldozers.

"You're quiet, Haydar," Baraat said as he started moving again.

"I was just thinking."

"I could see that you were deep in thought. Were you thinking about the days you worked the fields, or maybe the days you were busy hunting for treasure, for the Black Globe that you once told me about?"

"You don't need to remind me, my friend," Haydar said and again looked at the ravaged fields. "Those days are gone," he said softly, "and what's the difference if I would have found the Black Globe? It's all the same."

After a while he turned and glanced at Golandam and Bibigol. "I'm worried about them," he said to Baraat, "and think that Sangriz isn't a good place for them anymore. But I don't know what to do for them, either. I begged them to sell Abrash—what do they need to keep a horse for?—and gather their few belongings and move to the city to live with us, but they won't do it. If they'd moved, maybe Golandam wouldn't have lost her baby. Even now, after all that's happened, they don't want to leave Sangriz."

"It's not their fault, Haydar. How could they come and live in the city? They've lived all their lives in the village. It would be difficult for them in the city, plus the rent—you know how much one small room rents for. It's better for them to be in a quiet place after all they've gone through. Don't worry, Haydar. God is the solver of problems."

There was silence between them. The minibus kept going over bumps. Baraat took a last drag on his cigarette and threw the butt out the window. "Life is short, Amu Haydar," Baraat said. "Good or bad, it comes to an end. Of course, it's better to have a good life." He looked at Haydar out of the corner of his eye. "Isn't that right? . . . More than fifteen years ago I came to this part of the country and got this old bus. It seems like yesterday. How the days go by—just like the wind."

Haydar was listening but his mind was engaged with the past again, thinking about Jamal and the day he had come out to the pit where Haydar was digging in the hills. "Hey, Haydar," he'd called out. "You're digging so hard—have you come upon the treasure?" He had told Jamal about the Black Globe buried in the hills and watched Golandam run back to the village after she and Mehrangiz had brought him his lunch. And that was the day, in the evening, that Jamal had come with his mother and Mirza-ali and asked for Golandam's hand.

A dump truck with a load of bricks came toward the minibus. Baraat slowed down and pulled to the side of the road. The truck passed and the cloud of dust engulfing the minibus caused the passengers to cough and sneeze. Baraat shifted into first gear and the minibus started to move with a jolt but soon dropped into a pothole, sending the passengers, who had grabbed on to their seats, shaking from side to side.

Baraat maneuvered the bus around a few more bumps. "These no-good brick factory owners," he said bitterly, "they use this road day and night but won't throw a few loads of gravel over it. The cost wouldn't even equal one truckload of bricks."

Baraat drove slowly the rest of the way and soon they reached Sangriz. Bibigol, Golandam, and the rest of the passengers got off hurriedly and shook the dust from their clothes. Baraat climbed on top of the minibus and began to untie the load. Sayed Ayoub ran over and took the sacks of rice and flour, crates of Coca-Cola and cooking oil as Baraat handed them down, setting them aside to take to his shop. From the other side of the square, Mirza-ali and a couple of other elders came over to greet the travelers. Jaffar told his mother and Golandam to go home and that he would bring their belongings as soon as they were down from the top of the minibus.

It took Haydar a moment to recognize the frail old man following Mirza-ali as Amir Khan. His hands were shaking and his eyes were sunken and had no light in them. Haydar couldn't believe that Amir Khan, in the few months since the death of his son, had turned into this fragile while-haired man. He thought of the day after the martyrs had been buried and he had gone to Jamal's grave and seen Amir Khan kneeling at his son's tomb, grieving and calling out his name. It had torn at his heart and he had walked over to him to help him up.

"Don't disturb yourself, Khan," he had said. "Why don't you let me take you back home?"

"Oh, it's you," Amir Khan had said, raising his head. "God bless you, Haydar."

They walked together in silence out from among the graves and were by the village entrance when Amir Khan stopped. "I'm sorry, Haydar, sorry for all that came between us . . . I know I may have caused you some trouble—forgive me."

"It's all right, Khan," Haydar had said. "It's all right . . . don't disturb yourself."

After staying for a few days to make sure that things were okay with Golandam, Haydar went back to work at the Plasco factory and sent Mehrangiz to Sangriz to stay with Bibigol and Golandam for as long as needed. Jaffar asked his mother if he could stay a few days before going back to school, and she agreed as long as he wouldn't get behind in his studies.

Mirza-ali came almost every afternoon to visit, but his visits were usually short and he was quieter than usual. A couple days before Jaffar was to return to the city, Mirza-ali asked him to accompany him back to his home. On the way he told Jaffar how much he had respected Jamal and how sad he was for the way things had turned out for Golandam. He wanted Jaffar to know that he liked him very much and saw him as a smart young man who was concerned about his mother and his sister-in-law. It was nice that he had stayed at home for a few days to be with them. He told Jaffar that he shouldn't let the problems worry him and that, yes, life sometimes could be difficult, but a young man like him should never lose hope and do what he is supposed to do. He should go back to school before he got too far behind. At the same time he shouldn't forget that he was faced with more responsibility now, now that his older brother, God rest his soul, had left this world and left a young wife widowed.

Jaffar walked slowly alongside Mirza-ali and listened to the old man say that he knew what that responsibility meant, because that exact responsibility had fallen to him when he was young, close to Jaffar's age, maybe a couple years older, after his older brother had been killed in a tribal war and, like Jamal, left a young wife behind.

"I had to take responsibility on my young shoulders," Mirza-ali said and stopped for a moment to catch his breath. "And not just any responsibility, a moral one. I decided to marry my brother's wife and take care of the family, and we were very happy. That sort of thing is common, especially among us country folk. I hope you understand. Some of us have to grow up fast. It's not fair, but unfortunately that's the way life turns out sometimes."

Jaffar knew what the old man was trying to tell him but was too shy to say a word and only nodded.

"I know you and Golandam are very fond of each other. Which I'm sure will make everything much easier. But don't worry now. I'm talking about a year or so from now, after you're finished with school. By then, with God's help, you'll have a job in the city and can take your family there to live with you. In less than a month it will be the holy month of Moharam and Haydar will be here. Then I'll talk to him and Bibigol. I'm sure they'll be happy about it."

Jaffar nodded again. He had never thought about marriage or marrying Golandam, although he was sure he loved her and had ever since they were children.

He tried to overcome his shyness. "I don't know, Amu," he said, his thin voice sinking. "Why are these things happening, Amu? . . . Why? . . . Why did my brother have to die? Why did Golandam have to be ill? I wish things could be the way they were."

"I know, my son," Mirza-ali said, stopping and putting his arm around Jaffar's shoulders. "I'm sorry. Don't disturb yourself. Things will be better . . . Things will be better."

"All I want is for Golandam to be well," Jaffar said, choking.

"We all do, and she will be, God willing. Don't worry about that."

"A few times I've thought about quitting school," Jaffar said, tears in his eyes. "If my mother and Golandam weren't here, I would just go away—I would run away from this place."

"Oh, no. You must not think that way."

"Maybe it would be better if I got a job at one of the brick factories and took care of my mother and Golandam."

"No, no," Mirza-ali said. "Young man, you can't do that. There is no future in that. You have to finish school. You're a smart young man. You mustn't think that way. This will all pass, God willing." He squeezed Jaffar's shoulders. "Things will get better . . . You need to go to school and not worry about anything now. Go to school and do your best. I'll make sure that your mother and Golandam are all right while you're away. Haydar's wife is here now, and she'll take care of her."

Jaffar nodded and wiped his eyes.

After Jaffar returned to the city, Golandam did well for a while but then started to eat less and not sleep well and day by day got thinner and weaker. Bibigol didn't know what to do. She brewed different kinds of tea and made soup for her. She gave her the medicine they had prescribed at the clinic and listened to Samar and other village women who came to visit and give their advice. At one point she asked Sayed Ayoub to write a few prayer verses, which she sewed into small pieces of cloth and pinned on Golandam's clothing or hung around her neck. Numerous times she raised her head to the sky and asked God and the Prophet Mohammad to save her daughter-in-law.

Often, in the afternoon, Golandam wasn't able to stop herself from wandering outside the village or in the fields and around the brick factories. At times she talked to herself as if she were talking to Jamal. She would stop and think she saw him, his figure tall in front of her like a shadow, but when she reached out to embrace him, the shadow would escape from between her arms. Bibigol, not being able to stop her, and at times not wanting to stop her, thinking that it might in the end do her some good, would go with her. But Bibigol was happy that Marafi was always around and often went with her. He would limp along behind her, his satchel over his

200

shoulder. When she sat, he would sit beside her, and when she got up to move on, he would follow. They would often sit and watch the Afghan workers, turbans on their heads, crouch down and, with a continuous rhythmic movement, pick up a handful of moist dirt from a heap of clay, throw it into a brick crate divided into four rectangles, and then wet their hands in a water pail and smooth the tops of the bricks, sliding their palms over the surface in a circular motion. Barefoot boys, not more than nine or ten years old, their pants rolled up to their knees and their legs bamboo thin, would put down empty crates next to the men, pick up the filled crates, and carry them a few yards away to lay them in rows to dry out under the bright sun. Another group would pick up the dry bricks and carry them to the huge pyramid to be fired from underneath and cooked into bricks. Marafi and Golandam would sit for hours and watch.

Golandam would talk to Marafi about anything that came to her mind, saying that Jamal would tell her how much he loved her, how nice and comforting that was, and how much she missed him. She would tell him that she was troubled by what Jaffar was going through and was sorry for his unhappiness and the way he worried all the time—worried for her and for his mother—and hated to hear him talk about the war and wanting to go and fight the Iraqis to avenge the death of his brother. Another thing she told Marafi was how happy she would have been to have the baby, her last hope after Jamal's death.

She would ask Marafi what was in his heart, even though she knew he wouldn't be able to tell her. One day she asked him if he had ever thought about going away after falling in the well all those years ago. Marafi, she said, what happened in the well to make you the way you are? Was it true what people said, that in the bottom of that dark old well you saw jinns? Or did the jinns exchange the real Marafi with one of their sick little boys, because that's what jinns do whenever they have a chance—exchange their children with ours because they like human babies?

201

Part
Nine

1

It was Ashora, the tenth day of the month of Moharam, a day of mourning for Imam Hossein, the third Imam of the Shiites, who was son of Imam Ali and grandson of the Prophet Mohammad and was killed in a sectarian battle in the early days of Islam. A procession was under way. From early morning, the people of Sangriz had gathered outside the village, holding green-and-black banners to commemorate the day of martyrdom.

Cries of *Imam Hossein, Shah-e shahid*—Imam Hossein, king of martyrs—rose from the crowd. The banner carriers were in front, followed by *zangir zan* and *sine zan*, groups of men hitting their backs with chains and beating their chests with the palms of their hands. All were repeating the religious verses in unison after Sayed Ayoub. The children had their own small banners and chains and mimicked the adults. The women followed at the end with tears in their eyes.

The people were on their way to the nearby village of Chale-Sabz to watch the passion play of Imam Hossein. Before getting on the road, they stopped at the graveyard to pay their respects to their own martyrs—Jamal, Sarferaaz, and Hatam. The women held back Bibigol, Golandam, and Sarferaaz's mother so they wouldn't kneel down to caress the graves and torment themselves further. But it was Jaffar who suddenly cried out the name of his brother and threw himself on the grave. Haydar helped him up and tried to calm him down. Sayed Ayoub, realizing that emotions were running high, called out, "O Imam Hossein, king of martyrs, we're coming to you" and motioned to the banner carriers to go ahead.

In the outskirts of the village, Golandam stopped beside one of the brick factories, insisting that she didn't want to go to the passion play. Haydar, still shaken at seeing the women and Jaffar so upset in the cemetery, spoke to her without thinking: "When are you going to stop this?" he said. "We can't raise our heads in the village anymore. I swear to this holy day it's not good what you're doing, wandering around the brick factories."

Golandam stared out at the open plain without saying a word.

"Don't upset yourself, Haydar," Bibigol said. "You and Mehrangiz go ahead. You, too, Jaffar. I'll stay with Golandam for a while and then we'll go back home. She's tired and so am I. It's going to be a long walk to Chale-Sabz on this sunny and warm day. Maybe it's for the best that we return home and don't go."

Jaffar didn't know what to do or what to say to make things any easier. He was sorry for getting emotional at the grave and realized it must have made Golandam more upset. He wanted to help her but was at a loss to know what to say or how to comfort her.

The crowd slowly continued on its way, passing the piles of bricks and the huge pits filled with rainwater where the soil had been dug out and entering the narrow road that stretched out alongside the mountain. About half a kilometer further on, the stone columns of Persepolis came into view and then the huge stone steps leading up to the area of the ruins known as the Palace of Xerxes. The crowd, with their black-and-green banners, walked in single file beside the ancient wall and palace columns.

Haydar followed absentmindedly, without paying attention to the religious chants and cries. He glanced at the silent ruins and thought about the New Year, when people from all around the country would come to Persepolis to celebrate Nowruz and the arrival of spring as they had since ancient times. Only in the past couple of years, because of the overlapping of the religious month of Moharam and Iranian Nowruz, had the government discouraged celebration at the place that symbolized the old monarchy. Haydar remembered the time of Nowruz when he was ten or eleven years old and he and Jamal would ride their horses to Persepolis and rent them out to visitors. In the afternoon when they rode back home, they would joke about the city boys who were afraid of the horses and couldn't stay on a horse without being held.

As Haydar and the others reached the village of Chale-Sabz, they were met by people carrying banners and chanting verses who had come out from the village to welcome them. Tired and suffering from the heat, the travelers entered the square and joined the people who were already sitting on the ground in the shade of the village wall waiting for the passion play to start. Two large tents had been erected on the opposite side of the square, one flying a green flag and the other a red one.

The newcomers hadn't rested and their sweat hadn't yet dried when suddenly, to the sound of the horn and the drums, Shemr Zel Joshan, on horseback and in red armor, two long red feathers on either side of his helmet and waving a sword in the air, came in and circled the square several times. Soon he was joined by Ibn Sa'ad, also dressed for battle, who rode in from the opposite corner of the square carrying a lance.

"Oh, people of Kofe," Ibn Sa'ad yelled at the top of his voice, "from the right and from the left, come upon Imam Hossein."

A dozen men in red war outfits, some armed with swords and shields, others with bows and arrows, ran out of the red-flagged tent and assembled in front of it. Then the flap of the green-flagged tent was pulled aside and Imam Hossein, in a long beard, a green turban wrapped around his head, and a black cloak draped over his shoulders, walked slowly out of the tent looking bewildered and exhausted after returning from the battlefield and leaning on his sword to support himself. Cries rose from the audience seeing the Imam so tired and defeated.

Imam Hossein's family, men and women, young and old, dressed all in black, came out of the tent and gathered around him. As the horn and the drums played, the riders galloped around the square, and everyone looked through the dust kicked up by the horses' hooves toward the battle scene.

Imam Hossein recited his sorrowful story, saying that he was grandson of the Prophet Mohammad, son of Imam Ali, and the legitimate leader of Islam who had been wronged by those who were deviating from the teachings of God's Prophet. He called on the men of his family to fight the infidels. After everyone, crying, said good-bye to them, one by one they went into battle. Shemr Zel Joshan and Ibn Sa'ad shouted out their challenges to the enemy and killed whoever came forward to fight them with a slash of the swords, an arrow from their archers, or a strike of the lance. The women from Imam Hossein's camp, weeping and reciting mourning verses, ran to wrap their martyrs in bloodstained shrouds and lay them in front of the tent.

The Imam's family was tired and thirsty and the children cried out for water. Since the water canal had been diverted from their camp by the enemy, the Imam sent his brother Abbas to go and fetch water. When Abbas returned with both his arms cut off, the leather water bag hanging from his shoulders full of arrows and the last drop of water dripping from it, the cries of the audience rose higher and people hit their chests and foreheads with the palms of their hands and cursed the infidel enemy who had not shown the least pity for even the thirsty children.

As the battle went on, all the men from the Imam's family were killed, including the teenagers and the infant Ali Asghar, killed by a stray arrow. The only male who survived was the Imam's eldest son, Zayn al-Abidin, who was ill and too weak to be sent into the battle. By noontime the women and children of the family, wailing, had gathered around the Imam, while his sister Zainab tried to prevent him from going into battle alone. With her pleading and the insistence of the Imam that it was God's will that he go to the fight and be martyred, the audience totally lost themselves in the drama and the square of Chale-Sabz became the battlefield of Karbala.

Haydar was moved to tears by the exchange between Imam Hossein and his sister Zainab and wished he hadn't been impatient with Golandam.

In the square Imam Hossein entered the battle after saying his farewell to what was left of his family. A sword fight ensued. The Imam was in the heat of the fight when a roar came from somewhere, and the audience turned in the direction of the sound. A deep silence fell over the crowd. This was one of the high points of the passion play and delighted everyone, especially the children.

Two men dressed in dark suits, bowler hats, and dark sunglasses ran into one side of the square and kept looking back in fear. The two *farangiz*—Europeans—were an ambassador and his assistant who were on a hunting expedition far from Karbala where the Imam was fighting his enemies. The foreigners looked around in agitation, not knowing where to go or what to do. Suddenly there was another roar, and a lion, as yellow as the sun, with a fluffy mane and a long tail, ran into the square and chased after the two men. The lion pulled down the ambassador and stood above him ready to tear him apart. His assistant, shaken, managed to tell the ambassador that there was only one person in the whole world who could save him from the lion and that was Imam Hossein and he should call on him for help. When the Imam heard the plea for help, he left the battle scene and hurried to rescue the foreigners. The lion, upon seeing the Imam approaching, left the ambassador alone and ran to the Imam and lay down at his feet like a house cat. The foreigners, saved by what they considered a miracle, kissed the Imam's hand and, kneeling at his feet, expressed their wish to convert to Islam. The Imam happily acceded and welcomed them in the name of Allah and the Imam's grandfather, the Prophet Mohammad.

After the Imam and foreigners left, the lion roared and clawed the air and, before leaving the scene, went to the village head and received a few bills in reward, then went over to a few city people who had come to see the passion play and was similarly rewarded.

Imam Hossein returned to the fight but, after a few strokes, wounded, tired, and thirsty, struggled to support himself on his sword while the enemy's arrows rained down on him. He dragged himself to the platform set in the middle of the square and lay down on the bed. Shemr got off his horse, rolled up his sleeves, and, drawing his dagger, slowly approached the platform, crawling in a cowardly manner as if afraid that at any moment the Imam would stand and attack him. A few times he backed away, his hands shaking with fear. Finally he reached the platform, jumped on the bed, and sat on the Imam's chest. As Shemr held the dagger above the Imam, ready to kill him, the audience grew quiet, watching every move of Shemr's hand in anticipation of this familiar act as if they were going to witness it for the first time. Shemr grabbed the Imam's head with his free hand and pulled it up slightly, then brought down the dagger and held it to the Imam's neck. The Imam's legs wiggled. Then suddenly Shemr held up a head impaled on the tip of his dagger. At that exact moment the audience rushed toward the platform, chanting, *"Imam ma shahid shod . . . Imam ma shahid shod"*—Our Imam is martyred, our Imam is martyred— and lifted the bed with the Imam and Shemr, still holding the head aloft, on their shoulders. A group of men from the enemy army held up the heads of the other martyrs planted atop lances. The crowd made a procession around the square carrying the bed, everyone—men and women, young and old—crying and chant- ing, *"Imam ma shahid shod."*

Marafi, thinking that the beheadings and painted ceramic heads with wide, dark eyes and blood dripping down their necks were real, murmured his song and hung on to Jaffar as he limped along. Jaffar was tired and fed up with everything—the cries, the heat, the passion play. He wanted to run away from the commotion and the people who were tormenting themselves. He knew they were relat- ing the Imam's agony and sorrow of hundreds of years ago to their own and were sorry not only for the Imam and his family who were killed and abused by the infidels but for themselves as well. He could see it in their eyes. He could see it in the way they inflicted pain on themselves and grieved for the ancient deaths, year after year. He wished he had never come and had stayed behind with Golandam and his mother. He wished he were on Abrash riding away and leaving everything behind.

Haydar followed the crowd. The passion play, the martyrdom, and the grief of the mourners made him think of being at the grave the day after Jamal's burial and how people had been so moved that they started to beat their chests, circling Jamal's grave. He wished the passion play were over and they were on their way back to San- griz. He felt dizzy and was drenched in sweat. Raising his head to look up at the noon sky, he could see the hazy sun above him, so close it seemed to threaten to put everyone on fire and burn them all to ashes.

The crowd, after circling the square a few times, put the bed back down on the ground. Shemr took the ceramic head off the dagger and slid his dagger into its sheath. Imam Hossein's body was laid alongside the other martyrs. People went back to their places and sat down. The horn player played sorrowfully. The lion came back onto the scene and sat looking at the dead, then started to walk among them, moaning and touching each body softly, showing his grief by throwing straw and dirt over his head. People sat quietly, not a sound coming from anyone. It was as if they had exhausted themselves and were stunned by the deaths of the innocent Imam and his family, deaths that even a wild animal mourned.

Bibigol had tried but was unsuccessful in persuading Golandam to go back home. The brick factories were deserted because of the religious holiday. The trucks and digging machines were silent, and all the Afghan workers had gone to the city. She sat with Golandam for a while and then returned to the village to bring her food and water as she had done many times in the past.

Golandam couldn't sit still. She walked by the heaped-up dirt and the piles of bricks toward one of the abandoned kilns where there was a pit full of water where the village children liked to swim and play. She stood close to the rim and looked at the water, the noon sun reflecting off its cloudy surface. She felt dizzy for a moment and closed her eyes. When she opened them, she could see through the haze a human shape at the opposite edge of the pit, an image that seemed to fade. She blinked and looked again and saw it again, realizing it was a man. She didn't know if he had been following her or for how long he'd been standing there watching her. He started to walk into the water and come toward her. The water rose to his knees and then higher and higher as he came closer. She closed her eyes again, feeling the blazing sun on her face. When she opened them, he was in the middle of the pit, water rippling against his black-haired chest. He was holding something in his arms above the water. She squinted and shaded her eyes with the palm of her hand so she could see more clearly. He was holding a newborn infant. The umbilical cord was hanging down and touching the surface of the water. Her heart began to pound and she was about to turn when she heard his voice. "Come, Golandam," he said, smiling and beckoning to her. "Why are you standing there? Come, it's me, Jamal. Don't be afraid. Come to me. I've brought our son, our Jalal, the bright light of our lives. Come. Come and take him."

The rays of the sun reflecting over the water came sharply at her, making her blink and the image glide away momentarily. Uncertain and feeling her head spin, she inched closer to the edge of the pit. The closer she stepped, the more clearly she thought she saw Jamal's face and heard his voice, softly calling to her, "Come my beautiful . . . don't be afraid . . . come to me . . . here I am . . . good, closer, closer . . ."

At Chale-Sabz, the passion play was over. The lion had left the scene and Imam Hossein and the other martyrs rose, straightened their turbans, and shook off the dust. Someone chanted, "God's grace be upon Mohammad and the Imams and may they always be our protectors"—the sign that the play was over. Then people scattered to go home.

Haydar and the villagers, hungry and thirsty, started to walk back to Sangriz like a defeated army. The banner carriers had the poles on their shoulders and the ends of the banners dragged on the ground behind them. When they reached the ruins of Persepolis, they sat in the shade of the broken wall to rest. The water jars that the women had brought were passed around. Not far from where they were sitting, a couple of field rats ran out from between the stones and disappeared back into their holes.

Sayed Ayoub entertained his fellow villagers with stories about the ancient days. He said that where they were sitting had been the site of a Zoroastrian temple where a flame was kept burning day and night. Zoroaster was a prophet sent by Ahura Mazda with the message of Good Thoughts, Good Words, Good Deeds. That was long ago, many years before Mohammad became a prophet and our people became Moslims. The children gathered closer to listen. They always enjoyed having him tell about the battles of Imam Ali and Imam Hossein with the infidels or the stories from *The Epic of Kings* about Rostam, the hero of the Iranian wars against the enemies, and how he fought the demons who could move mountains.

212

Sometimes Sayed would tell them about the things that had happened in Sangriz before the children were born.

Sayed Ayoub took off his green hat and wiped his forehead. Then he pointed to the stone columns of the palace ruins. "Yes," he said in his deep voice, "everything has its time. Everything has its era. Its highs and lows. Look at this amazing place. At one time King Jamshid walked the grand halls of this palace. Where has all its might gone? . . . Gone to dust. To nothing, leaving behind only these crumbled columns, arches, and walls . . ."

He shook his head. "These lines from the poet Omar Khayyám say it best," he told them, before reciting a stanza from the fabled poem.

> The mighty a palace against the heavens threw
> And came here the ancient plain to view
> A ringdove flies up to the fortress wall

(The children all looked to the top of the wall.)

> She sings coo, coo—Where oh where are you?

"Yes," Sayed Ayoub went on. "All is gone. Gone to dust. Nothing is eternal in this world except the Almighty. No king, no amir, no khan, no sultan, and no ordinary man . . . All who enter this world will have to leave it. One day Cyrus the Great and Xerxes walked upon this land and built this mighty palace, another day Alexander came along and tumbled it to the ground. Then came the Arabs and then the Mongolians to establish their empires . . . But they're all gone. Gone to dust . . . as we will all be . . .

"It's said that when Alexander conquered this palace, he was so moved by its magnificence that he knelt down and kissed its steps. It was a gesture that softened the rage of the king's men. And it was one of Darius's lovers who guided him to the place where the king's treasure was hidden—O the enemy within is far worse than the enemy without. But Alexander was after something else, something more precious than any palace or treasure of kings or the love of any woman. He was after *aab-e zendagi*—the water of life. So he set fire to this palace, and it's said that it went on burning for forty days and nights with such a dark smoke that no one could see the

213

mountains behind. Then he headed for India in search of the water of life, not knowing that he would lose his life in vain."

Listening to Sayed Ayoub, Haydar thought of all the stories he had heard about treasure, especially the Black Globe that, for years, he had searched for in the hills, hills that were now being leveled to make bricks.

Sayed Ayoub turned to Marafi. "Give me your book, son," he said. "*The Epic of Kings*. I'll read one of the heroic stories."

Marafi took the old book from his satchel and handed it to him. Sayed Ayoub opened the book to the story of King Zahhak, who was known as Zahhak Mar be Dush—the king with snakes on his shoulders. He cleared his throat and started to recite the story of Zahhak, the king who killed his own father and took the throne. Zahhak was visited by a stranger, who was none other than the devil. The stranger offered to help the king keep his kingdom. All he requested was to be allowed to kiss the king's shoulders. After a while two snakes grew from the spots he had kissed. Again the devil came to the king, this time as a physician, and said that to keep the snakes from hurting the king, the brains of two young men must be fed to them every night. Zahhak was able to rule for a thousand years, a reign that devastated the country, with generations of young men killed to protect him from snakes and many families forced into exile to flee his brutality, until a man named Kaveh Ahangar—Kaveh the Blacksmith—who had lost his two young sons to the snakes, decided on revenge. He made a banner out of his blacksmith's apron and marched to the palace with all the citizens following. Kaveh sent for Farydoun, the prince whose father had been killed by Zahhak. Farydoun killed Zahhak and his devastating rule was over.

Sayed Ayoub was in the midst of reciting when suddenly he stopped and leafed through the pages. "There are pages missing," he said to Marafi. "How did that happen?"

Marafi was troubled by the question. A tragic expression showered down over his features as he pointed toward Sangriz and went on muttering. It was Mirza-ali who calmed him down and then related the story of the jeep that had stopped in front of the Gypsy Danial's tent late one afternoon and the man and woman who had torn the pages from the book.

Sayed Ayoub shook his head in dismay and handed the book back to Marafi. As they sat, still tired and passing the water jar around, there came a howling from the ruins that startled everyone. Someone said it was a dog, possibly a wild dog. Someone else said that it was a wolf, maybe a pack of wolves. A couple of the men said that they had heard it a few times before when they had been passing the ruins. Soon they heard the howl again, louder this time, which caused an agitation among the villagers, especially the women and children. Quickly they all rose and headed down the road, some people continuing to look as they went.

When they got close to Sangriz, the boys pulled off their shirts and noisily ran to jump in one of the pits filled with water to cool off but suddenly stopped. The crowd hesitated at first and then, realizing something was wrong, rushed ahead. Haydar pushed his way past the children and saw on the top of the water the fan of long hair as black as Hajar al Aswad—the black stone of Mecca—spread wide over the muddy water.

2

Haydar was waist deep in the grave he was digging and, as he shoveled out the dirt, surveyed the scene around him.

He saw the sun, a halo of dust around it, at the highest peak of the mountain and about to gather up its last spikes of light.

He saw Bibigol, crumpled down by Golandam's body.

He saw Mehrangiz, with her hand on Bibigol's shoulder.

He saw Sayed Ayoub, his hands held up to the sky, turning his prayer beads.

He saw Amir Khan and his wife beside the grave of their son, Sarferaaz.

He saw Mirza-ali, his head bent, hitting the ground with his walking stick, his old dog, Gorgi, and his grandson at his side.

He saw Marafi, waving his arms like a bird spreading its wings to fly but with its legs tied to the ground.

He saw Jaffar at the edge of the cemetery, walking away from Sangriz and not looking back.

He saw the women, all in black, gathered together in silence.

Haydar kept digging and wouldn't let anyone help him. It was as if all the pain of the world had gathered inside him. He could hear the pounding of his heart like the heart of the whole world inside his chest. He kept digging and shoveling out the dirt.

"O people . . . ," he cried out. "People of Sangriz, come. Come gather around . . . Haydar Ganji the treasure hunter is calling to you. Come—come and see. Come and see the seeker of the Black Globe about to bury his treasure."

CENSORSHIP LETTER

The letter that follows lists the corrections that the Iranian government requested before the original publication of the novel in 1997. In some cases the lines in question are also supplied and are indicated [in square brackets] with my comments. As explained in the preface to this edition, the lines and page numbers used in the letter refer to a mock-up and do not correspond to the pages in the novel as it was published in Persian or to the present, revised edition in English.

In the name of God

Number _____
Date 8/5/75 [7/29/96]
Enclosure _____

The Islamic Republic of Iran
The Ministry of Culture and Islamic Guidance

Honorable Head of Navid Publications of Shiraz
With greetings

We sincerely inform you that the publication and distribution of the book *Sangriz* is subject to the corrections as listed in the following.

The Special Office of Books
[no signature]

The list of changes needed for the book

1. The beginning sentence of the book, "It's not obvious from what direction the wind is blowing . . . ," refers to the victory of the revolution, the imposed war, and the years of the holy defense. Delete. [This was the epigraph—the lines from a poem by Manouchehr Atashi—and was deleted.]

2. Page 21, lines 1–7, delete - the first line should of course be deleted and the rest of the lines corrected.
[The lines were: "Jamal's gaze sought Golandam's. Although many glances had passed between them, it was as if he were seeing her for the first time, and a feverish warmth rushed to his heart. For a moment he felt dizzy and was afraid of being thrown from the horse right in front of the women's eyes, but then he broke off his gaze and dug his heels into the horse's sides. *Yal-lah*, he called, and Abrash sped away."]

3. Page 25, lines 11 and 12, delete or correct.
["What did you say is broken? The *dog arm*? What sort of thing is this? It doesn't look anything like a dog's arm"—in reference to an automobile part.]

4. Page 27, line 13, delete, and the following lines must somehow be corrected.
["Jamal passed the group of women and girls on the road without paying much attention to Golandam, whose eyes were seeking him."]

5. Page 28, to line 4 of page 29, the whole page should be deleted or somehow corrected.
[The problem appeared to center around this passage: "He pushed one end of the hose into the tank of the minibus and started to suck on the other end of the hose. As soon as he felt the flow of gas, he quickly took it out of his mouth and pushed it into the motorcycle's tank . . ."]

6. Page 40, delete the last line.
["Were you going to put the treasure between your mother's legs?"]

7. Page 54, the whole page, the relationship between Jaffar and Golandam should be corrected.
[This was the scene at the primary school when the teachers tease Jaffar, urging him to tell them which one of the schoolgirls he likes.]

8. Page 55, line 9, delete.
["You sneaky devil, didn't we see you yesterday in the corner of the school yard holding Golandam's hand?"]

9. Pages 56, 57, and 58, all these pages should be corrected.
   [Relates to Jaffar and Golandam traveling to the city and visiting his school, eating ice cream, holding hands, and later playing in the park.]

10. Page 60, line 15 to the end of the page, delete or correct.
    [Scene in which a group of people come out of the mosque throwing stones and bricks at a movie theater and injure Bibigol.]

11. Page 82, lines 9, 13, and 14, delete.
    ["Golandam was in front. With each step, water splashed over the rim of the pot and dripped over her shoulders and chest . . . Goodarz was about to say something when Sarferaaz, Amir Khan's son, noticed Goodarz's attention and broke the silence. 'You're too late, Goodarz,' he said. 'She's going to be warming up Jamal's bed any day now.'"]

12. Page 86, line 17, delete the expression "dog shit."

13. Page 86, line 20, delete the expression "son of a bitch."

14. Page 99 from line 2 to the last line of page 100 and the first paragraph of page 101, delete.
    [Section where Jaffar witnesses Haydar and Mehrangiz making love inside a mosquito net.]

15. Page 108, lines 1–8, delete.
    ["Haydar, looking at Mehrangiz, would pay attention to see the slightest change in her and would see the tiredness and loneliness in her eyes. He wanted her, he wanted to hold her tight in his arms. Wanted to brush her hair and kiss her. Mehrangiz looked back at him, wishing she could break down the glass with her fists, free her husband, hug him, comfort him, and take him away with her."]

16. Page 109, lines 8 and 9, delete.
    ["Am I a donkey brain to put my ass in front of a raging bull? For what, for the stupid people of Sangriz?"]

17. Page 110, line 16, delete the expression "son of a dog."

18. Page 111, line 10, delete the expression "son of a dog."

19. Page 112, lines 14 and 15, delete.
["But as you know, the Rahbaris are related to a well-established mullah. And they say that the mullahs are taking control of everything."]

20. Page 120, line 3, delete or correct.
["A woman with long, straw-colored hair and eyes the color of the sky made every head turn as she got out of the car."]

21. Page 136, lines 11–13 and the last line on the page, delete.
["Everyone looked at Golandam. Most of them were seeing her naked for the first time. She was tall with dark eyes, fair skin, a long neck, and shapely breasts. She looked like a beautiful and perfect marble statue standing to be admired. Some of the women sighed as if remembering their younger days."]

22. Page 137, lines 2–4, delete.
[Passage describing women and girls dancing at the wedding.]

23. Page 143, lines 1–4, delete.
[The scene of beautifying the bride.]

24. Page 144, lines 3, 18, and 19, delete.
[Description of how Golandam feels inside her wedding dress and her thoughts of being alone with Jamal in the wedding chamber.]

25. Page 146, [no line number provided], this again relates to Golandam and Jaffar's relation and must somehow be modified.
[Scene in which Golandam is remembering Jaffar and the spring picnic when the young boys and girls laughed and played in a field.]

26. Page 147, line 4, delete.
["Her heart was beating harder under her breasts."]

27. From page 153 to the end of the book, there is negativity about the front and the war that the writer must altogether correct.

28. Page 154, line 2 [no comment given].
[Passages relating to the war.]

29. Page 167, on this page the carrying of the martyrs' bodies to the village is described very badly and must be corrected.

30. Page 168, lines 4 and 5, again, the same negative description of the front must be deleted or corrected.

31. Page 169, the whole page, again, the negative description of the front must be deleted or corrected.

32. Pages 175, 176, 177, on all these pages the fate of the martyr's wife and her wandering in the fields are portrayed very undesirably and must be deleted.

33. Page 178, again relating to the fate of the martyr's wife; must be corrected.

34. Pages 181 and 182, last lines, negative description relating to going to the front; delete.

35. Page 183, last two lines, an insult to the Koran, delete.
   [One of these lines was "The Arabic words from a loudspeaker hovered insistently over the patients in the clinic yard."]

36. Page 184, bad-mouthing the situation of the cities at the time of the war; delete.

37. Page 187, again, the mention of the shortages and problems during the war is from a negative point of view, delete.

38. Page 191, the fate of the martyr's wife is described negatively, delete.

39. Page 204, the death of the martyr's wife and her falling in the water, delete.

40. Page 205, the mention of the fate of the martyr's wife, delete.

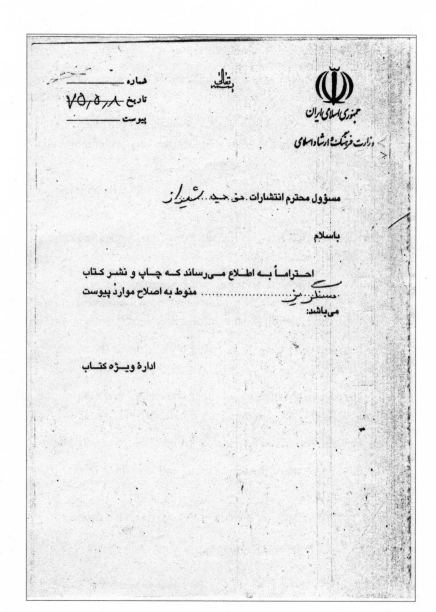

بسمه تعالی

جمهوری اسلامی ایران

وزارت فرهنگ و ارشاد اسلامی

مسؤول محترم انتشارات حق حیه شمیراز

باسلام

احتراماً بـه اطـلاع مـی‌رساند کـه چـاپ و نشـر کتاب
مستطر میزا .... منوط به اصلاح موارد پیوست
می‌باشد:

ادارهٔ ویـژه کتـاب

224

توضیحات	سطر	صفحه	ردیف
... جمله ابتدا ... به آخر اصلاح شود و ... باشد ... حذف شود	جمله اول سطر		۱
... حذف گردد. از سطر اول حذف و سطر بعد اصلاح گردد	۷ تا ۱۷	۲۱	۲
حذف یا اصلاح شود.	۱۱، ۱۲	۲۵	۳
حذف گردد و سطور بعد بهمان اصلاح شود.	۱۳	۲۷	۴
صفحه ۲۸ تا سطر ۴ صفحه ۲۹ کل این جمله حذف یا اصلاح شود.			۵
حذف شود.	سطر آخر	۴۰	۶
ارتباط جمله با ... اصلاح شود.	کل صفحه	۸۴	۷
حذف شود.	۹	۸۸	۸
اصلاح شود.	کل صفحه	۵۲، ۵۷، ۵۸	۹
حذف یا اصلاح شود.	۱۵ تا آخر	۶۰	۱۰
حذف شود.	۹، ۱۳، ۱۴	۸۲	۱۱
کل آدرس حذف شود.	۱۷	۸۶	۱۲
کل آدرس حذف شود.	۲۰	۸۶	۱۳
از ۲ سطر آخر تا ... کل حذف شود و پاراگراف اول صفحه ... حذف شود		۹۹	۱۴
حذف شود.	۸ تا	۱۰۸	۱۵
~	۸ تا ۹	۱۰۹	۱۶
عبارت بدرستی حذف شود.	۱۶	۱۱۰	۱۷
~	۱۰	۱۱۱	۱۸
حذف شود.	۱۵ تا ۱۶	۱۱۲	۱۹
حذف یا اصلاح شود.	۳	۱۲۰	۲۰
۱۱ تا ۱۳ و سطر آخر حذف شود.		۱۳۶	۲۱
حذف شود.	۶ تا ۲۷	۱۷۷	۲۲
~	۱ تا ۴	۱۶۴	۲۳
۳ و سطر ۱۸ تا ۱۹ حذف شود.		۱۴۴	۲۴
باز بیا ارتباط جمله ... انداز اشاره شده و باید سبب ... اصلاح گردد		۱۶۲	۲۵
حذف گردد.	۴	۱۶۷	۲۶
از صفحه ۱۵۲ تا پایان کتاب که مطالب سفر در مورد جبهه و جنگ ... آورده شده باید ...		۱۵۲	۲۷
	۲	۱۵۴	۲۸
در این قسمت انتقال منزه سند ... داده با تشکیل حیلی بجا اصلاح کرده است		۱۶۲	۲۹
باز مطالب منفی در مورد جبهه علت حذف شود یا اصلاح	۴، ۵	۱۲۸	۳۰
~	کل صفحه	۱۶۹	۳۱
در این ... علت ... ترتیب ... اصلاح یا حذف شود		۱۷۲، ۱۷۵، ۱۷۶	۳۲
اصلاح یا حذف شود.		۱۷۸	۳۳

ردیف	صفحه	سطر	توضیحات
۳۴	۱۸۱و۱۸۲	سطر آخر	مطالب منفی در مورد رفتن به جبهه حذف شود.
۳۵	۱۸۳	دو سطر آخر	۲ مورد در همین سطر. حذف شود.
۳۶	۱۸۴		بهتر این از جمله دوم از رمان کتاب حذف شود.
۳۷	۱۸۷		با در مسائلات و نارسائی ها ی ... با ... ... مطرح سده حذف
۳۸	۱۹۱		ذکر عاشتی همسر پشید بشکل منفی مطرح سده حذف شود.
۳۹	۲۰۴		نشست ... همسر شود. و آقتدن ( ) و در ... حذف شود.
۴۰	۲۰۵		ذکر عاشتیت همسر شود حذف شود.